The Highlander's Wild Heart

JOAN BORBA

A SPICY CELTIC ROMANCE SERIES

Printed in the United States of America

First Printing, 2025

ISBN 979-8-9923930-1-9

Chapter 1

Instead of the end of her life as she knew it, May 15 should have been a typical Friday afternoon for Hannah Vander Dussen.

She should have arrived at home before her husband, Lawrence, and changed out of the silk twill Prada suit she had worn to work into yoga pants. Hannah should have headed to the Guru Studio for an early Pilates class, then picked up her daughter, Charli, from a friend's house before stopping off to grab some takeout from Umai. Mother and daughter should have gotten back home right about the time Lawrence Vander Dussen was pulling his Audi into their cavernous garage next to her Mercedes SUV, and the three of them should have enjoyed planning their weekend over sushi.

In an alternate reality to the one Hannah expected, she opened the door to the master bedroom of her posh Pacific Palisades home to find a slim brunette straddling Lawrence. Although her breasts were a few cup sizes smaller than Hannah's, they bobbed pertly as she bounced on top of Hannah's husband.

"I'm sor—wait. Who ...?" Hannah sputtered as she tried to make sense of the scene. For an insane moment, she realized, she had been about to apologize for walking in on them.

Lawrence's eyes, which had been trained on the woman who was still astride him, though she had stopped bouncing, shifted to his wife. "Hannah," he said in a calm, almost conversational tone, "you're home early."

Though Hannah tried to match Lawrence's composure, a wave of nausea hit. She scrambled for the master bathroom, making it to the toilet just in time. When there was nothing left inside her but a cold emptiness, she splashed water on her face and rinsed her mouth. As she dabbed her lips with a hand towel, Hannah avoided looking at the woman reflected in the mirror. None of this seemed real, and she wasn't ready to face what she might see in her own eyes.

Steeling herself with a deep breath, Hannah returned to the bedroom to find her husband's playmate had climbed off him, though she remained on the bed beside him. Hannah's eyes narrowed as she pinned them on the woman.

"I know you," Hannah mocked her, wishing she could stop sounding so damned shocked, wishing, really, that this entire spectacle was a bad dream. "We met two weeks ago at the partners' luncheon for the new associates."

The woman might have at least tried to look embarrassed, even if she wasn't. The only thing she managed to do was bow her lips into a smirky pout and nod her head.

Hannah's gaze swung back to Lawrence. "So, what is this? Did HR introduce some new orientation program?"

"This is Mackenzie." Lawrence sounded annoyed as he sat up. "And it's not what it seems." He pulled on a pair of jogging pants from a tousled heap of clothing on the floor.

As Hannah tried to puzzle out what possible explanation Lawrence had that didn't add up to infidelity, he muttered something to Mackenzie about letting herself out. She hadn't moved an inch, not even to cover herself with Hannah's Millesimo sheet. Lawrence thrust a bundle of clothing at her, giving her a grim nod. Then, he stalked out the door, hooking Hannah's arm as he went, and dragged her down the stairs to his study.

Hannah fired off incredulous questions as they went. However, it wasn't until he had shut the door and poured himself a bourbon from the well-stocked bar in the corner that he deigned to speak.

"Calm down," he chastened her, tossing back his drink and pouring himself another. "There's no need for an embarrassing scene."

Hannah's jaw dropped. "No need for an embarrassing scene?" she repeated. Did he not see how absurd this was? "I walked in on you having sex in our bed—with another woman."

The look he gave her brimmed with disdain. "If you're concerned about sexual harassment, there's no need to worry." He took a sip of his second drink instead of downing it in one shot. "Mackenzie doesn't report to me. She works for Jerome."

"You think that's the issue?" An incredulous huff of a laugh spluttered from Hannah's mouth. "I just found out you're having an affair. And, what you were doing—whenever I've brought up trying anything other than the same missionary position we've done since our wedding night, you shut me down."

Lawrence's jaw muscles clenched as he studied her for a moment. "You weren't meant to see that." His words came out low and insolent. "And besides, my wife isn't a harlot. I don't expect anything from you other than normal, respectable marital relations."

"Maybe that's at the root of this problem," Hannah grimaced, seizing on what might be the reason her husband felt the need to have sex with another woman after all these years. "It's only natural for you to be curious about trying different things, but trying them with someone else isn't the answer. I'm your wife. We should experiment together."

A disgusted smirk twisted on Lawrence's lips. "Don't be crude. Everything is fine between us the way it is."

"My God!" Hannah exclaimed, stunned with Lawrence's inability to see his unfaithfulness as a symptom things were anything other than fine. "Have I been so oblivious that you think we'll go on with you cheating on me?"

"It's not like it's the first time." His voice was dull, almost resigned. Turning from her, he moved toward the bar. "It's been going on since we were undergrads." Lifting the cover from the ice bucket, Lawrence plucked up ice cubes with a set of silver tongs and plunked them into a second glass.

Hannah watched him pour another drink as she processed his words. She had heard them and knew what they meant; however, it took a moment before she believed them.

Memories flooded her brain, a million little signs she had written off without hesitation over the years, ones that should have tipped her off to her husband's infidelities. She had never confronted him outright, though once or twice she had asked questions about where he had been or how he had known a particular woman who had looked at him with disturbing familiarity. After he had explained away her suspicions with semi-believable rationalizations a few times—"I was working late and figured it would be easier to sleep at the office," or, "Her parents are old friends of the family"—Hannah had taken to coming up with explanations on her own whenever doubts arose. After a while, it had become an automatic reaction, and she had stopped registering her misgivings altogether. Now, as clarity settled on her like a curtain on the final act of her marriage, Hannah began shaking.

She didn't notice Lawrence stride across the room toward her. Even when he held out the glass of bourbon to her, she didn't realize he had come to stand in front of her until he spoke.

"Here. Drink this, for God's sake. It'll calm you down."

The sound of his voice drew her attention to the glass he held out to her. Still shaking, Hannah focused on it, then looked up at Lawrence. His brows were knit, though he looked more agitated than concerned.

Calm ... down.

The words echoed in Hannah's head.

Suddenly, unable to stand one more minute near her husband, Hannah leapt from her seat. She thrust her arm in an angry arc, knocking the drink from Lawrence's hand.

Hannah rushed from the room and hurried through the corridor, as Lawrence beckoned, calling enraged commands to come back, trailing behind her. She had parked in the driveway, hadn't even opened the garage door because she had planned on leaving again to go to Pilates. As she raced toward the front door, she scooped up her purse and car keys from the console in the entryway where she had dropped them less than thirty minutes earlier. Had it only been less than an hour since her world had begun to crumble? She was out of the house and in her Mercedes before she knew it. Because her trembling hadn't stopped, she fumbled to start the SUV as it seemed to have kicked up a few notches. She ended up jabbing at the keyless ignition button several times before hitting it right and hearing the engine purr to life.

She might have caught a glimpse of Lawrence standing in the front doorway as she backed up the Mercedes in a quick maneuver to turn around. She realized she couldn't be sure and couldn't have cared less. Right now, she needed to get as far away from him as possible.

The tears didn't come until Hannah was on CA-1, driving along the coast and heading for Santa Monica. She brushed them away with one shaking hand, though she kept the other clutched around the steering wheel in a death grip.

Wouldn't a car wreck be the perfect ending to this perfect day?

Chapter 2

As the miles sped by, a buzzing, almost comforting numbness, crept over her. When Hannah arrived at her destination, she didn't remember the drive there. Wobbling on her feet and her shoulders shuddering, Hannah made her way from the apartment complex's parking lot to her best friend's third-floor apartment. When Grace opened the door, Hannah's face crumpled.

"Gracieeee," she sobbed.

Without hesitation, Grace's arms were around her, drawing her close and pulling her inside. "Hannah! What's wrong, honey?" Grace asked with confused concern.

Hannah's attempt at explaining came out in equal amounts of words and non-verbal noises. It didn't help that she had to stop and sniff every few seconds to keep her nose from running. And to make matters worse, a fresh wave of tears started just when she thought she had her emotions under control.

Grace listened for a moment, her eyebrows drawn together, then went to the bathroom to retrieve a box of tissues, allowing Hannah to blather on. When she returned, Grace smoothed Hannah's long, sandy brown hair from her face and blotted her tears from her blue eyes.

The tender care from her friend seemed to do the trick of calming Hannah enough to speak. At least the waterworks had let up and her sobs had given way to hiccupping, jerky breaths.

"Okay," Grace coaxed when Hannah's breathing leveled out. "Now, tell me what's going on."

"It's Lawrence." Hannah paused, afraid the crying would start again. "I caught him in bed with another woman."

Grace's eyes became wide. "He's having an affair?"

"Not just one," Hannah sniffed, taking charge of the tissues herself and wiping her nose. "Apparently he's been sleeping around since college."

"That son of a bitch," Grace cursed, murder blazing in her eyes. "How could he do this to you and Charli?"

Hannah coughed a mirthless chuckle. "He has compartmentalized his life quite nicely," she despaired. "He's kept his successful lawyer wife and brilliant, beautiful daughter with his Pacific Palisades mansion, sports car, and country club membership here—" she thrust out her right hand, palm up, "—and kept his skanks here." Her left hand came up, demonstrating the distance Lawrence kept between his two lives.

"Skanks?" Grace arched an eyebrow.

Shoulders shrugging, Hannah huffed a sigh. "I heard it from Charli. I'm guessing from the context, I used it correctly."

"Mmmm." Grace shook her head and gave Hannah a grim smirk. "I think he's the 'skank' in this tragedy."

The lump lodged in Hannah's throat began expanding again. She couldn't disagree; Lawrence was as much at fault as any of the women he had slept with. Even more, she thought, since he had likely used his money and power to entice them into bed. Plus, although he was within a stone's throw of his forties, Lawrence still had his polished prep-school looks. There wasn't a trace of silver threading through his dark blond hair, and only the slightest lines creased his face, near his eyes. He kept himself in shape, too. His attractiveness coupled with his position and wealth would be a difficult combination for most women to resist.

"Well, what are you going to do?" Grace's question broke into Hannah's thoughts.

Hannah was picking at her trousers, plucking the silk between her finger and thumb, and letting it drop in a soothing repetitive motion. At last, she sighed. "The marriage is over. No amount of counseling or talking things through will bring back my trust in him."

"So, you're leaving him?"

"Of course. How can I stay married to a man I can't trust?" Fresh tears brimmed in Hannah's eyes.

"I can only imagine how hard a decision this is." Grace handed Hannah a fresh tissue. "But it's not the end of your life—only the end of one chapter of it."

"A huge chapter," Hannah sniffed as she blotted tears from the corner of each eye. "We started dating our first year in college. At this point, Lawrence and I have been together almost half of my life."

"And now, it's time to get on with the next half," Grace doted, her tone taking an upbeat turn. "You've spent almost two decades compromising and doing things 'Hairy Larry's way.' I think the best thing you can do to move forward is start planning what you'll do without him, things to make your life better."

"What? Like wag more, bark less?" Hannah faltered, eyeing her friend with uncertainty. "Eat healthier?"

Grace groaned a bit. "Sure. Why not? But try to come up with some out-of-the-box things. Stuff you wouldn't or couldn't do when you were tied to Lawrence."

"Such as?"

Shrugging, Grace's brows dipped. "I don't know. It's not my list; it's yours."

"List?" Hannah matched Grace's bemused frown. "What list? I can't think of anything I couldn't have done married."

"There are loads of things single women can do that married ones can't," Grace assured her. "Give it some time and some thought. I bet you'll come up with plenty of things to fill a bucket list."

"A bucket list." Hannah blew an amused breath from her nose.

"Right—a Divorce Bucket List." Grace beamed. "A list of all the things to improve your life. Things that make you light up."

When Hannah continued to look unsure, Grace encouraged her, "I know I've heard you talk about traveling more. Why not pick a place and put it on your DBL?"

It was true. Lawrence was a workaholic. He had inherited the Type A drive from his father, along with a sobering fortune when the older Vander Dussen died. The money, added to Lawrence's income as partner in a law firm and Hannah's paycheck from the Los Angeles City Attorney's Office, meant they could have traveled extensively throughout the years. But they rarely had. Lawrence always had multiple cases going at any given time—and multiple mistresses, Hannah now realized. Although she had brought up the possibility of taking trips a few times a year, Lawrence had always claimed to have a conflict with his schedule. As a result, they hadn't gone anywhere, just the two of them or as a family, for longer than a three- or four-day weekend.

"Maybe you're right," Hannah acquiesced, trying to see the silver lining Grace was presenting. "Right now, though, all I can think about is Charli and the next twenty-four hours."

Inside her purse, Hannah's cell phone trilled with a text message. When she pulled out the phone, her daughter's name appeared on the screen, as if conjured by Hannah's speaking her name.

"Terrific," she moped, exasperated with herself. "I was supposed to pick up Charli from Jessica's house twenty minutes ago."

"What are you going to tell her?" Grace asked.

"I don't know," Hannah admitted. "Maybe nothing right now. We have to go home tonight, and I don't see Lawrence agreeing to move out." The corners of her lips turned down. "I'm not sure how he's going to take this. However we move forward, I hope he at least agrees we have to make Charli's best interest the priority."

Grace's eyebrows went up. "Good luck." She didn't sound optimistic.

"Thanks. I'll need it," Hannah said, deadpan, knowing it was true.

As Grace walked Hannah to her car, her arm went around Hannah's shoulder, and she pulled her close in a side-hug.

"You know I'm here for you, bestie," she reminded her when they reached the parking lot. "Whatever you need, whenever you need it, all you have to do is call."

"I know. Thank you." Hannah turned to squeeze Grace tight. "I don't know what I would do without you."

"You'd figure it out, but you wouldn't have as much fun," Grace reassured her with a cheeky smile.

Chapter 3

When Hannah pulled up to the curb at Charli's friend's house, she put on her game face. Whatever turn their lives were about to take, she was determined to shield her daughter from the worst of it.

Charli had been watching for her. She was out Jessica's front door, her backpack slung over one shoulder, and coming down the walkway before Hannah had a chance to put the Mercedes in park.

"Hi, sweetheart. How was your day?" Hannah asked, noting she had forced a bit too much cheer into her voice. Hoping Charli would think it was because she felt bad for running late, she added, "Sorry I wasn't here on time. Things kind of spiraled out of control this afternoon and my schedule fell apart."

"It's okay," Charli replied, sounding unconcerned as she buckled herself into the passenger's seat. "Jessica's mom invited me to stay for dinner, but I didn't want to miss sushi night."

Hannah cringed. There was another dropped ball— normally, she would have called in their order so it would be ready when they arrived at Umai. "Right. Do me a favor. Will you, sweetie?" she asked as she swung the SUV around in a wide U-turn. "Call the restaurant and place our order. I didn't think to do it myself before … um, before I left the office."

Though Charli gave her a curious look, she took her cell phone from her backpack and found Umai's number in her phone's contacts.

As Charli rattled off their typical to-go order of a salmon teriyaki bento box for Lawrence and an assortment of sushi rolls for Hannah and herself, Hannah grimaced. Although Hannah doubted Lawrence would willingly leave their home, she wasn't sure if he would be at the house when they got there. She was in the process of choosing which excuse she would give if Lawrence ended up missing sushi night—Stuck in traffic? Working? Late golf game with a client?—when Charli ended the call. She opened her texts and began thumb-typing, and at the same time started chattering to Hannah.

"So, OMG, Riley said the worst thing to Jessica today." Charli was a master at multi-tasking, at least when it came to texting while holding up her end in a verbal conversation. "She said if Jessica makes one misstep, Riley will make sure she gets tossed out on her ear because Jessica is a scholarship student and she's, like, supposed to show her gratitude for even being allowed in our school by towing the line or something. Can you believe that?" Charli flashed Hannah an irritated sideways glance before she went back to texting.

"If it were anyone else, I'd say no. But considering Riley lives up to her 'mean girl' reputation, it's not surprising," Hannah carried on the conversation, glad to have her daughter's junior high drama take center stage for the moment. "What did Jessica say?"

Charli gave a derisive snort. "Jessica's too nice to say anything. She just looked down at her feet while Riley was ranting, so I said, 'Leave her alone, Riley, you bee-atch—'"

"Charli!" Hannah cut a sharp look at her daughter, who shrugged and put on a defensive expression.

"Well, it's true. But I didn't say anything else to her. I just dragged Jessica out of the cafeteria and told her she should tell the counselor im-me-di-ate-ly, because, you know, they're always going on nooooon-stop—" Charli dragged out her words in her typical dramatic fashion, "—about bullying and they tell us to report even a whiff of it." Charli's thumbs stopped working and she turned to Hannah. "Mom? If Jessica doesn't report it, should I?"

"Maybe it was only a snarky comment, and you could let it pass instead of getting into Jessica and Riley's business." Flipping on the turn signal, Hannah considered the situation for a moment. "Is it part of the Honor Code to report those types of comments?"

Charli looked thoughtful. "It's part of the Honor Code, because it has to do with a negative comment relating to social or economic status."

"Will Jessica find out if you report it?" Hannah asked.

"Maybe," Charli surmised, her face falling. "Then Jessica and Riley will both be mad at me for being a snitch. The school always says it's confidential, but things have a way of leaking out."

"Hmmm ..." While Hannah pulled into a parking space at Umai, she gave her daughter's dilemma some thought. Switching off the ignition, she faced her daughter. "I think you should talk to Jessica about it again and recommend she report it. Tell her to insist on confidentiality if it's important to her. If she says no, tell her you should report it because it's mandatory under the Honor Code. It's a tough situation you're in, but you have a good head on your shoulders. I trust you." Hannah brushed Charli's long, wavy hair, a shade lighter than her own, away from her face and tucked a strand of it behind her ear. "You'll figure it out."

When they arrived home, the garage door was open, and Hannah's heart fell when she saw Lawrence's car in the garage. She wished she had opened the garage door when she had come home that afternoon. At least then she would have seen Lawrence's car and known he was home. She might have seen Mackenzie's car, too, parked in Hannah's spot, she thought uncomfortably. Although she wouldn't have jumped to the conclusion he was upstairs in their bedroom under a junior associate, she might not have been taken off guard so fully.

Entering the house through the door from the garage, Hannah and Charlie passed through the mud room into the kitchen to find Lawrence sitting at the table. A soda can sat next to a glass half-filled with melting ice in front of him, and he was reading something on his laptop. When Hannah walked by, she saw he was perusing the stocks section of *The Wall Street Journal*. Her jaw clenched. How could he be sitting there doing something as normal as reading an online paper when their marriage was crumbling around them?

Lawrence looked up when Hannah and Charli walked in, beaming his brightest smile at his daughter. "Hi, Peanut! How was school?"

Hannah's stomach knotted.

"Ugh! You don't want to know," Charli griped, rolling her eyes as she deposited a takeout bag onto the granite countertop of the island in the center of the kitchen. Then, she made her way to the table, where she slid her backpack from her shoulder onto a chair and gave Lawrence a peck on the cheek.

"That bad, huh?" he quipped, closing his laptop.

"Eh," Charli shrugged. "The usual."

Hannah was busy unpacking their takeout meal, while keeping watch on her daughter and husband from the corner of her eye. When Lawrence slid out the chair next to him and offered it to Charli, Hannah couldn't resist intervening.

"Charli, sweetheart, why don't you take your backpack up to your room and change before dinner?" It amazed Hannah how casual she sounded when her insides were a twisted, buzzing mess.

"Sure, Mom," Charli chirped, grabbing her pack and stopping long enough to hug Lawrence around the neck.

"You want me to kick your butt in Harry Potter Clue later?" she teased Lawrence.

He grinned at her. "I'd like to see you try," he dared, giving her nose a tweak.

Watching the two of them together made Hannah's heart ache. For being such a colossal disappointment as a husband, Lawrence was a good father to Charli. Hannah only had a moment of second-guessing her decision; when the picture popped into her head of Mackenzie riding Lawrence like a petting zoo pony, it shored up her resolve. This wasn't the type of relationship she wanted to model for her daughter.

Hannah took three plates from the cupboard and brought them to the table, biding her time as Charli's footsteps pounded up the stairs. When she felt their daughter was out of earshot, she spoke up. "I won't ask you to leave, but I think it would be best if one of us moves into the guest room, until we get this sorted out."

Lawrence leveled a measured gaze on her. "That's a bit extreme. Don't you think?"

The afternoon's drama had drained Hannah's energy, and she felt as if she was still in shock. She had nothing left to put toward arguing with Lawrence. "Fine," she returned, concentrating on laying out the wooden chopsticks just-so. "I'll move some of my things from our room after dinner." As she turned to start bringing the cartons of food to the table, Lawrence caught her wrist and tugged her back.

"This is ridiculous. There's nothing to sort out. It won't happen again. There's no need for either of us to go anywhere."

As Hannah looked into her husband's blue-green eyes, ones so like her daughter's, she read the hidden truth. He wouldn't bring another woman into their bed again; of that, she was certain. But she was equally certain he wouldn't stop cheating. He would just be more careful not to get caught.

"I need some space, Lawrence," she relented, pulling her wrist from his grip. "And some distance from you. When I said we need to sort this out, I meant we need to start figuring out how to end this marriage without traumatizing Charli. You've already started unraveling our relationship. The only thing left is to disentangle ourselves from it and move on."

"Great," Lawrence conceded, his tone flat. "And if Charli asks why you're staying in the guest room?"

If they could avoid telling their daughter anything yet, that would be the way Hannah would choose to go. Still, she knew better. With a weary sigh, she uttered, "We'll explain I've chosen to move into the guest room because we're having some problems with our marriage."

The look on Lawrence's face was the one he wore when he was winding up for an argument. Before he could say anything, Charli appeared in the doorway, her eyes wide and brimming with tears.

"Wh-what's going on?" Her voice came out small, through trembling lips. "Are you getting a divorce?"

Hannah's heart fell. There was no telling how much of their conversation their daughter had heard but, obviously, it was enough.

Without missing a beat, Lawrence sprang from the table and went to Charli, his expression reassuring and conciliatory, a complete change from the contentious mask he had worn only seconds before. "No! We would never do that to you," he assured her, his arm going around Charli's shoulder. He turned and locked his eyes on Hannah's. "Your mom just needs some time to think things through before she moves back into our bedroom."

Her stomach in knots, Hannah stared back at him. *So much for not using our kid to manipulate me into staying married to a lying, cheating bastard.*

She came forward to put her arm around Charli's other shoulder. Drawing her away from Lawrence and toward the table, she explained, "We're having a few problems, nothing to do with you, so we don't want you to worry about a thing. Okay?" She sat Charli down in a chair and wiped away a tear that had tumbled down her cheek.

Charli looked uncertain but nodded.

Relieved, Hannah forced her lips to curve up the slightest bit. "Okay. Who wants sushi?"

As she transferred their takeout dinner from the counter to the table, the rest of Hannah's dwindling energy drained away. At least Lawrence had the sense to strike up a conversation with Charli about the girls' field hockey tryouts at school. It kept both of them occupied enough that they didn't notice Hannah spent the meal picking at the food on her plate and staring out the window.

By the time dinner was over, Charli was back to her sweet, cheerful self, though a bit subdued. Still, when she took her plate to the sink, she said, "Thanks for dinner, Mom," then followed Lawrence into the family room for their Harry Potter Clue showdown.

Running on autopilot, Hannah collected the detritus of cardboard and styrofoam boxes littering the table. She dumped them into the trash before stacking Lawrence's and her plates in the sink with Charli's. The dishes could wait until tomorrow—or next week, for all Hannah cared at the moment. Right now, the only thing she wanted to do was crawl into the guest bed and fall into a black, dreamless sleep.

Chapter 4

For the first few days of the weeks that followed, Hannah walked around in a daze. Unable to focus her thoughts, she took a week off from work, citing a family emergency. In the state she was in, she wouldn't be of use to anyone needing her legal assistance. She spent some of the time wondering how she could have been so blind, then moved to mourning the future she had thought was planned and secure.

Soon, however, Hannah started thinking of the possibility of a different future. As much as she didn't want to hurt Charli, she knew she needed a new life. A real life. As a mother, Hannah was confident she modeled being a strong, capable person at work. On the other hand, she also realized she modeled being a Stepford wife in her marriage. It wasn't what she wanted for Charli's future with a partner.

The change Hannah's new awareness sparked took Lawrence off guard. One day, he came home to find she had moved the last of her things into the guest room. She had been sneaking them out, a few things at a time so as not to be obvious to Charli. Today, however, Charli had gone home with Jessica after school and was staying the night, and Hannah had made the most of the opportunity. When Lawrence saw the half-empty closet and that she had cleared her side of the vanity in the bathroom, he stormed into the kitchen, furious.

"What the hell is going on?" he demanded.

Hannah looked up from the salad she was preparing for herself and saw he hadn't gotten past taking off his jacket before he had come stomping back down the stairs. The top button of his shirt was undone and, though loosened, his tie was still knotted around his neck. She put her attention back on the tomato she was slicing and in an even, calm voice, replied, "What do you mean?"

"I'm not in the mood for games!" The fact that he had begun shouting was bizarre, although he had been raising his voice a lot more lately, especially when they argued, which—in itself— was surreal. For all the years of their marriage, they had rarely argued, and Hannah had never shouted or screamed. But she was finished being the obedient, compliant wife.

Setting down the knife, Hannah leveled her gaze on Lawrence. "If you're referring to my things being cleared from the master bedroom, it's no game. You've been acting like me moving to the guest room is a temporary thing, but it's not. It never has been. I told you our marriage was over the night I moved in there."

"You only moved in there to think things through," he protested, his jaw clenched.

"That's what we told Charli," Hannah corrected, then caught herself. "No, actually that's what *you* told Charli. I only let it go without saying anything because I wanted to protect her." With a jerk, she picked up a cruet filled with poppyseed vinaigrette and gave it an aggressive shake.

"And how is breaking up her home protecting her?" Lawrence's words were still tinged with anger.

Hannah's eyes flashed and she set down the salad dressing with a thump. Coming around the island to face Lawrence, she declared, "I'll tell you how. It's me showing my daughter it's not okay for anyone to treat their spouse like a doormat. It's me showing her a woman doesn't have to stay with anyone who lies to her and cheats on her." Her fists came to her hips, and she leaned in to deliver her final blow. "It's me standing up for myself and for what I want. And what I want is to be out of this marriage and to move on. I'm protecting her from ending up in this exact situation."

Oddly enough, after all the arguments they had had over the past few weeks—both petty and serious alike— this fight seemed to lift a weight from Hannah's shoulders. Her heart pounded, with excitement, not anxiety, and she felt liberated. The experience appeared to have set her free, and in more ways than one. She watched a succession of emotions chase across Lawrence's face. Anger to confusion to comprehension, then resignation.

"I didn't honestly think it would come to this." Lawrence shoved his hands into his trouser pockets, deflating a bit. "I thought, with time, things would even out and we'd be back to normal after a week or so."

"It's been almost a month," Hannah pointed out. "I don't need more time to think about it. There's no coming back from this, Lawrence."

"So, our marriage is really over." It sounded as if this was the first time he realized they were true.

"Yes. It is." She reached out and placed her hand on his arm.

He shrugged. "What now?"

Although she was relieved they seemed to be moving out of the limbo they had lived in for more than three weeks, Hannah didn't have a ready answer to Lawrence's question. She had thought about the next steps only once or twice and had a preference for which direction to take. Before now, however, Lawrence hadn't been open to discussing a divorce.

"I think we both agree it would be best to find a way to proceed that affects Charli as little as possible."

Lawrence nodded. "Of course. Parents splitting up is tough enough on kids. There's no sense in making it any harder."

"Then why don't we forgo seeking separate counsel and work through the details of a dissolution with a mediator?" Hannah didn't want to engage in ugly, acrimonious litigation. She wanted out of the marriage. If given a choice, using a professional mediator was how she wanted to deal with the divorce.

It came as a relief when Lawrence nodded again. "I think a mediator is a good idea. One of the guys at the firm, a family law specialist, has a shortlist of mediators he works with. I'll get some names and we can schedule an appointment."

The thought occurred to Hannah she might want to dig up a few mediators' names herself, ones that weren't tied to her husband's law firm, but she let it go. This was the most progress she and Lawrence had made, and she didn't want to jeopardize this tentative truce they seemed to have forged. "Okay. And in the meantime, we can make some decisions and write up a preliminary agreement regarding the usual issues. Of course we'll share custody of Charli, and it shouldn't be too difficult to list community and separate property."

"Right," Lawrence responded, studying her with an unreadable expression. "A list of community property and valuation is something we can start on right away." He turned to go back upstairs, adding, "I'll change and get to work on it."

Later, Hannah sat on the bed in the guest room with a pen and legal pad and began listing her personal property. She intended on also writing her own list of community property so she and Lawrence could compare notes and make sure they were on the same page. However, after jotting down only a few items, she found her mind wandering, and this time it wasn't because of the fog of misery she had been living in. She felt like the weight of the world had been lifted off her shoulders. This was it. If things went smoothly, she could be free to start a new life in a few months.

Of course, that was if she and Lawrence agreed on everything. Considering the circumstances and her husband's competitive need-to-win nature, complete agreement might not be likely. But Hannah had already decided her independence and Charli's well-being were more important than fighting tooth and nail over everything. She had no doubt Lawrence would pay more than reasonable child support as well as spousal support for herself. And she knew they could come to an agreement on dividing the community property. Lawrence had made investments he thought she didn't know about, like the Phillips Building in downtown L.A. he had acquired during the recession with partners in a consortium. They had made a killing on it, and she suspected he had a stake in a new high rise going up near the Staples Center. Everything he made on it would legally be half hers. Yet, if he was cooperative and generous enough, she didn't see any reason to drag him through a legal battle just to get her fair share.

The thought of giving up what would be a large fortune to settle for a smaller but still sizable one didn't trouble Hannah. Even if she walked away with child and spousal support, and half of their bank and joint investment accounts, she would be a rich woman. And that was without half of the money she would have coming from the sale of their house. With no mortgage on it, their home would add another two to three million to her net worth. With her financial future covered, maybe it was time she thought about the rest of her future. Grace had encouraged her to make a list of the things she wanted to do once she was a single woman again. Right now, it seemed like a great idea.

Flipping to a fresh page in her notepad, Hannah scrawled Divorce Bucket List in her artful cursive hand across the top. At first, she drew a blank. It had been so long since she had complete control of her life, since she hadn't had to defer to Lawrence's schedule and his wishes. She didn't know what on Earth she wanted to do once she was independent and free. Remembering she had told Grace she wanted to eat healthier, she jotted down, "Eat more omega-3 fatty acids."

She crinkled her nose. Although omegas might be good for her heart, Hannah suspected health supplements weren't what Grace had in mind.

"Okay. Let's try again," she announced to the empty room. She had been toying with taking an early retirement from the City Attorney's Office. This seemed like the perfect time to do it. At thirty-eight, she could make a fresh start anywhere, but it would be nice to have some time off and get used to her new single life first. On the second line of her list, she wrote, "Retire."

With a grin, she nodded. Now she was rolling. The next three items came in quick succession with hardly any thought:

Trade in (and trade up) my Mercedes.

Go hiking in Scotland.

Have sex with a stranger.

The last one surprised her. Had it popped out as a subconscious reaction to Lawrence's cheating? Or had it been hiding in there all along? Although Lawrence wasn't the only man she had been with, he was the only one she had been with for almost two decades.

The notion excited her and she wondered what Lawrence would think. He would, no doubt, find her desires obscene. Lawrence was the king of patronization when it came to all things wifely. And he didn't subscribe to the adage of, "What's good for the goose is good for the gander." He had a different set of rules for himself than he had for her, and it was usually his way or the highway.

Well, the days of letting Lawrence dictate decisions for her were over. She was doing this—doing everything on her bucket list, starting with supplements for her health and continuing on down the line. She could let her boss know next week about her plans to retire and would call a travel agency tomorrow to book a trip to Scotland in the spring. Her divorce should be final by then and, if she waited until May, Charli would be out of school. She could stay with Hannah's mother, Charlotte, for whom Charli had been named, and Hannah could take her time and go on a few walking tours in the Land of the Scots.

And who knew? She might just meet a sexy Scottish stranger to help her mark off number five on her bucket list.

Chapter 5

Strolling into the expansive hotel bar, Hannah looked around, drinking in the twenty-first century opulence and posh decor. It had taken almost eight months to finalize her divorce, and this trip did more than check off one of her Bucket List items. It also served as a reward for making it through mediation without both Hannah and Lawrence retreating to their neutral corners and retaining separate legal counsel. Although she had made some concessions, Lawrence had agreed to almost everything she had asked for, and had signed over the house to her free and clear. Even having given up her claim on the investments and accounts Lawrence thought she didn't know about, Hannah was still wealthy by anyone's standards.

Now, a slow smile formed on Hannah's lips. So. This was the Munro. With its high wood ceiling and matching wood wainscoting set off against the shimmering eggshell walls, antique mirrors, and flowing gray Thai silk draperies, its opulence could have been intimidating. Somehow, however, it presented a welcoming warmth.

Treating herself to a drink here could be considered a reward in itself. But Hannah had booked herself into the Prestige Hotel in Edinburgh, Scotland, which housed the Munro, for a three-week stay, and that was the real reward.

Throughout the bar's sumptuous space, customers filled the seating area which consisted of a group of tables clustered near large and small banquettes lining two walls with floor-to-ceiling windows offering uninterrupted views of a picturesque Scottish garden. And more people sat on stools at the bar. It, too, was a masterpiece of reclaimed oak wood which was wide enough to double as a runway for small aircraft. As Hannah scanned the patrons seated at it, her eyes lingered a bit longer on the male clientele than on the women. After all, there was Bucket List Item Number Five to see to.

"Come on, Hannah, you can do it," she counseled herself under her breath. "Rip off the bandage. Tell the first hot guy you see that you want to fuck him."

She had counted on the conversation buzzing throughout the bar and seating area to keep anyone from hearing her little pep talk to herself. Waitstaff were milling around, serving drinks and appetizers; a pretty server with heavily lined eyes stopped and gave Hannah a quizzical look.

"Sorry, ma'am? Would ya like something to drink?" she asked in a melodic Scottish brogue.

When Hannah shook her head, her face warming, and said she would order her drink at the bar, the woman said she could serve Hannah at the bar top.

"Sure. Thank you," Hannah replied, knowing the sooner she had a drink, the sooner she could relax and get on with her mission. "How about a glass of Belhaven Ale?"

"Comin' right up." The server smiled and pointed Hannah toward an empty stool at the bar. "I'll bring it over to ya."

As Hannah made her way to the bar, she caught sight of herself in the antique glass mirror behind it. She had taken her time getting dressed for this occasion in a floral, Zac Posen short swing dress, a white Tory Burch shrug sweater, and Christian Louboutin high heels.

Not bad, she thought, appraising her trim five-foot-two-inch form. *Bernadette from* Big Bang Theory *from the knees up, and sexy rocker chick from the knees down.*

The server met Hannah at the bar, leaning past her to set a tall glass of rich copper ale on the bar top. Hannah thanked her, asked to start a tab, then took a deep sip of the nutty, spicy brew and let her mind wander through her first full day in Scotland.

It had been wonderful. She had booked a trip with a walking tour and had started the city hike at St. Giles. After it, Hannah had walked the Royal Mile, took a guided tour of Edinburgh Castle, and finished at Holyrood Palace. It had been a perfect first day, leaving her happy and energized and free from the winds of the past.

And ready to plunge into your future, her inner voice reminded her.

Not that she had forgotten. It was why she had come into the Munro this evening—for the express purpose of taking a Scottish hunk back to her hotel room.

Lifting her glass to her lips, she murmured, "Might as well jump in with both feet."

After taking a fortifying gulp of ale, she spotted a group of men and made a beeline for them. When she beamed a friendly smile and called out, "Hi!" their response was to stare at her chest.

A hot prickling tingle crept up her neck. Following an awkward silence that couldn't have been as long as it felt, she politely excused herself and went back to the bar alone to nurse her drink. Maybe she was rushing things, Hannah thought, and decided not to approach anyone else, at least for the moment.

As she took a consoling drink of her ale, she spotted the bartender a few feet away. He looked well over six feet tall and was gorgeous, with dark brown eyes and a chiseled jaw. He wore his dark hair cut shorter on the sides and in the back and his thick, longer locks on top combed back. Hannah's eyes traveled down. The way his Ermenegildo Zegna bespoke suit vest hugged his physique, it had her picturing a hard, flat stomach and six-pack abs. She couldn't stop herself from murmuring an appreciative, "Mm-mmm ...." He was definitely a modern-day pin-up-worthy beast straight out of her fantasies.

Bartenders were always open and pleasant, she mused. Maybe striking up a conversation with this one would be a good way to ease herself into talking with strangers.

As he finished filling a glass from one of the custom engraved beer taps behind the bar, Hannah spoke up.

"Hi, I'm Hannah." She gave him a toned-down version of the smile she had given the group of men.

"Knox." He pointed to his name tag. "Are ye staying at the hotel, or are ya just in to the Munro for the evening?"

"I'm here on vacation," she told him, his friendly manner already putting her at ease. "I booked one of those hiking and walking tours."

He nodded. "Ah. Is it one of the group tours, then?"

"No. I'm here alone." Hannah shook her head.

"Oh?" Knox wrinkled his brow. "I thought ye were meeting some friends." He lifted his chin toward the group of men Hannah had approached earlier.

Hannah chuckled. "No, they were strangers. I went up to them in hopes of striking up a conversation, but they looked at me like I was a girl on display in a window in Amsterdam."

Knox threw back his head and laughed. "Yir a funny lass. Ya think ye look like a hooker? I've got to say, I have known a lot of hookers in my life, and I can assure ye, ya don't look or act like one."

"Um ... okay. Thanks?"

Knox's comment about knowing a lot of hookers took Hannah off guard, as had his observation that she didn't look like one. It also surprised her to realize she felt a fizz of jealousy. Why that was, she didn't know. She had barely met the man. Why should she care how many women he had been with?

Just in time to diffuse the uncomfortable moment, a server arrived at the bar and presented Knox with a drink order. Thankfully, he changed the subject as he went to work filling it.

"So yir on a walking tour alone?" Knox asked as he mixed a martini. "Edinburgh can be a romantic place to visit with a husband or boyfriend."

"I'm sure it is." Was this polite conversation, or was the bartender fishing for details of her situation? "I don't have either one, though. I'm divorced, actually."

"I'm sorry to hear it." His expression had sobered a bit, though it didn't quite match his words. "It can be tough being on yer own again, especially if ye were married for a long time." He poured another beer from the tap for the server standing patiently by.

Hannah shrugged. "Yeah. It's strange to be suddenly single after almost twenty years, but it was for the best, for both my daughter and me." As easy as it was to talk with this man, Hannah didn't want to get into the gory details, especially in front of the server, whose deferential manner toward Knox Hannah couldn't help noticing. As she waited for Knox to load the drinks onto her tray, she stood politely, almost at attention.

Knox gave Hannah a knowing nod. "Being a single parent adds an extra level of difficulty to the mix." He handed the order ticket back to the server with the final drink, and she thanked him and strode away.

"You sound as if you know what it's like." Hannah kept her eyes on Knox as she took a drink of her ale. With the server gone, she was feeling a little bolder.

Knox hesitated for a moment, the indecisive look flitting across his face so quickly, Hannah couldn't be sure she had really seen it. "I do," he revealed. "I have two boys. Sam's twenty-seven and Stuart's twenty-four. Their mam—my wife—passed away when they were still in primary school."

Hannah's heart fell. Divorce was one thing. As tough as it had been, she had had a choice, and had had time to get used to the idea of stepping away from marriage. How tragic was it to have a spouse taken away? At such a young age, and to have to go through it while raising two young children, to boot.

"It must have been so difficult. I'm so sorry." She had to restrain herself from reaching across the bar to touch Knox's hand. It took effort, too, not to ask if his wife's death had been sudden or had come after an illness. Having just met the man, neither question felt appropriate.

"Thank you." Knox had begun taking barware from the dishwasher under the bar, and when he turned from placing two glasses on the shelf behind him, his expression was unreadable. "I don't know why I told ye all that, and I certainly dnna mean to put a damper on our conversation. What do ya say we change the subject?"

Hannah nodded, eager for a change in subject. Listening to Knox speak, something had caught her attention, and this seemed like the perfect opportunity to ask him about it. "Where are you from?"

When Knox raised his eyebrows, she laughed. "I know you're Scottish, but why does your accent sound a little different?"

He grinned, the twinkle returning to his brown eyes. "Ah, yir not just a braw-looking lassie, yir a clever one too. I'm not from Edinburgh; I'm from Glasgow. And, by the way, yir the one with the accent, not me."

"Ha. Point taken." Hannah laughed again, happy the conversation was back on more comfortable ground. "Say something Glaswegian and let me see if understand."

"Happenin? Yir peach?" Knox asked.

Hannah's brow knit. "I'm sorry?"

"I asked you how you are, and if everything's good."

"Really? Do another!" Hannah exclaimed, clapping.

"Yir yaldi. You wint tae come to ma bit cos I've goat an empty ra morra 'n a fancy a swally?" He paused, giving Hannah an expectant look. "Did ye understand any of that?"

"Not a word," Hannah replied, mesmerized. "What did you say?"

"I said yir excited. l asked ye to come to my house and have a drink. Glaswegians have a lot of their own sayin's, and we 'ave a tendency to shorten words. I've moderated the way I speak over the years because people wouldn't understand me otherwise, even here in Edinburgh."

"That, I believe," Hannah blinked in amazement.

When another member of the waitstaff signaled Knox, he held up a finger to Hannah. "Pard'n me for a moment," he said with a wink that made Hannah's stomach flip.

She watched him talk to the waiter and wondered whether Knox was the manager. He wasn't wearing a uniform, like the rest of the staff were. There was an air of authority about him, too, and it seemed the waiters and waitresses were coming to him with issues in addition to drink orders. When he turned from talking with the waiter, Knox caught Hannah looking at him and smiled. He held her gaze as he strode back to his station behind the bar.

"Ye had another question?" he asked. "Or do ya want another drink?"

"I have more questions," she answered with a mischievous smile. "And for every incorrect answer, you have to remove an article of clothing."

Knox laughed. "Sounds good to me. But don't ask too many questions because I don't have my new boxer shorts on."

"Right. I bet your boxers are designer. You could probably give Cristiano Ronaldo a run for his money in Armani briefs." Since she was still nursing her first drink of the evening, Hannah knew this flirtatious side must not have been buried too deep beneath the surface.

"Not quite. Maybe Ronaldo's father," Knox said with a crooked grin.

Hannah laughed. She found his self-deprecating manner charming. "Well, then, maybe I can question you again another time. It'll give you a chance to make sure you have on appropriate undergarments."

Knox lifted his chin. "The customer is always right."

Hannah shifted on her seat. Something in the way he was looking at her felt a little too good. "I guess I should call it a night," she acquiesced, slipping from her bar stool. "I'm going to head back upstairs. Can you charge my drink to my room?" She held her breath, waiting for him to ask her for her room number.

Instead, Knox smiled, his eyes twinkling in a playful way she was already beginning to enjoy. "No worries. It's on me. 'ave a good night."

Smiling, Hannah ducked her head and thanked him. She wished him a good night, too, and made her way through the bar and out into the lobby. As she went, the thought that Knox would do just fine for a one-night stand flitted across her mind; then, she batted it away. First, she was supposed to have sex with a stranger, and for having just met the man, she felt like she knew him too well to call him a stranger. Second, she was staying at the Prestige for two weeks of her visit to Scotland. Aside from the fact that he may have only been nice to her because it was part of his job, it would be awkward to see him several more times after having a rendezvous with him.

And, there was a third reason Hannah felt she should avoid having sex with Knox the Bartender. If she went to bed with him, she was fairly certain she would end up wanting more than one night.

Chapter 6

Hannah's second day of hiking in Scotland took her twelve lovely, lengthy miles up and down the hills of Ben Ledi. It was a long trek, but she was determined to check off her Bucket List Item Number Four. And, as far as the list was concerned, she was also resolute about not chickening out again when it came to Item Number Five. She was so set on seeing it through, she hadn't even changed out of her hiking clothes before she hit the bar, and not only to save time. She also wanted to switch things up from the previous night. After all, Hannah had spent a lot of time getting ready the night before, and it had ended up being a bust. Tonight, long before she walked into the Munro still wearing a light sweater, shorts, and her hiking boots, she had decided this would be the night she would sleep with a stranger.

As she took a seat at the far end of the bar, Hannah spotted Knox chatting with a customer in a business suit. Knox was wearing Giorgio Armani pants and jacket, and Hannah decided he must be a manager after all. Either that, or bartenders earned a better living here than in the

States. However Knox managed to dress so well, he was definitely dreamy, Hannah mused, then snapped herself out of it. No. He was the bartender, and she had already ruled him out as a possibility. Besides, he was working. She needed to focus on the customers.

After ordering a drink from the second bartender working the bar, Hannah looked around. It shouldn't be hard to find someone. Beautiful people were all around her, sitting in small groups on cream-colored pebbled-leather chairs and loveseats, and standing in clusters near the massive terrace doors. Some of the men and women wore business suits; some had on casual attire and jeans. She certainly had a lot to choose from.

Just proposition the first hot guy by himself, she mentally instructed herself.

Right then, Hannah's eyes landed on a tall, red-haired man taking a seat at the bar, a few stools down from her.

Hannah's brows shot up. *Uh-oh, gorgeous ginger sighting.*

Yowza, he was hot. Another hunky, handsome man straight out of her many masturbating fantasies. Before she could lose her nerve, she picked up her half-full glass and started making her way toward the sexy Scot.

As she went, she muttered encouraging self-talk under her breath. "Be confident. If he rejects you, it's okay. This Bucket List is just your goofy way of moving forward. There's no right or wrong result. Being here is a win. You came to Scotland to hike and have sex. Now, go do this shit!"

Stepping close to the redhead, Hannah asked, "Is this seat taken?"

Inside, she groaned. *What an original line.*

To her relief, he smiled. "I was savin' it for ya." He slid the bar stool next to him out for her and she sat down.

"You look like a Viking," Hannah blurted. "You're very attractive." She was going to have to figure out some way to sensor her thoughts, instead of letting them slip out of her mouth the minute they popped into her head.

He smiled again; however, his ice-blue eyes amused under arched brows. "So are you."

"Thanks." The conversation stalled for an uncomfortable beat before Hannah remembered her manners. "I'm Hannah."

The man took her hand and gave it a soft squeeze instead of shaking it in greeting. "Nice to meet ya. I'm Eric."

"What a coincidence." Eric the Viking. The chances of her fantasies coming true tonight were getting better and better.

"Pardon?" Eric frowned.

Hannah shook her head. "Ur, nothing. Sorry. What are you drinking?"

"Scottish ale." He held up his pint glass.

"Is it good?" Hannah cringed. God, her pre-teen daughter was better at flirting than Hannah was.

Eric didn't seem to notice. "Yeh, it's good." Then he leaned in, resting an elbow on the bar top. "So, yir American?"

Okay. Now the conversation was going somewhere.

"Yes."

"Are ya here on business, or fir pleasure?" Eric's tone and the look in his eye laced the question with double meaning.

Hannah hesitated for a moment. "For pleasure." *Orgasmic pleasure, hopefully.* "I'm touring the country, mainly taking hiking journeys. I walked through the Old Town and New Town yesterday, and today a guide took me to into the hills for a longer hike."

"Great. Are ya enjoying it yirself?"

"Yes. Scotland is a beautiful country." Hannah took a sip from her glass, buying time to think of something smart or funny to say.

Before she came up with anything, Eric asked, "What part o' the States do ya hail from?"

She smiled. "I'm from L.A."

"L.A.? Sexy, California girl."

When Eric grinned, looking as if he had struck the jackpot, Hannah cheered inside. Things were going well.

Until he started singing.

"I wish they all could be California girls..."

Hannah's smile froze on her face. She glanced around, hoping no one was paying attention.

Grinning, Knox appeared and took Hannah's empty glass, replacing it with a fresh Belhaven Ale.

Terrific. No one else seemed to be watching except for the hot bartender. But good Lord, was the man going to sing the entire song?

Hannah continued to hold her smile as Eric took a breath then broke into the second verse. The ache in her cheeks told her she wasn't quite pulling off looking pleased or impressed. When he hit a sour note, she managed to keep herself from cringing.

So, he sings off-key. I can live with it in exchange for a combustible night of passion, she bargained with herself.

Maybe if she kept drinking, she and Eric the Red could get drunk and happy together. Or, what if she could distract him? She had watched Grace divert a man's attention by leaning in and touching him. It was worth a try.

Shifting her smile from pained to suggestive, she leaned in and pressed her hand to Eric's leg. When she began dragging her hand up and down his thigh, he stopped singing and snapped his head down to look at her. Surprise and lust mingled in his eyes.

She slid from her barstool to step closer and gave him a peck on his lips.

Eric responded by enthusiastically returning her kiss, slipping his Scottish ale-soaked tongue inside her mouth.

This is it, Hannah thought, a jolt of nerves sparking through her. There was no question Eric was attracted to her—with her hand still planted on his upper thigh, she had a better than good idea of how attracted. She broke the kiss, pulling back a little, and looked up at him through her lashes.

"Wow. Ya must have really liked the song." He chuckled.

"You do have other qualities I admire," she cooed, giving his leg a squeeze. Then she leaned in, placing her lips near his ear and whispered, "Do you want to come upstairs with me to my room?"

Eric's reply came without hesitation. "Hell yeah!" He lifted the ale glass to his lips and drained it before grabbing Hannah's hand, then hesitated before leading her away from the bar.

"I've been called a spendthrift. It's not true, but this is an expensive bar." He gave a regretful grimace and nodded at their drink glasses.

For a moment, Hannah wasn't sure what to say. At last, she shrugged and signaled Knox to charge the drinks to her room.

"It's fine," she told Eric. "I put the drinks on my tab." Lowering her voice, she added, "Now let's go to my room and get naked."

She didn't know what he meant when he replied, "Brill!" From his enthusiasm, and the way his eyes darkened at her suggestion, she guessed it wasn't a bad thing.

When Hannah turned to thank Knox and say, "Goodnight," something unreadable passed across his face. Although he nodded, he didn't return her smile, and she thought there was a hint of stranger danger in the look he gave her. After two decades of seeking macho male approval from a boyfriend who then became her husband, Hannah bristled at Knox's apparent warning. She stopped short of telling him where he could shove his disapproving looks and took Eric's hand to lead him out of the bar.

Once upstairs, getting into Hannah's room proved challenging, with Eric nuzzling her neck from behind and pawing at her with his huge hands. As she fumbled with the keycard, she speculated what might be in store for her. She thought she had heard the size of a man's hands was a sign of a generous endowment. Or was it the feet?

After the hotel door closed behind them, Eric dove in for a wet kiss. It took almost all of Hannah's concentration to keep from feeling like she was being licked by a Great Dane. Instead, she tried to focus on the erotic aspect of having sex with a stranger. He was so tall, his cock-strained jeans rubbed against her stomach, almost to her chest. As he continued to sloppily French kiss her, he cupped his massive hands over her breasts, massaging them like he was kneading bread. It felt strange. And yet—also strange—it turned her on.

"Ya have very nice breasts, Hannah," he moaned, squeezing one, then the other over and over.

She mumbled an embarrassed, "Thank you," then turned around, bringing her hand to her mouth to muffle a giggle. She had thought anything said in a Scottish accent would be drool-worthy. Now she knew different. There was nothing sexy about the way Eric had rolled the "r" for what seemed like forever, and he had pronounced it "breests." As she went to retrieve a condom from the drawer, she had to command herself to stop laughing.

"Eric, honey," she told him over her shoulder. "I like dirty talk. You can call them 'tits.'"

"Okay, baby." His voice dropping to a growl. "I'm dyin' to see yir tits."

When she turned back around to find Eric watching her like a hungry bear looking at a deer, her heart pounded an extra-hard beat. *Shit. This was happening.* She took a breath and reminded herself she had taken a rape safe class. And, she had researched the strict U.K. and Scottish laws about the purchase and use of knives in Scotland before buying a knife. It was stashed in the nightstand drawer next to the bed. Now she was facing the reality of the situation she had gotten herself into; however, her nerves started to get the better of her. But she had come this far and had gotten a strange man up to her room. It was now or never. She needed to get out of her comfort zone and into her erogenous zone. Biting at the edge of her lip, Hannah dove in, kicking off her boots and stripping off her shorts before flinging them aside.

Eric was tearing off his clothes, too, dropping them on the floor as he came toward Hannah.

As Hannah pulled her sweater over her head, Eric's lips spread in a wolfish smile. "Oh yeah, lemme see those luscious California tits."

To his obvious delight, she gave a coy smile and flicked open the clasp on the front of her bra.

When he had removed every stitch of clothing and stood before her completely nude, he palmed his cock. "This is all fir you, baby, and it can't wait to fuck ya."

Hannah took a moment to admire Eric, all of him. He was fit, that was for sure, and she marveled at how turned on she was by the thatch of orange hair surrounding his enormous erection. It had to be all those damned romance novels. *The Highlander Hunk. The Ginger Laird Takes a Virgin Bride. The Devil Highlander Marries a Shy Widow.* Reading those books was a guilty pleasure, but now the fantasies they had inspired were coming to life.

She jumped onto the bed, propping herself up on her elbow, and curled her index finger, inviting Eric to join her.

He obliged, lying down on his back, fisting his cock. When he saw Hannah licking her lips, he enticed her, "Ye like my stonking cock, baby? Kiss it."

Although this was her dirty-sex-with-a-stranger-one-night-stand bucket list item, Hannah had set a few ground rules for herself. No penises in or near her mouth or exchanging body fluids without protection. She took the condom out of the wrapper and slid it over Eric's swollen cock.

"I can't wait," she purred. "My pussy is going to love having this big cock inside it."

"Yeah, sexy dirty talk," he exhaled, her words seeming to make him harder, if it was possible.

Hannah's girlfriends had told her their typical one-night stands were quick and dirty, and that was fine with her. She pushed herself forward on her knees, straddling Eric, and began to slide over the head of his erection, then stopped. Would she be able to take it all in?

Eric frowned. "What's wrong?"

"Nothing," she assured him, slipping a saucy smile onto her lips as she pulled open the nightstand drawer and retrieved a bottle of lube. "You're just so big. I want to make sure we're both comfortable."

Eric grinned. It didn't matter who the man was, it never hurt to feed their egos.

Hannah made a show of pouring lubricant from the bottle into her palm and rubbing them together, then she slid both hands up and down Eric's erection. God, he was huge. And so hard.

Eric's breathing deepened and he groaned. "Hannah, let's chivvy along."

She could only guess what he meant and moved to straddle Eric's pelvis again. Guiding his cock, she slowly pushed herself down. After taking it all inside her, Hannah gave out a little moan.

Eric grunted, "Fuck yeah. Ride me, California girl."

Starting out slow, then picking up the pace, Hannah pumped herself up and down. Her girlfriends had advised her to pick a young guy if she ever wanted to have good, easy, anonymous sex, because she would only need to chase her own orgasm. No worries about satisfying him— he would get there no matter what. She hoped it was true, because she felt the first waves of pleasure rippling through her core. *Yeeeees, Eric, or Red, or whoever you are.*

"Fuck yes!" Hannah moaned as her orgasm overtook her, and Eric grunted his release.

"Bloody cracking!" Eric cried.

As she slumped off him, Hannah bit her lip, hoping the people in the rooms on either side of hers wouldn't complain about the noise.

Eric pulled Hannah to him, spooning her, and they laid together for a long time. When Hannah began to feel drowsy, she knew it was time to get Eric going. Maybe number five on her Bucket List was a one-night stand but to be perfectly accurate, she had wanted a one-fuck stand. She had no interest in sleepovers with strangers. Hoping he would follow her lead, she got up and cleaned herself off. She put on her underwear and began sorting through the clothes strewn around the room. When she realized Eric hadn't budged, she steeled herself, then spoke up.

"Um, thank you… Eric." Awkward! "I don't want to be rude, but can you get dressed and go? I've had a long day, and I need to wake up early tomorrow for another hike."

Although he looked stricken, at least he sat up and retrieved his underwear from the end of the bed. "Yir shitting me. A kiss and a tickle and that's it?" He pulled on his jeans and began looking around for his shirt.

"No, not at all. I really had fun. You're a handsome, sexy guy." Hannah had no problem sounding sincere. She did think he was sexy and good-looking; the problem was, she didn't want him there anymore. "I had a really long day and need to call it a night."

Eric looked up. He had found his shoes and was seated on the edge of the bed, putting them on. "How long are ya staying in town? I'd like to see ya again before ya leave for the States."

"Another booty call?" Hannah gave a nervous chuckle.

"Sorry?"

"Do you want to see me again for another quick shag?" That might not be so bad, Hannah reasoned. After all, the man had given her the first orgasm she had had in decades.

"For whatever ya want. I don't even know yer last name. Can we exchange information?" Eric stood, dressed now, but looking bedraggled.

"Sure, I'm Hannah Vander Dussen. What 's your last name?"

"McGregor. I'm Eric McGregor." Eric held out his hand.

Hannah shook it. "Nice to, um, meet you, Eric McGregor."

They both laughed.

"I'll give you my cell number, and I'll take yours."

"Super." Eric grinned, sliding his arms into his jacket sleeves. "When can I see ya again?" He combed his fingers through his copper hair in a self-conscious gesture.

Hannah paused, trying to think of the best way to put this. With Eric still in her room, she was in a vulnerable position. She didn't know anything about him. What's more, she didn't want to hurt his feelings, or lead him on.

Ladies and gentlemen of the jury...

She put on her best lawyerly, friend-of-the-people smile. "Do you mind if I don't make any promises about specific dates or times? We can play it by ear. I had a great time, but I'm here for a short vacation and don't want to make too many plans separately from what I've already scheduled."

Stormy anger flooded Eric's face. "What the fuck, Hannah? Ya bring me up here fer some dirty talk and a quick shag. Then ye say, 'Fuck you,' stick yer boot in my ass, and kick me out the door? Are all American girls this flaky and slutty? Or is it only the California girls who act like whores?" He gave a derisive snort and added, "Ya sure handled yerself like a real professional tonight."

Stunned, Hannah froze, unsure she had heard him correctly. When she realized she hadn't misunderstood him, her own anger surged.

"Get out!" she demanded, pointing at the door. When he didn't move, she grabbed her keycard and rushed out the door herself, into the hallway. After Eric's outburst, she might be safer outside instead of alone with him in her room.

Eric followed her out, a contrite expression in place of the enraged one he had worn seconds earlier. "Sorry. Sorry," he apologized, his tone placating. "That was stupid of me. I didn't mean any of those things. I just like ya. A lot. Here." He began scribbling on a Prestige Hotel notepad he had taken from the table near the door. "I'm leaving my mobile number on this paper." He held the pad out to her. When Hannah didn't take it, he stepped back inside the door and set it on the table where she could see it. "Please call me if ye have some free time and want to see me again."

Hannah blinked hard, holding back fearful tears. "Just go," she said in a near whisper.

She felt his eyes on her as he walked past, and she refused to meet his gaze.

After the elevator doors pinged shut and Hannah saw the hallway was clear, she went back into her room. She twisted the lock, engaged the deadbolt, and slid the security chain into place before turning and leaning back against the door.

What the fuck? What was that?

"That was fucking a stranger," she answered her mind's question aloud.

As she changed into her nightgown, she reminded herself she had known sex with a stranger would be risky when she had put it on her Bucket List. Now she was questioning whether the reward was worth it. The orgasm had been, well, orgasmic, and it would have been worth it if Eric the Red hadn't turned into a psycho. Was she wrong thinking sex was the only expectation when you invited a stranger from a bar to your hotel room? She hadn't treated him badly or made promises, and she would not let him manipulate her into feeling ashamed.

No. If anything, after this, Hannah was more determined than ever to take back control of her life, and that included her sex life. She would do what she wanted, when she wanted, and who she wanted. And if she wanted to behave in ways she had only read and fantasized about, then she was damned well going to do it.

Crawling into the rumpled bed, feeling the crisp cool sheets on her skin, Hannah decided to try to get a good night's sleep and forget the evening. Or at least forget Eric's meltdown. She would chalk it all up to a crazy experience she had at age thirty-eight instead of in her twenties.

Chapter 7

After a night spent tossing and turning between snatches of fitful sleep, Hannah awoke a bit groggy. Hours into the early morning, she had gone back and forth, beating herself up one minute, justifying her actions the next over what had happened with Eric. Was she really so naïve to think a one-night stand with a random stranger could be handled neatly with no hassles? Was it too much to assume Eric should have understood her intentions and been on the same page; no questions asked? On the other hand, she had objectified him. Hannah couldn't deny it or defend her actions. She had fallen asleep knowing if the issue was on trial and she was the prosecutor, Eric the jury, the defendant would have walked. No question.

Today, however, Hannah's intention was to stay out of her head and enjoy the beauty of her third day of hiking through the Edinburgh countryside. Her guide, Annie, an experienced hiker and Edinburgh enthusiast, had told her to plan on hiking near the water's edge of the East Lothian coast. The drive out would be a bit longer, and the hike a bit shorter than her previous hikes.

There would be less history and more scenery, and Annie assured her the seaside vistas were worth it.

As it turned out, Annie was right. When they arrived at the trailhead, Annie and Hannah started out on a rough path up a green hill. It was steep, but the stones jutting out here and there from the hard-packed earth created a natural staircase of sorts. It offered a sturdy place for hikers to get a foothold and continue upward. At the top, the gorgeous green chessboard of Scottish farmland was visible on one side, the stunning sea on the other. Two trails wound down from the pinnacle, and Annie led Hannah down the one leading to the sea. At the bottom, they walked along a sodden gravel path, still wet from the rainstorm the night before. The path took them through a short narrow passage, man-made of what appeared to be stones taken from the hill they had just descended. When they emerged on the other side, Hannah found they were on the beach, powerful waves crashing onto the rocks and sand only yards away. The sea's mighty intensity was breathtaking, and Hannah found herself mesmerized by the rolling of the surf.

After strolling along the beach for a while, Annie guided Hannah up a set of stone steps which took them to a proper sidewalk that led into a village built on a small fist of land jutting out into the harbor. She allowed Hannah more time at an iron railing to watch the undulating water as it threw itself against the wall below them, as if the sea had followed them and was trying to get their attention. When Hannah's stomach growled loud enough to be heard over the din of the waves, Annie suggested they continue on into the village for a bite to eat at a pub she knew of. It turned out to be a darling establishment, no larger than a cottage, with quaint stone walls and simple, handmade tables and chairs. The dim interior was lit by a fixture over the bar, supplemented by the daylight streaming in through a few small windows on the exterior wall. The friendly old man behind the bar asked if they were in for dinner or a pint.

When Annie replied, "A bit o' both," he told them to take a seat where they wanted.

"Will ya be havin' dark or light today?" he said in an accent so thick Hannah almost didn't understand what he had asked.

Annie told him they would love a pint of "the light," and the bartender said he would send out their drinks and food.

As they sat down, Hannah wrinkled her brow and leaned toward Annie. "How does he know what we want? We haven't seen a menu."

Annie pointed to a chalkboard near the door they had come through. "Clive likes to keep things simple. His wife is the cook, and she only makes one thing every day, all day long."

Hannah's gaze followed Annie's pointing finger to find the days of the week listed on the chalkboard, along with one item next to each day. Today's offering was fish and chips.

"So I'm guessing there's no wine list," Hannah chuckled.

With a smile, Annie shook her head. "No beer list, either," she added. "He's got Dark Island—a dark ale, obviously—on tap, and Belhaven is his light ale."

Belhaven wasn't actually a light beer, but considering it was her drink of choice, Hannah had no complaints.

Clive brought their drinks over straight away and assured them their meal would be coming soon.

While they sipped at their beers and waited for their food, Annie inquired, "I don't mean to pry, but ya've been awfully quiet today. Is anything wrong?"

Hannah took an extra-long drink, studying Annie as she did. The guide was as perceptive as she was knowledgeable. The first day out, she had told Hannah to ask as many questions as she would like, while also assuring her not to feel obligated to talk at all. As easy as Annie was to talk to, Hannah had kept an ongoing conversation throughout their first two hikes that made Charli look introverted by comparison. It was no wonder Annie had noticed Hannah's silence today.

"Nothing's wrong," Hannah answered, not quite managing a smile as she set down her glass. "Just trying to stop the self-deprecating tape running through my brain and focus on all this lovely scenery." She looked past Annie, out the wavy glass of the window set deep in the stone wall behind her, to the distant beach and the sea beyond. "The panoramic views and light breezes have made today's hike seem like it's right out of a travel film."

Annie pressed her lips into a sympathetic smile. "Well, that's why ya're 'ere—to enjoy the surroundings. Sorry yer troubles are takin' away from it."

"Not at all—no worries." Hannah brightened, then shifted the focus to Annie. "I am curious about you, though, if it's not too intrusive. I know we Americans have a reputation for 'TMI' and asking personal questions that would seem inappropriate to you Brits."

"Ask away." Annie grinned, holding up her hands, palms-up. "Anythin'. I'm an open book."

"Okay." Hannah took a drink of ale. "Your website mentions you graduated from St. Andrew's University with an Art History degree. How did you go from there to here?"

"My two best friends at uni and I used to spend our free time takin' hikes around the countryside. We used to conjure up scenarios of what our work lives would look like if we could find a way to incorporate hikin' with a job. In our last year, we committed to makin' a business out of it."

Annie's eyes were sparkling as she recounted starting her business. She paused to sip from her glass before going on.

"After graduatin', we all took on low payin', flexible jobs, lived together in a wet, rottin' flat." Although she made a face, the underlying amusement told Hannah she hadn't truly minded it much. "We saved our money and started our business on the side as soon as we could. After a couple o' years, we were able to do it full time. At first, my parents thought it was a horrible idea. Now that we're successful, they think startin' this business was the most brilliant concept ever." Annie chuckled.

"And your two best friends became your business partners." Hannah posed the question as a statement.

Annie nodded.

"I saw their pics on your website. You're very pretty. They're both good looking."

Annie's smile turned coy. "Yeah, they are."

"You know what I'm going to ask, don't you?" Hannah couldn't keep herself from beaming.

Annie laughed. "I s'ppose I do. I've never hooked up with either of them, if that's what you're gettin' at. My partners are my business partners, and each other's partners."

"Oh, I see." Hannah understood, only mildly disappointed to find there was only business between Annie and her attractive coworkers. With no dirty details to pursue behind the scenes of the hiking tours business, Hannah shifted the focus to Annie's college years. "Did you attend the University of St. Andrew's when the Duke and Duchess of Cambridge were there?"

"Yes. I was a couple o' years behind 'em."

"Did you ever see them around campus? You should have pursued the Prince." Hannah waggled her eyebrows.

Annie blew an amused puff of air through her nose. "Yes, I did see 'em, but 1 didn't know 'em. They had a lot of security, and most o' the students respected 'eir privacy." She paused when a plump, white-haired woman bustled from the kitchen and set two plates of fish and chips on the table. After thanking her, Annie went on.

"Besides, I didn't run in their posh circles. I did take some classes with Kate because we were both readin' for a Master of Arts degree in Art History. I never spoke to 'er, though." She plucked up a thick potato spear and took a bite. "As far as pursuin' the Prince, I would have been more inclined to pursue Kate than William, if it were possible."

"Gosh, Annie, that was the second insensitive remark I made about your personal life." Warmth flooded Hannah's cheeks. "I should know better than to make assumptions. Please forgive me."

"Nothin' to forgive," Annie assured, her tone sincere as she shook malt vinegar onto her chips. "I said ya could ask me anythin', and I meant it."

As they ate in silence for a moment, Hannah wondered if she should open up to Annie about her personal life. It might do her some good, she decided, to talk about the things going on that had brought her to Scotland, if not a few of the things she had experienced once here.

At last, she started, "I guess I'm just a hopeless romantic, although I should be the most cynical person around. I thought I'd achieved my perfect, happy ending, but I was kidding myself. I wound up leaving my jerk-off husband, and this trip is a reward to myself after the divorce was finalized."

Annie gave a sympathetic nod. "Right. Separatin' and divorcin' is emotionally drainin'. But when someone 'as the courage to push themselves into something unknown because 'eir gut tells 'em it's a healthier choice, it's amazing what they can do. Would ya have taken this trip when you were married?"

"Ha. Great question," Hannah quipped, popping a bite of fish into her mouth. She washed it down with a swallow of ale before she responded, "The answer is no. I wouldn't have. I would have been too busy with my daughter, my husband's to-do lists, my job. My ex wouldn't let me travel alone either, although he was big on guilt trips." Hannah gave Annie a half-smiling apology for the corny line. "I do feel embarrassed saying things like, 'He wouldn't let me.' It makes me sound like a passive child. I should say, 'I didn't allow myself to travel alone,' because the truth is, I had control over my own life. I made choices. I have to take responsibility for those choices."

Hannah's thoughts took a quick detour to Eric and what had happened the night before, but she refused to let them linger there.

"No one can make another person feel bad without their consent," she continued. "The divorce has had some positive results, though. My ex spends a lot more time with our daughter now, and he and I interact much more in an adult/adult way rather than adult/child or even traditional husband/wife manner."

"Talkin' about it is a sure sign ya've grown personally through the experience," Annie commented, looking impressed.

Hannah sighed. "Growth and wisdom aren't coming fast enough for me," she said with a wry smirk. "Still, I've pushed myself in many ways in my personal life that continue to surprise me. I'm not sure the decisions I've made, even recently, have been for the best. For me and for others, but I'm learning in the process."

When a scene from the previous night flashed through Hannah's mind again, she decided to focus on something more upbeat.

Brightening, she continued to banter on, "I'm moving from L.A. to New York after this trip. My ex-husband's been promoted. He'll be heading up his firm's entire real estate transactional and litigation departments, so he'll be moving to the main office in Manhattan." Although Lawrence didn't have to work, he liked the rainmaking aspect of his job. And there was no doubt he loved the prestige and power that were perks of becoming the youngest head partner at the firm. The timing was right for both him and Hannah. She was more than ready for a big lifestyle change.

"And, since it's important to me for my daughter, Charli, to be close to her father," she went on, "we've decided to move to New York, too. I'm looking forward to what this new chapter will bring."

"Progress!" Annie exclaimed. "Good for you. I think it was your Benjamin Franklin who said, 'Without continual growth and progress, such words as improvement, achievement, and success 'ave no meaning.'"

"It was," Hannah confirmed with a smile. "And I can see why some of the testimonials on your website claim you and your partners should charge for therapy fees."

Annie laughed. "We discussed whether we should post those testimonials or not. We didn't want potential customers to think we're sanctimonious asses or that we give out unsolicited advice."

"Those testimonials are what inspired me to book with your company," Hannah admitted.

"Good. Then I'm glad we posted 'em." Annie held up her glass. "Ere's to positive feedback."

Hannah touched her glass to Annie's. "And to personal growth through experiencing the untouched beauty of Scotland's magnificent hiking trails."

"We've got plenty of those lined up for ya," Annie confirmed, wiping her fingers with a paper napkin. "And speakin' of which, we'd better get started hikin' back to the car. I promised to have ya back to the hotel no later'an six, and I mean to keep my word."

"It doesn't matter what time I return." Hannah waived away Annie's concern. "I have no plans this evening, only packing the things I'll be taking on the next part of the trip. What time did you say we'll need to leave to catch the train?"

"I'll pick you up at noon," Annie affirmed as she counted out bills from her wallet to pay for their meal. "And Caesar and Henry'll meet you in Glasgow. The walks you signed up for there are both city hikes. One takes you along the Mural Trail and the other is a tour of the historical churches in the city." She grinned and lifted a brow. "If the colorful urban art doesn't take your mind off your worries, you'll surely find peace in the gorgeous Gothic churches."

Hannah nodded, rising from her chair to follow Annie out of the pub. If there was one thing she was ready for, it was moving forward. And getting some peace of mind while she was at it would be a nice bonus.

Chapter 8

The low drone of conversation hummed over soothing strains of classical music as Hannah took a furtive peek around the Munro from the bar's entrance. Upon returning from her coastal hike, she had decided to have a quick bite before going to her room to pack, but she wasn't up for a dramatic confrontation. The tense knots in her shoulders relaxed when she confirmed Eric was nowhere in sight.

Spotting Knox behind the bar, Hannah strolled over and sat on a stool across from him.

"Good evening." His greeting was pleasant and professional. "Can I get ya a Belhaven Ale, or something else?"

"You remembered what I drink?" A warm tingle of surprise fizzled through her.

"Yir hard to forget." An unreadable look sparked in his eye.

"Thanks." Unsure how to interpret his words and his expression, Hannah fumbled a bit to respond. "Uh, yes. An ale would be nice."

When Knox took a fresh glass and stepped to the taps to pour her drink, Hannah considered him. It seemed just looking at the guy made her wet. But why? He wasn't her type. Then again, what about tall, dark, handsome, and Scottish wasn't her type? And he was always so nice to her, chatting her up, remembering she favored Belhaven Ale. Of course, it was likely he was required to be friendly to all the guests.

You've had your fling, she told herself when he set her drink down in front of her. *Just enjoy the rest of the trip and forget about the bartender.*

"Would ya like some food?" Knox busied himself wiping down the counter as he spoke.

When she answered, "Yes, please," he motioned to a server, who was at her side in seconds with a menu.

As Hannah looked over the list of options, debating between ordering a salad and an appetizer or an actual meal, the back of her neck began to prickle. Out of the corner of her eye, she found Eric standing a few feet away, a dozen red roses in his hand.

Oh God. Noooooo.

As soon as she turned and noticed him, he began to sing.

"You gotta go and get angry at all of my honesty ..."

Before he could mangle Justin Bieber the way he had the Beach Boys, Hannah sprang up from her seat and interrupted him. "Eric—please. Stop singing."

Still he continued on with his musical apology, either ignoring her pleas or unable to hear her over his caterwauling.

Unwilling to let him manipulate her into spending a minute more with him, she took another stab at stopping him. "Please, Eric. Don't do this. If you don't leave, I will."

As Eric continued singing his heart out, Hannah cast a pleading glance at Knox. It appeared he was trying to keep from laughing.

Catching the desperate look Hannah was giving him, Knox sobered and stepped in. "Hey, mate," he started, his tone forceful enough to get Eric's attention. When he stopped singing, Knox continued, "The lady doesn't want ya pestering her. Yir going t'ave to leave her alone."

Eric's jaw went taught and his nostrils flared. When he spoke, he aimed his loud words, dripping with anger, at Hannah. "Ya seemed to like it when I sang to ya before. Or was that all part of the fake personality ya created to get a quick shag, ya bloody bitch? You and yer dirty sex talk. Yir a fucking whore!"

Eric's words hit too close to home for Hannah's comfort. Even so, his verbal attack felt like a physical slap. They left her stunned, and she couldn't believe he was saying these awful things to her. Realizing the bar had gone quiet, Hannah looked around and found the rest of the crowd watching them with curiosity. Her tongue tied, Hannah was grateful when Knox responded.

"Right. That's it. Yir done." His arms folded across his chest as if he were holding himself back, Knox gestured with his chin toward the door. "Ya need to leave."

Slowly, Eric shifted his gaze from glaring at Hannah to regarding Knox. "But I sang to 'er and brought 'er flowers. I thought she liked me." Eric locked his eyes on Hannah again and implored, "I thought we had a special connection."

By then, Knox had come around from behind the bar to face Eric. It reminded Hannah of two giants from The Game of Thrones matching off.

"The problem with grand gestures, ya know," Knox said in an even tone, "is for them to work, both sides have to be on the same page. Hannah obviously doesn't feel the way you do. Ya have to get over it. And no one would blame her for not liking ya if they heard the bollocks ya just spewed."

"But I love 'er."

At that, Hannah's head shot back as if someone had smashed her in her forehead with a two-by-four. Eric's despairing claim stunned her even further.

"Okay, that's it," Knox warned, clearly at his limit. "Now ya sound like a nutter." He nudged Eric toward the door. "Go home and lick yer wounds. Ya aren't welcome here for a few weeks. Ya need to cool off. And don't try to contact Hannah or get in touch with her again."

Knox gestured to a shorter man who hurried over. He looked as wide as he was tall and appeared to be all muscle.

"Michael is goin'ta walk ya to yer car," Knox told Eric. "Mind what I told ya. Don't do anything stupid, anything yir going to regret. I don't want to have to get the police involved. I will, though, if ya keep coming in to bother the guests."

As Michael walked Eric to the door, Knox motioned a nearby server over and whispered something into her ear.

The sight of Eric trudging away, clutching the roses, his shoulders slumped, was the final straw for Hannah.

"God—I made such a mess of things." Tears filled her eyes and one spilled over to roll down her face. She slumped onto a barstool and buried her face in her hands. "I'd go back to my room, but I'm too humiliated to walk past everyone."

Knox touched her shoulder, the light pressure and warmth comforting. "You can go to yer room, lass. And don't worry about yer drink. It's on the house. Don't feel ya have to leave, though. Look around."

Hannah lifted her head, avoiding Knox's gaze, and picked up a cocktail napkin. As she dabbed it to her eyes, she peeked around the room.

"See?" Knox swept his hand toward the crowd around them. "Everyone is back to minding themselves. Why not finish yer drink and have something to eat? That wanker won't be back, but I'll keep watch and make sure he doesn't approach ya again. Ya have my word. Ye'll be long gone by the time he's allowed back into the hotel again." The concern in his dark eyes was reassuring enough to bring a weak smile to Hannah's face.

As he walked back to his station behind the bar, he went on, "Ya don't have to stay here, either, if ya really want to go back to your room. Don't feel any pressure to do anything ya don't want to do."

Hannah shook her head. "No. I'll stay and finish my drink. But I'm not hungry. I've lost my appetite."

The corners of Knox's mouth curved in a sympathetic smile. "I'll have Wendy bring ya a platter of starters. Ya can pick at them. Eat what ya want and leave the rest."

"Okay, I guess," Hannah acquiesced. Whether Knox was only doing his job or not, it felt good to have someone taking care of her for a change.

As she nibbled at the appetizers and sipped at her drink, Hannah sat facing the bar with her back to the room. Although conversation was buzzing at a normal pace, she still didn't want to risk catching someone looking at her with curious interest. After her glass was empty and she had made as much of a dent in the hors d'oeuvres as she could, Hannah made her way down the bar to where Knox stood sorting through drink tickets. When she sat down in front of him, he looked up.

"Is everything alright? Was there a problem with the starters?"

"No. The food was great, thank you," she assured him, managing what she hoped was a believable smile. "I wanted to ask you a quick question."

With a nod, he set the tickets aside. "Right. Ask away."

Hannah bit her lip, then plunged in. "Last night when I walked out of here with that guy, Eric, you gave me a 'stranger danger' look."

Knox's brow furrowed. "Stranger danger?"

"It's something they tell kids in the States. It means to be wary of adults and people you don't know. After what happened, I thought maybe you knew something about Eric. Is he a known stalker? A criminal or something?"

"Ah. I see." Crossing his forearms on the bar, Knox leaned forward, holding Hannah's gaze. "No. I've seen him in here a few times. It wasn't a stranger danger look I gave ya last night, though. I dinna know anything about him, and I certainly don't know anything about his personal life."

Hannah dropped her eyes, feeling a bit embarrassed. "Oh. Okay. I must have misread your expression."

"You dinna."

Looking up again, Hannah frowned. "What do you mean?"

"I mean, you dinna misread my expression." Leaning closer, Knox dropped his voice so only Hannah could hear him. "But it wasn't a stranger danger look, as you put it. It put me out when you took off with him because I was hoping we could get to know each other better. I guess I was jealous." A self-conscious smile spread on his face. "Maybe ya have an effect on male Scots, because I thought we had a connection, too."

Hannah sat gaping at him, her mouth open like a fish out of water gasping for air.

Seeing her speechless, Knox's smile softened. "It seems you've had too much, ah, excitement, for tonight. I just don't want ya to think yir misreading things."

"Oh. I ... don't know what to say," Hannah sputtered, finding her voice.

"You don't have to say anything. Sorry to lay that on ya," Knox whispered, drawing back to stand up. "I've got to get back to work. Ya should go to bed. Get some sleep," he told her. "Everything will seem better in the morning.

Although Hannah opened her mouth to speak, she wasn't sure what to say.

Knox smiled at her, although she couldn't tell if it was the one he put on for customers, or if there was meaning behind it. "Have a good evening, Hannah. Enjoy the rest of your trip." And with that, he gathered up the drink tickets and walked to the cash register at the other end of the bar.

Dumbfounded, Hannah watched him go. This, she decided as she rose from the barstool to leave, had certainly been a night of surprises.

Chapter 9

The following morning, Hannah was awake early. Although she had planned on packing the night before, she found the hike earlier the day before had added to the unexpected events of the evening, sapping all her energy. She had followed Knox's advice instead and gone straight to bed. Surprisingly, her sleep had been restful. Before the alarm on her phone went off, she was out of bed and ordering room service for breakfast. While she dressed and packed, she sipped at the strong, hot coffee, then sat down to write a note to Knox. As she wrote, Hannah ate a scone and nibbled on the berries served on the side. With that task complete, she called the front desk to check out, then went to the lobby and found the concierge.

"Good morning," Hannah greeted the woman standing at the desk studying papers in a binder. "Since the bar is closed for a few more hours, I'd like to leave this with you. It's a note for Knox, the bartender." She held out the cream-colored Prestige Hotel envelope she had found in the desk drawer of her room along with the stationery she had written her message on.

The woman's eyes slid from her paperwork to the envelope, then up to Hannah's face. "Knox Munro? You'll have to take it to the administrative offices behind the lobby."

Hannah's brows dipped. "No. The bartender, Knox. The one who was working in the bar last night."

A knowing smirk appeared on the concierge's lips. "Yes. That's him. He works in the administrative offices during the day. Women *fall—*" her fingers twitched, making air quotes, "—for the *bartender—*" more air quotes, "—all the time. You can leave the note with his assistant." Her eyes dropped back to her binder.

Disconcerted, Hannah stood there for a moment. "Okay. Thank you," she replied to the top of the woman's head.

Turning, Hannah moved in the general direction of the front desk, the concierge's condescending response giving her second thoughts about leaving the note. She checked the time on her phone and, seeing as she still had thirty minutes before Annie would arrive to pick her up, she made up her mind. Apparently, people were bitchy around the world. It wasn't just an L.A. thing. Good to know. Hannah decided to get over it, leave the note, and have another coffee. It would give her a chance to psych herself up about seeing Glasgow and the famous Highlands she had been reading about forever.

As she approached the door set back in a corner near the front desk, Hannah spotted the brass placard above it, engraved with the words "Administrative Offices." When she tried the knob, it was locked, so she pressed the button below a small speaker next to the door. Within seconds, a woman's voice spoke through the intercom.

"May I help you?"

"Yes," Hannah replied. "I'm Hannah Vander Dussen. I've just checked out and I'd like to leave a note for Knox. The bartender from the Munro. Can you give it to him for me, please?"

There was a brief silence, then the woman said coolly, "One moment."

It turned out to be a long moment. After what seemed like an eternity, Hannah looked at her cellphone. It had only been five minutes. With a sigh, she decided she would wait another five minutes before leaving. Her gaze sweeping up, Hannah noticed a security camera over the door, its unblinking eye trained on her. She shifted uneasily and looked away. What was this? TSA? If the woman behind the door hadn't forgotten her, could she look forward to a strip search before being allowed to leave her note? Hannah's brow lifted in a speculative arch. Come to think of it, she wouldn't mind Knox performing a full-body search.

Just then, the door opened, and heat flooded Hannah's cheeks when she saw Knox himself standing on the other side.

"Hannah. Is anything wrong?" His dark eyes clouded with concern. "Are you alright?"

"No, I'm fine," Hannah affirmed when she regained her voice. "I just wanted to leave a note for you. I'm leaving soon for your hometown."

Knox's expression softened. "Ah, I see. Come in. We can talk in my office."

His office? Since when did bartenders have offices?

"I don't want to bother you," Hannah commented, following him through the foyer of the administrative offices. With Carrara marble mosaic tile floors and what looked like antiques furnishing the waiting area, the offices were as posh and elegant as the rest of the hotel.

"It's no bother. Can I get ya something? Would ya like a cup of coffee? Or tea?"

"Coffee, please."

Knox stopped beside a desk in front of a hallway with offices on either side. An older, gray-haired woman with a confident air of efficiency sat behind it.

"Justine, please bring Hannah a coffee." He turned to Hannah. "How d'ya take it?"

When she told him she liked her coffee with a little milk, he directed Justine, "A coffee with milk, please. And nothing for me, thank ya. We'll be in my office."

Knox led Hannah down the hallway to the corner office at the end. Like the rest of the administrative area and the hotel beyond, the spacious room was luxurious. Plus, the views of the manicured gardens and the stone wall running around the perimeter of the property lent the office an Old-World appeal, adding a charming nuance to it all. It was a space, however, where a lot of work was obviously done. In addition to the desktop computer and the laptop on the gigantic antique Venezia desk, stacks of files and paperwork cluttered it.

"This is a nice office for a bartender," Hannah remarked, taking everything in. "Are you also a manager?"

"I own the hotel." Knox gestured for her to take a seat on the antique Venezia sofa, angled across from the desk in the perfect spot to enjoy the garden view. Instead of sitting beside her or taking one of the chairs upholstered in gray silk facing the sofa, he leaned back against the desk, his legs crossed at the ankles. "I work in the bar when we're short staffed."

That explained a lot, and it left Hannah at a loss for words.

"Oh. I didn't know."

"No reason ya would." Knox crossed his arms. "Ya mentioned a note?"

Before Hannah could hand it over, Justine came in with a silver tray bearing a matching silver coffee service. Next to it sat a miniature silver pitcher and a porcelain cup and saucer decorated with a pretty pink rose pattern. Justine had also included a slim silver vase holding a single delicate pink rose that matched the pattern on the china. With practiced care, she set it on the ornate cherry wood side table next to Hannah.

After thanking his secretary and dismissing her with instructions he wasn't to be disturbed, Knox came and sat next to Hannah. He poured her coffee, added milk, and stirred it with a silver spoon, so delicate and small it looked almost silly in his big hand. When he handed the cup to her, he inquired again, "So. The note?"

"Yes. I wanted to leave a note for you." Hannah produced it and gave it to him. "God, I've mentioned this note so many times to so many people this morning, you'd think it was the Magna Carta."

She took a sip of coffee as she watched him open it and read it.

"I wasn't expecting to give it to you in person." She bit at her lip, unsure why she felt compelled to explain.

When Knox finished reading and looked up with a serious expression, Hannah cringed inside. She had the uncomfortable feeling of being an awkward teen-aged girl asking a boy to the Sadie Hawkins dance. She pinched her lips together between her teeth to keep from saying anything to add to her embarrassment.

"First of all," Knox began, breaking the silence and saving her from herself, "ya have nothing to apologize for. I didn't do anything for ya I wouldn't have done fir any guest receiving unwanted attention in the bar. That guy was out of line when he said those vile things to ya, and ya have nothing to feel guilty about." He paused and gave her a pointed look as if to assure himself she understood him. "Secondly," he went on, the serious edge slipping from his tone, "did ya mean what ya wrote about wanting to see me again next week when ya come back through Edinburgh?"

Hannah took another sip of coffee, and swallowed, before mumbling, "Yes."

Knox smiled. "And yir leaving today fir Glasgow?"

When Hannah nodded, he asked, "Where are ya staying?"

"I'm staying at the Prestige Hotel there, too." Her voice was coming out so small and quiet, she could only hope Knox heard her.

He did. His smile brightening, he concurred, "Of course ya are. It's the best hotel in the city."

"I suppose you own it, too." Hannah smirked. It should have occurred to her right away, but Knox was so full of surprises, she was having a hard time keeping up.

"I suppose I do." A twinkle lit Knox's eyes and he tilted his head a bit, as if an idea had just struck him. "I need to go to Glasgow to check on some things there. Would ya feel I'm being too forward if I asked ya to have dinner with me tomorrow night? The hotel has an excellent restaurant, if yir interested."

Hannah's heart thumped a happy beat. "Yes. Of course I'd like to have dinner with you." She struggled to merely look pleased instead of grinning like a fool.

Apparently, Knox had no reservations about showing his level of joy at the prospect of a date with Hannah. His face lit up and he beamed. "Good. The restaurant is called 'Francesca.' I'll meet ya there at 9:00 p.m. tomorrow night. How does that sound?"

"It sounds great," Hannah confirmed, certain her heart couldn't take this level of happiness. When the ornate vintage clock on Knox's desk began chiming the noon hour, Hannah remembered her plans. "I should get going," she admitted, regretting not coming to find Knox sooner. Oh well. At least she would be seeing him again soon.

Taking Hannah's hand, Knox offered to walk her out. She felt a little moment of triumph when they walked by the concierge desk and Air Quote Girl's jaw dropped. It was a struggle, but Hannah managed to keep her eyes straight ahead and her expression composed.

Annie was waiting at the valet area when they came through the hotel doors. The bellhop had already loaded Hannah's luggage into Annie's Kia Sportage so, once Hannah had introduced Knox to Annie, the women were ready to go. Before Hannah stepped into Annie's car, Knox pulled her closer and kissed her lips. Although it was quicker than Hannah would have liked, it was still heated and full of promise.

"I'll see ya tomorrow night," Knox whispered before letting her go.

A shiver tingled through Hannah's body. With a meaningful smile, she squeezed his hand. "I can't wait."

Chapter 10

T he only way Hannah managed to get any sleep the night she arrived in Glasgow, she was certain, was the walking tour. Right after picking her up at the train station and driving her to the hotel, Caesar and Henry took her on a city hike. In addition to being as attractive in person as their online pictures promised, they were friendly, knowledgeable, and talkative. They filled her in on local history, hot spots for live music, and they took her to the outskirts of the city center shopping district.

"In case ya want to do a bit o' walkin' and shoppin' on yer own," Henry explained.

Between the interesting turn her morning had taken and the journey to Glasgow, the afternoon hike did Hannah in. By the time her guides returned her to the hotel, she was exhausted. After a hot shower and a simple room-service dinner of hairst bree—a delicious vegetable soup with tiny chunks of lamb—and a miniature loaf of crusty brown bread, Hannah sent Charli a short text to see when she woke up. Although it would be early morning in California, Hannah had promised to text at least every day, and she hadn't missed a check-in yet. Then, she got into bed and turned out the light, falling asleep practically before her head hit the pillow.

The following evening, when she walked into the Francesca, Hannah was glad she had turned in early the night before. She had gotten the rest she needed for her hike along the Glasgow Mural Trail and the evening ahead with Knox. She cast an anxious look around as she stepped through the restaurant's entrance. There was no seating, and people were lined up waiting for tables. When the hostess, a pretty, slender Asian woman, behind the rostrum saw her, she asked, "Hannah?"

"Yes."

The woman nodded and beckoned Hannah to follow her. "Right this way."

Ah, the perks of knowing the hotel's owner.

A surge of satisfaction fought with slight self-consciousness as Hannah nudged her way through the crowd, some casting envious glances at her. The hostess led Hannah through the bustling restaurant to a back room.

When the woman opened the door, Hannah found Knox seated at a table in a private room, studying his cellphone screen. He looked up and smiled, then placed the phone in his pocket and stood to come to her. Taking her hands, he gave Hannah a European greeting, a kiss on both cheeks. Her entire body tingled at his touch.

So. Knox Munro was as charming as she had remembered, and even more striking, if it was possible. She took in his impeccable Armani suit, Versace tie and Stefano and Mario shoes. The man liked his Italian designers, and she couldn't say she disapproved. And how had she forgotten how handsome he was? It hit her like a tidal wave every time she saw him again, leaving her feeling a bit off kilter.

"Thank you, Edith," Knox said to the hostess. "Can you ask Sandy to give us a few minutes before she takes our orders?

"Certainly, Mr. Munro," Edith replied as she stepped from the room.

Once the door had closed, Knox turned back to Hannah, setting her Oroton clutch aside and taking both her hands in his. He stepped back and took her in, giving an appreciative nod at her red Christian Dior haute couture cocktail dress and Valentino poudre 'Rockstud ' t-strap pumps. Although it was the first time she had worn the ensemble anywhere, it wasn't new. She had bought it for a wedding anniversary dinner, had spent an entire day shopping for the perfect outfit. When Lawrence saw her in it, however, he had insisted she change.

"Your bosoms are too big to wear something that low cut," he had remarked, his tone suggesting she should know better. "I want you to look like my wife, not like a trollop."

So she had changed into a black Chanel outfit he approved of. After all, the point of wearing the dress was to please him.

Now, however, there was no doubt. Knox thoroughly approved of the dress. He slid his hands along her upper arms, a dark, hungry look in his eyes. "May I kiss you?" he asked.

When Hannah nodded, he bent to brush his mouth against hers. When his tongue swiped gently across the seam of her lips, she opened them and let him in. He stroked at the inside of her mouth, exploring in surges of gentle thrusts and tantalizing retreats, giving Hannah the opportunity to do some exploring of her own. It was the sexiest kiss she had ever had.

God, I'm in trouble.

No sooner had the thought drifted through her muddled mind, than Knox pulled Hannah closer, tightening his grip on her waist, and deepening the kiss. Pressed against his body, embraced in his strong arms and her head swimming from the effects of his skilled tongue, Hannah lost all track of time and space. Nothing registered, not her past, not her future, only this amazing moment and equally amazing kiss. It felt too good, heating her core and igniting her blood, the inferno moving through her body and into her private parts.

There was no question. The man could kiss.

After what seemed like forever, both Hannah and Knox broke apart at the same time.

"I've been wantin' to kiss ya since I first saw ya." Knox exhaled, heat still smoldering in his eyes. "But I wasn't expectin' to get this carried away in the first few minutes of seeing ya tonight."

Hannah gave him a coy smirk. "In case it wasn't obvious, I enjoyed it too."

Knox smiled and moved to pull out a chair. "Please have a seat. I've ordered champagne for us, unless ya prefer something else?"

"Champagne is great," Hannah concurred as she sat down.

Pulling a bottle of Dom Perignon Rosé from the ice bucket sitting on a stand next to the table, Knox opened it like the expert he was. He popped the cork without spilling a drop, then poured a glass for each of them. They toasted to a wonderful evening, locking eyes and holding each other's gaze as they drank.

As if on cue, Sandy came in with menus. When Hannah got a look at the number of different choices, all described in such delicious, tempting ways, she declared, "I'm not sure what to order. Everything sounds so good."

"Everything *is* good," Sandy assured her.

Hannah looked to Knox, perplexed. "What do you recommend?"

"Do ya have any food allergies?" he asked, looking thoughtful. "Or any foods ya want to try or prefer to avoid?"

"Not really." Hannah shook her head. "Do you mind ordering for me? Since you know the menu so well."

They settled on the tasting menu, to allow Hannah to try a bit of everything, and Sandy and another server were back within minutes, delivering the first course.

Over warm oysters with spinach, garlic, and ginger on a parsley salad, Hannah and Knox engaged in easy conversation. They talked about favorite books, authors, and poets—his was Dryden, and he gave an appreciative nod when she told him hers was Thoreau. All the typical first date get-to-know-you topics were covered, like movies they had seen and funny experiences, and Hannah told him about retiring early from the city attorney's office. Knox revealed that, in addition to owning the Prestige hotels with a partner, he also had a stake in the family whiskey business.

"Our Scotch whiskey is becoming one of our most successful enterprises. It's especially popular with the Americans," Knox informed Hannah with a sparkle of pride in his eyes.

They also talked more about the personal things they already knew about each other. Knox revealed a bit more about his wife, and that she had died of ovarian cancer. Hannah expressed her sympathy again. When he told her his sons had been the grounding elements that kept him going, Hannah told him all about Charli. She told him how wanting the best for her daughter had given her the courage to walk away from a toxic marriage.

"She's the light of my life, and I want to set a good example and give her a strong foundation for a successful, happy future," Hannah confided.

"It's why we do what we do, isn't it?" Knox agreed. "It's gratifying to build a successful business, but the best part is the legacy for my boys."

"Do they work in the hotel business, too?" Hannah asked.

"Stuart's pursuing a law degree at University," Knox shared, unable to hide his paternal pride. "And Sam works for the family whiskey company. They're both good lads, and I'm proud of them. I'm hoping to bring Sam into the Prestige Hotel soon, on the management side. He worries about nepotism and wants to learn the ropes before he gets more responsibility, so he works in the bar here at night in the summer."

"So, your last name, Munro, is the same as the bar in Edinburgh."

"Yes. The bars and restaurants are all family names. This restaurant is named Francesca, after mi mam. The bar here is named the Holiday, for my business partner, Thomas Holiday, and the dining restaurant of the Prestige in Edinburgh is named for his mam, the Janet."

Hannah cocked her head. "Your mom is Francesca? Her name doesn't sound very Scottish."

"Mi mam's Italian. She was a foreign exchange student here, and she and mi da fell in love. She went home when her term was through, then came back a few years later, and they got married."

The story was delightful and romantic. Just as Hannah was about to comment on it, she realized Sandy was bringing in more food. With a frown, she recounted the dishes that seemed to have come non-stop the entire time she and Knox had been talking.

She cast a hapless gaze at the long platter Sandy set down. It was decorated with chocolate mousse and whipped cream swirls garlanding Calimyrna figs and pistachio nuts. Scattered among the dollops of mousse and cream were a selection of small almond-dough cups holding different types of homemade gelatos—strawberry, chocolate, vanilla, Neapolitan, fig, and pistachio. The final course? Hopefully. Hannah was beyond stuffed.

She looked at Knox. "I've kind of lost track, but isn't this about the twentieth course?"

"No, sweetheart," he told her with a chuckle. "There are only seven courses in the tasting menu."

"*Only* seven?"

Her reaction made him laugh again. "Eat as much or as little as ya like, no pressure. Ya *are* hiking during the day, though."

Hannah snickered. "I'd have to climb the Matterhorn to burn off tonight's dinner. Don't get me wrong. Everything is very delicious. It's impossible not to indulge too much."

As Sandy made a quiet exit, Hannah scooped up a spoonful of the mousse and looked at Knox. "This is nice. I'm having such a good time, and you're so easy to talk to. I'd probably tell you anything and everything, my silliest, most embarrassing secrets, and wouldn't think twice."

Knox lifted an eyebrow and leaned in. "Oh, really? What silly, embarrassing secrets could a delightful lass like you be keeping?"

Hannah's lips curved in a coy smile. Maybe the wine had gone to her head, or maybe Knox was as easy to talk to as she had thought. Before she could think better of it, Hannah spilled the entire story about her infamous bucket list.

"So getting together with that kid at the bar was part of yir Bucket List?" Knox sounded as if he was trying to control his astonishment.

"Well, first, he's not a kid," Hannah hedged, regretting spilling this particular secret. It wasn't exactly first-date information. "I'm sure he's got to be in his mid-twenties, at least. And, second, yes— it was number five on my Bucket List, but it's finished. I tossed the list already. It was a bad idea, and I'm not going to do it again. Eric wasn't an object to use and throw away. Just because he's male, it doesn't mean it was acceptable for me to toy with his feelings. I wouldn't appreciate it if a man treated me that way, so I shouldn't be a hypocrite."

"He's an adult, and he said some contemptible things to ya. You shouldn't make excuses for him," Knox argued. Then his expression shifted. "You are a barrister, though, and ya specialize in prosecuting criminal cases. Ya understand human behavior. It was foolish to have taken such a chance."

When Hannah told him about her research into the knife and weapon laws in the U.K., and about the Rape Safe class she took with Grace, Knox's expression changed. His displeased concern dissolved into laughter.

"At least ya were prepared, then," he chortled, wiping his eyes with his napkin.

Hannah couldn't stop herself from laughing, too. When she thought about it, the whole thing did seem kind of bizarre.

Once their laughter died away, Knox let a beat of silence pass before he said, "I've got to wonder, though, and ya can tell me to fuck off if it's too personal, but why would ya have sex with a stranger on yir bucket list? Were things between you and your ex-husband less than... satisfying?"

His question made Hannah's mouth go dry. Although she had claimed she wouldn't hesitate to reveal to him every secret she had, this part of her past was humiliating. She didn't want Knox to see her as the people-pleasing doormat whose husband felt the need to screw other women. She dropped her eyes from his and tried to think of a way to answer.

"Yes, you could say that," Hannah replied at last in a subdued tone. "Not that we had sex often. He got his, um, satisfaction outside of the marriage." A low hum began ringing in her ears at the admission. What would Knox think of her now?

Setting his plate aside, he reached across the table to lift her chin, forcing her to meet his eyes. "There's nothing to be ashamed of. It sounds like yir ex-husband was a controlling wanker. Whatever his issues, they never had anything to do with you. It's more likely they had more to do with his psychoses than his sexual proclivities."

Hannah shifted in her seat. "It's nice of you to say—"

"It's not just kindness and courtesy," Knox insisted, dropping his fingers from her face to clasp her hand. "I'm trying to find out what makes ya tick. Can I ask ya another question?"

Unsure what he would come up with next, Hannah agreed anyway. "Okay."

"When it came to sex, did ya like taking direction from him, yir ex?"

Although she hadn't known what to expect, the question took Hannah off-guard. "I, well... is that necessary for you to know?" she stammered.

His expression shifted and his grip on her hand loosened the slightest bit. "I don't want to push ya to talk about it if it's uncomfortable and, as I said, if it's none of my business ..."

Hannah expelled a despairing sigh. As the Brits said, in for a penny, in for a pound. "As a matter of fact, I did," she blurted before she could stop herself. "Oh God, this is so embarrassing. Yeah, I liked it when he dominated me in bed. But when I wanted to try different things, you know, to explore, even to talk about doing something new, he was disgusted with me."

"As I said. Wanker." Knox gave a decisive nod. "Sex is, or should be, an important part of everyone's lives. There's no shame in discussing it openly." He eyed her for a moment, then added, "To be honest, I think you're somewhat of a sexual submissive, but maybe it's just wishful thinking on my part."

Crinkling her brow, Hannah questioned, "Sexual submissive? Do you mean like BDSM?"

Amused, Knox smiled. "No, not hard core BDSM. I don't get off on whipping women—well, ya do have a tight, wee round ass I'd like to spank some time. In general, though, it's not my thing. I'm not a sadist. I don't get off on sharing or exhibitionism. What I feel you should know is that I like to dominate in the bedroom.

But I wouldn't push you into anything you don't want because of your bad past experiences."

In the bedroom? A thrill sizzled through Hannah's core. If that was where this evening was headed, the discomfort and embarrassing questions were worth it. Her lips curving in a coy smile, she teased, "And you're telling me this because ...?"

With a grin, Knox pushed his chair back from the table, his long, muscled legs spread wide. Patting his leg, he gestured for Hannah to come closer.

Without hesitation, she stood and came to him.

He pulled her down onto one of his legs, closing her in with his other one. Fixing her with an intentional gaze, one of Knox's hands slid behind her back while he reached up with the other to smooth her hair back from her face.

Tiny chills shot through her as his fingers drifted down her cheek and her neck, then traced a feather-light path across her collar bone and further down between her breasts.

"I'm telling you this," he said, his voice low, "because I'm attracted to ya. And I flatter myself that you're attracted to me, as well." He lightly pressed his palm to her torso and smoothed it down her stomach, coming to rest on her thigh, which he gave a gentle squeeze.

All the while, Hannah gazed into his eyes, trying to concentrate on his words instead of his tantalizing touch.

She smiled weakly and gave a slight nod. "Even though I was attracted to you from the beginning, I didn't pursue it because I didn't think it was mutual. I thought you were only being nice to me because it was part of your job. On a sexual level … I don't have much experience interacting with men. I've only ever had intercourse with one man, other than my ex." She wasn't sure how she had managed a coherent sentence, let alone saying so much with a gorgeous, sexy Scot staring deep into her eyes.

When she admitted to only having been with two men, Knox cocked his head. "Truly?"

"Truly," Hannah echoed. "That's why it's strange how easy it's been tonight for me to be this open with you. Overwhelming, really, but you're gorgeous and honest and unbelievably sexy."

Knox studied her for a moment, an indecisive expression on his face. He looked as if he might have more to say. Instead, he took a lock of her hair in his fingers. "I think I've talked more with you tonight than I've talked with anyone in the past year." His hand moved to cup the back of her head. He pulled her face toward his until their foreheads were touching. "I don't want to converse anymore. The only thing I want right now is this."

And then his lips were on hers.

Hannah opened her mouth, and they breathed into each other, exchanging deep kisses. With each one, her desire and desperation grew, making her feel like she would expire if she didn't savor his mouth completely. He tasted of wine and chocolate and sex. Glorious.

Knox was devouring her. He moved to kiss the back of her ear while his fingers traced the neckline of her dress and found their way to her breasts. He pressed soft kisses along her neck as his thumbs rubbed against her nipples, and they stiffened under his touch.

"You have a beautiful body," Knox murmured against her skin. "I love your breasts."

This time, hearing it from Knox, the compliment didn't sound as absurd as it had coming from Eric. In Knox's deep, delicious voice, coming out in a ragged whisper, it was erotic.

"Thank you," Hannah managed, her words strangled with need.

Knox continued kissing his way down her neck, slowly massaging them as he went, stopping to dip his tongue in the hollow at the base of her throat.

She moaned with pleasure, her fingers sliding into his hair and curling to clutch fistfuls of it.

"Take yir dress down and take yirself out of yir bra," he instructed her. "Show yir breasts to me."

Giving it no thought, Hannah pushed one side of her dress down, then the other, and pulled her bra straps down in turn. Sliding her dress down a bit further, she brought her breasts out of the cups of her bra and displayed them to Knox.

His breath hitched and became heavy, and his eyes darkened. "You're beautiful—even better than the fantasies I've been having about ya non-stop." He cupped her breasts, gave a gentle tug on one of her nipples and brought his mouth down to suck on it. Then he replaced his mouth with his fingers and massaged the wet nub while he moved to kiss and suckle her other nipple.

Hannah's stomach flipped and her hips began rocking as Knox continued to play with her breasts and suck on her nipples. How had she not known it was possible to feel this good? A small whimper escaped when he stopped and looked up at her.

"Your nipples are so pink and pretty. They're beggin' me to keep sucking on them. Do ya want me to keep doin' this, Hannah?"

"God, yes," Hannah moaned, throwing her head back. Everything he did and said made her wet and only heightened her need.

Knox dropped one more gentle kiss on her nipple then, looking as if it was the last thing he wanted to do, he pulled her bra straps back into place. "I want to touch you more, too, sweetheart. It's becoming apparent how impatient I am when it comes to touching you."

Bemused, she fixed him with a puzzled look. "Then, why are you stopping?"

Continuing to pull her clothing back into place, he responded, "Because this isn't the place I want to continue touching you. I'd like ya in my bed tonight. I have a house here in Glasgow. Sam, Stuart, and I live there, but I also keep a room here at the hotel to use when I'm on short trips. The room's available for us tonight, if you'd like. Or we could both go to yir room if it would make ya feel more comfortable. Only if it's what ya want, though.

You can go back to your room alone, and there'll be no hard feelings." As he spoke, Knox's earnest intensity waned, and he seemed to slip off onto a tangent.

Amused, Hannah said, "You're rambling. That's what I'm supposed to do."

"I'm going on about it like a boy who's crushin' on the cutest girl in prim'ry school," he said with a self-deprecating chuckle. "I guess it's obvious I'm trying to get into yir knickers."

Hannah laughed. "Well, I thought it was pretty obvious I'd like you to get into my knickers—you mean my panties, right?"

There was relief in his smile when Knox confirmed, "Yes. Exactly." Lacing his fingers with hers, Knox brought her hand to his lips and pressed a kiss to it before looking into her eyes with a heated gaze. "So. I suppose the only thing left to decide is yir room or mine."

Chapter 11

When Knox held the door of his suite open, Hannah stepped inside and looked around. It looked like a small, upscale apartment, with the nighttime Glasgow skyline framed in the large windows.

"So. This is your *fuck pad*," Hannah affirmed, taking in the basic yet tasteful furnishings.

"This is where I work. It's generally not a good idea to mix business with pleasure—in case things don't work out," Knox quipped, taking off his suit jacket.

Warmth crept across Hannah's cheeks. "I was just trying to make a joke. Not a funny one, apparently."

A smile stole onto Knox's face as he draped his jacket on the back of a stool near the breakfast bar separating the kitchenette from the larger living space. "I like yir jokes. I should have laughed. Sorry. Usually, I'm hard to offend," he assured her, coming to stand in front of her and clasping her hands in his. "But I wanted you to know this isn't my *fuck pad*. I don't bring women here. You're the first, and if ya want, I can make this place a birdhouse just for you and me."

A warm, unfamiliar feeling bloomed in Hannah's chest, catching in her throat when she realized it was what it felt like to be special to someone. It had been a long time since anyone had made her feel that way. Unable to speak, she could only smile at Knox and hope he understood what his words meant to her.

He gave her hands a gentle squeeze and the way he gazed back at her told her he did. "I've already got a few sex toys." One eyebrow twitching up, he looked around the suite. "We can always fill it up with more, if ya like. I think a sex swing would fit perfectly over there." He smirked and pointed to a corner of the room.

Hannah's delighted laugh was genuine. God, he was so out of her league. How was someone this attractive and sexually sophisticated interested in her?

When he looked back at her, heat flickered in his eyes and his amusement faded. "I'd like ya to stay for the night, but ya can leave at any point, and ya can say no to anything I ask ya to do. Do you understand?"

Still not quite trusting herself to speak, Hannah nodded.

He brought his hands to her shoulders and rubbed them lightly. "I need to hear you say it, sweetheart." Although he gave her a small smile, his tone was serious.

"Yes," Hannah said, quiet and clear. "I understand. I don't have to do anything I don't want to do. I'll say no to anything I feel uncomfortable with, and I can leave whenever I want to."

With a satisfied nod, Knox leaned down and placed his lips near her ear, sending shivers prickling through her body when he declared, "I'm going to kiss you now."

Hannah's body reacted on its own, her arms reaching up to slide around Knox's neck, and her head tilting up to bring her mouth to his.

After one brief but burning kiss, he moved her dress and bra aside and brought his lips to her nipple. With aching gentleness, he kissed and sucked on it while he pulled the other side of her dress and bra aside, then moved to kiss and suck on the other nipple. It was the sexiest thing anyone had ever done, Hannah thought, including full-blown, full-penetration sex. Electricity tingled from Hannah's breasts to her core and her nipples came to tight points.

With impressive self-control, Knox stepped back and gave Hannah a peck on the mouth. "Stay there. Don't move. I want to enjoy you as ya are right now."

As Hannah stood with her breasts naked and on display, Knox watched her. With anyone else, she might have felt self-conscious. Somehow, with Knox, it was a turn on.

After a moment, he went into the bathroom. When he returned, he took off his tie and belt, poured himself a glass of ice water, and drank it.

All the while, Hannah stood still, naked to the waist watching him, feeling herself getting hotter and more aroused by the second. For the life of her, she didn't understand how this gorgeous man, straight out of her romance hero fantasies, was affecting her without touching her. He was making her want to get to the sex part ASAP, and she was having a hard time remaining motionless.

When she began to squirm, Knox directed, "Don't fidget. Pull your shoulders back."

She did as he told her, and the smoldering heat in his eyes flared. "I like the way you look. It's sexy as fuck."

His words turned her on even more, sending a surge of desire racing through her. He came closer, holding the glass of water. Her breath hitched when he touched it to the side of one breast, then brought it to her face and caressed her cheek with it.

"Are you thirsty?" he asked in a low growl. "Do you want a drink of water?"

Her eyes locked on his, Hannah responded, "Yes. Please."

Knox brought the glass to her lips. "Drink," he instructed, serving her like she was a helpless child.

After she had swallowed a few mouthfuls of water, Knox took the glass back to the kitchen and returned, bringing a chair with him. He strode to the middle of the room and took a seat, where he continued to watch Hannah for a few moments more. At last, he beckoned her over. "Come here, baby. Serve up yir tits to me."

Fighting her eagerness, Hannah walked to him, leaned down, and put one nipple in Knox's mouth.

He began sucking. When he didn't move his hands from the arms of the chair, she started to pull away. He stopped her. "Not yet," then continued to suck at her nipple harder.

Hannah let out a whimper, thrilling at the smallest bit of exquisite pain edging the pleasure. At her reaction, Knox gave her nipple a tiny bite and sucked harder.

After a moment, he looked up. "Now the other one."

Cupping her other breast, Hannah brought the nipple to Knox's lips, and he began suckling it. When she whimpered again, he sucked harder.

Hannah caught her breath and felt her body beginning to combust.

When she was on the brink of losing herself, Knox stopped. "Take your clothes off for me, but keep yir heels on," he continued to direct her. "Take your time," he said slowly with a dark gleam in his eye. "I want to enjoy this."

She stood and began with her dress, peeling it off her body in unhurried, deliberate movements. She left her thong panties in place while she removed her bra. Then she walked across the room, where she bent over and placed her clothes in a neat pile across a chair. Turning, she found Knox watching her, lust burning in his eyes. She returned to stand in front of him before placing her palms on her sides and taking her time to glide her hands down her own body. Her thumbs hooked in the lacy strings of the thong, slipping them off. The entire time, her eyes remained locked on Knox, and she marveled at how sexy he made her feel. Without saying a word, she walked back across the room to place her panties with her other clothes, then returned to stand in front of Knox.

"Gorgeous." His words came out with a ragged edge.

Hannah's eyes dropped to his lap, where she could see his growing erection. The sight of it made her bolder. She went to him and knelt to unbutton his pants, bringing herself closer to the huge bulge straining beneath the fabric of his trousers.

He watched her draw the zipper down, and smiled when she opened his pants to reveal Emporio Armani briefs, the brand she had teased him about a few days earlier.

"Someone was confident," she teased, stroking the firm length of him.

"Like I said—lots of wishful thinking when it comes to you."

Hannah returned his smile as she took out his cock and caressed it. He kept his eyes on her as she kissed his stiff shaft, then began licking the smooth, silken tip. Gradually, she began sucking on the head, then took more of his cock into her mouth and sucked, softly at first, then harder. She heard his breathing quicken and start to come in heavy, excited bursts.

At last, he tensed, and took Hannah by the shoulders, stopping in time. "My cock feels good in your mouth, but I want to eat your pussy now," he commanded, drawing her upright. "Go sit on the bed."

She followed his instructions, and once she was seated, Knox stood, put himself back inside his trousers and did them up, then he came to her. He looked at her with such hunger, she felt heat pooling between her legs. It was all she could do to wait for him to tell her what to do next.

Knox, it seemed, was in much more control than she was. At the very least, he was savoring every moment. He bent and palmed her ass, squeezed and stroked, before bringing his hands to the top of her thighs.

"Spread your legs." When he spoke, Knox still sounded commanding, although his voice had grown husky. Bringing this confident, sexy man to that point made Hannah feel powerful and treasured, even, in a way she had never felt before.

While she spread her legs for him, Hannah remained seated upright. She wanted to watch him do the things she had only fantasized about and was pleased when Knox nodded and affirmed, "Good girl."

He took a slow swipe over the seam of her vulva with his tongue while his fingers teased her clitoris.

"You're so wet, sweetheart. You taste delicious," he complimented, before taking one side of her vulva in his mouth and sucking excruciatingly slow. Then he moved to the other side, sucking while continuing to play with her clit. The man was a freaking genius with his mouth.

"Knox," Hannah gasped when she felt on the brink of climax. "I'm going to come."

He stopped. "Not yet. You have to wait for me," he told her, calm and matter-of-fact, as if instructing her on the proper way to mix a martini. "You can't come until I say you can. Lie down on the bed."

"Are you going to take your clothes off?" Hannah asked as she slipped off her heels and pushed herself back on the bed. "I want to see what you look like."

"I'll undress in a minute," Knox replied. "First, put yir head on the pillow and grab the slats on the headboard behind ya."

Hannah did as she was told, eager to please Knox while watching his every move.

"Good." He nodded and gave her a trace of a smile. "Now pull yir knees up and spread your legs as far as you can." He watched her move into position, looking at her like a starving man with a feast laid out before him. His eyes traced every inch of her, taking her all in. "You knock me out, Hannah, all wet and sexy and waiting for me."

Only then did he begin removing his clothes, in no hurry, his eyes practically singeing her skin as they skimmed over her body.

She watched as he removed his shirt, took in his broad shoulders, toned arms, and tufts of hair on his chest. A dark line of it trailed down his flat belly, disappearing into the waistband of his trousers. Soon enough, she saw where that pleasure trail led when he removed his pants and the Armani briefs to reveal a mass of lovely black pubic hair and the thick, long erection standing at attention just for her. Hands down, he was the most beautiful man Hannah had ever seen.

As she took him all in, Hannah's body reacted on its own. With a firm grip on the headboard, her hips began wiggling, and her torso undulated up and down. "I can't wait any longer. Please fuck me," she begged. "Please let me get on top and we can fuck each other hard."

He didn't move, only gave her an indulgent look. "Be patient. The anticipation of pleasure is pleasure itself," he cajoled.

Hannah groaned. "For you, maybe, because you're more of a Scottish-Italian god than a human being. But I'm dying here."

Knox climbed on the bed beside her and began massaging and suckling her breasts. "Stop wiggling," he demanded when she couldn't hold still.

"If you don't fuck me soon, like now, I'm going to spontaneously combust!" Hannah heard the whining in her voice and didn't care. He had brought her right to the edge more than once. She was certain she would lose her mind if he didn't get inside of her soon.

"Hush," Knox soothed, looking as if he was trying to keep from smiling. He placed his hand flat on her stomach to hold her in place and kissed his way down her body, then began to suck on her hip bone. Sliding his hand from her stomach, he found her nipple and pinched it while he brought his other hand beneath her bottom. With gentle pressure, he lifted up to give himself better access to her hips.

"Oh ... holy shit," Hannah gasped.

At last, seeming to know how far he could push her, Knox tore himself away from tormenting Hannah's writhing body. As she lay gasping in air, he took a condom from his nightstand and ripped it open with his teeth.

Hannah watched him roll it down his cock, feeling her pulse speed up as he rubbed lube over himself.

"You can 't come until you hear me start to come," he instructed her, his words low and controlled. "If you don't wait, I'll torture you by sucking on your clit next time and won't let you come at all."

There's going to be a next time? an excited voice in Hannah's head squealed. *Woo hoo!*

"As turned on as I am, I don't know if I can come in this position—on the bottom," Hannah teased.

Knox planted a hand on either side of her, hovering his chiseled, magnificent body inches over hers. "You can, and ya will," he growled, holding her gaze with his. "I'll get you there. The only thing I want to hear from this point on is you moaning and screaming my name when you come. If you say another word, I'm going to put a gag in your mouth."

Hannah's nipples tightened and the warm ache in her core pulsed hard and strong at his threat. She contemplated talking back once more so he would follow through with gagging her, then wondered if something was wrong with her. Immediately, though, her thoughts splintered and faded away when Knox pressed against her opening and slowly guided the head of his cock inside her.

When he entered her, she sucked in a breath as he began thrusting into her in an exquisite rhythm. In and out, Knox penetrated, moving one hand down to massage her clit with his thumb.

Sparks and pulses of tiny climaxes tingled through her, adding to the pleasurable friction inside her. If there was a Heaven, this had to be it. She wanted it to go on forever and, at the same time, was afraid she couldn't last. In a desperate attempt to control her body, she commanded her mind to think of something else. Multiplication tables. Yes. That helped. While Knox continued pumping in and out of her and massaging her folds with his thumb, Hannah began on "one times one." Before she had made it halfway through the two's, however, he began nibbling at her neck, sucking and biting. Her eyelids began fluttering, and she had to start over on the ones again.

Thankfully, it wasn't long before Knox's breathing became shallower and more erratic. The strokes of his pumping slowed and seemed to intensify. Anticipating his orgasm, Hannah let go and allowed her own climax to come.

"Knox!" she screamed, as she felt his seed shooting into the condom. They crested the peak together, and it seemed to go on and on for them both. She had never experienced anything like it before and was on such a different level of awareness, she couldn't be sure she heard him call out her name.

Best. Sex. Ever.

Afterward, they lay together, spent. Hannah stroked Knox's hair, and he held her close, giving her soft kisses on her neck now and then.

At last, Knox got out of bed and went into the bathroom while Hannah lay drowsing, wrapped in a cocoon of satisfied bliss. She heard him in the other room, water running, the muffled sounds of him moving about. When he came back to the bedroom, he had removed the condom and had cleaned himself up. He brought two hand towels with him, one damp and one warm and dry, which he used to clean Hannah with tender care. After putting the towels back in the bathroom, he returned to the bed, flicked off the light, and got under the covers. He manhandled her into a spooning position, with her back and bottom pressed against his chest and stomach.

"You're the sexiest thing I've ever had the opportunity to have in my life, Hannah Vander Dussen," he whispered into her ear.

She smiled and snuggled back into him. Too exhausted to answer, she hoped he knew the feeling was mutual.

He placed his lips on her temple and planted a lingering kiss there as Hannah drifted off into the dreamless sleep of a contented and satisfied woman.

Chapter 12

When the alarm on Hanna's phone went off the following morning, she lifted her head from the pillow and looked around the room, groggy and confused. Her phone wasn't on the bedside table, where she usually kept it, and she was alone in Knox's room.

Dragging herself out of bed, she padded into the suite's living area, to the small island separating the kitchenette from the rest of the room. She blearily looked around for any sign of Knox. He was nowhere to be seen. There was, however, a folded paper with her name on it on the countertop next to her phone. Turning off the alarm, she sent a quick text to Henry. She wanted to let him know she was going to skip their morning hike and would catch up with him the next day. Then, she opened the note and read it.

Hannah,

I had to get an early start on work this morning. I hope you don't mind and don't think it too presumptuous of me—I had the porter bring your things from your room.

If it doesn't interfere with your plans, I'd love to spend the day and evening with you before you leave for Inverness. My number is below. Call or text me when you wake up.

He had signed the bottom of the page "xx, Knox" and written his cell number under his name.

Her heart beat a happy rhythm, spreading warm joy through her chest as she glanced around and saw her luggage in a neat stack near the door. She had spent a wonderful fantasy night with him and hadn't wanted it to end. Apparently, he felt the same way.

After programming Knox's number into her contacts, she texted him.

Good morning.

Three trailing dots appeared right away, followed by his quick answer.

Good morning sweetheart. How did u sleep?

Hannah's cheeks prickled with heat as she composed her reply. They had only gotten snatches of sleep throughout the night. Knox had woken her for round two only a couple of hours after they had fallen asleep, and when she got up later to use the bathroom, he was awake again. Round three had been even more amazing than rounds one and two.

Hannah: Very well, thank u...xcept an overbearing man kept me up most of the night doing nasty and wonderful things to me.

Knox: Overbearing? Nasty things? Give me his name and I'll make sure he's tossed into the River Clyde with cement boots on.

Hannah: Sounds harsh. Very American gansta of u. Maybe he should get a spanking from me instead.

Knox: Not happening—even from a superb lass from LA. Do you want to go for a hike and a picnic with me today?

Hannah grinned. At least she would get to hike today, even if it wasn't with Henry.

Hannah: Sure. ur a hiker?

Knox: I'm not a complete couch potato.

Hannah: I saw ur abs—not a couch potato. Just assumed u got it from an indoor gym.

Knox: I may not be one of your dreamy Highlanders, but I'm a Scot, and we like the outdoors.

Hannah: Oh, ur definitely dreamy-worthy

Knox: Ah?

Hannah: Even if ur a Lowlander.

Knox: Brat. I'll make you pay for that.

Hannah: Promise?

A spurt of adrenalin jetted through Hannah's body as she sent her replies. It turned out this flirting thing was easy—at least it was with Knox.

Knox: I'll come back to our room and get you in an hour.

Our room? Hannah bit at the corner of her lip, trying to keep her delighted grin under control.

Hannah: I'll be ready.

When Hannah emerged from the bedroom after showering and dressing, breakfast had been delivered and laid out on the kitchen counter: coffee, tea, pastries, hard boiled eggs, and fruit. She poured herself a cup of coffee and popped a chunk of melon into her mouth while she texted Charli. It would be midday in California, so she was likely to catch her daughter at a good time.

Hope ur having a great time! I'm off on a hike today with a new friend. C u in about a week! xoxo, Mom

Charli's immediate response was a string of emojis.

As Hannah was downing the last of her coffee, a knock sounded at the door and Knox came in.

"You don't have to knock," Hannah chided him good-naturedly as she came to him. "This *is* your place." She reached up to greet him with a kiss, unable to miss how amazing he looked in his casual jeans, black t-shirt, and trail shoes. Somehow, he managed to look like a GQ guy posing for an REI catalog.

"I wanted to respect your privacy," he told her after indulging in a sweet, sexy, slow French kiss.

"Good idea," Hannah teased, trying to regain her equilibrium. "I wouldn't want you to see me naked."

A wicked spark gleamed in his eye. "It wouldn't be a good idea, if we actually want to accomplish anything outside of this room today. Are you ready for our hike? Did you get enough to eat?" He cast a glance over her head toward the breakfast he had ordered for her.

"In spite of swearing off food after last night's feast, yes," Hannah replied. "I enjoyed a danish and some fruit and coffee. Did you have breakfast?"

"I did, and I've got a picnic in here for our lunch." Knox lifted up the backpack he was carrying to show her.

"The food and wine in here probably weighs more than you. I like that ya're such a cute, wee thing." He laughed.

"I like that you're a big, huge giant," Hannah countered. "In fact, I love everything about you—you're perfect."

"High praise from someone who's perfect herself," Knox said with appreciation, then bent to kiss her once more. "Now, let's head out."

Knox drove her in his big Range Rover through the bustling city, past towering skyscrapers, into the outlying area with ubiquitous and interesting architecture. In less than fifteen minutes, they had passed into the picturesque countryside. Soon they were pulling into a dirt lot next to a scenic lake surrounded by trees and green, rolling hills. After stepping from the SUV and retrieving the pack from the back seat, Knox came around to open the passenger door for Hannah and gave her a quick kiss.

As he helped her from the Ranger Rover, Hannah took in the trees and lush, rolling hills surrounding the lake. "It's magnificent," she said with amazement, her eyes on the water. "It's a loch, right? I know it's Gaelic for 'lake,' or it's derived from the Gaelic. I don't know one loch from another, though."

Impressed, Knox nodded. "You're right, and this is Loch Lomand. It's the largest inland stretch of fresh water in Great Britain. I spent a lot of time here growing up, with my family and friends, and my boys and I have camped on Inchmurrin, one of Loch Lomand's islands. It's the biggest fresh-water island in the British Isles."

An uneasy chill shot through Hannah, and she pushed it aside. It had to be the bracing air combined with their late night. She pointed to people canoeing and kayaking on the lake. "Do you do that?

"Och, not in years," he chuckled, as he locked up the SUV and took her hand. "When I was younger, my friends and I hit each other so many times over the head with canoe paddles, it's a wonder we have any brain cells left."

"Boys." Hannah laughed and rolled her eyes.

"We'll hike about three miles along the edge of the loch," Knox directed, slinging the backpack over one shoulder. With his free hand, he pointed toward the water's edge. "There's a quiet, pretty place on a hill with a view where we can have our picnic."

"Sounds delightful," Hannah replied, glancing around the parking area. An odd feeling had crept up on her, and she couldn't quite put her finger on what was at the bottom of it. When Knox squeezed her hand and asked if she was ready, she brought her attention back to him. He was looking down at her with those penetrating brown eyes, and she couldn't help but smile when she looked up at him. She felt at ease with Knox, so safe. With a nod from Hannah, they set off.

They hiked in companionable silence for about half an hour. It was as perfect of a hiking day as they could have asked for. Puffy intermittent clouds drifted on the breeze across the sky. Most were white and billowy, however, and didn't seem to threaten rain. Even with the sun playing hide and seek behind the clouds, it was still more than just warm, especially for Hannah who had to put some effort into keeping up with Knox's long strides. Once he noticed her scurrying to keep up, he slowed down his pace for her.

As they moved away from the motor craft, canoes, and jet skis, the lake took on a different appearance. It narrowed, almost resembling a river, though it didn't seem to flow in any particular direction. The sounds of voices from other hikers and those playing on the lake receded, and soon it felt like they had left civilization behind. Knox still had ahold of Hannah's hand, and he kept a firm grip on it as he led her up a hill punctuated by trees. An osprey gliding over the water cried out as they moved away from the shoreline, it's piercing call bringing back Hannah's apprehension.

It's just the jarring stillness, she told herself as Knox led her up the trail. And a little anticipation, she had to allow. She enjoyed having Knox all to herself way too much.

Right about the time she was opening her mouth to ask how much further he was taking her, they emerged from the trees into a crescent-shaped clearing. The beautiful turquoise lake lay in front of them.

Hannah's jaw almost dropped. "This is a perfect spot for a picnic."

Knox, busy taking things from his pack only smiled and spread out a blanket. As Hannah watched, he laid out utensils, water, food, wine, and glasses.

Kneeling beside him, Hannah snatched a wine glass and held it up. "Real glass?" she marveled.

With a nod, Knox worked the corkscrew and pulled the cork from the bottle. "Of course," he affirmed, filling her glass halfway. "The taste of wine suffers too much with plastic."

Hannah shrugged and took a sip of her wine. She had to admit the smooth, fruity flavor seemed richer, more pronounced than she would have expected. Maybe it was their glorious surroundings; maybe it was the wonderful company. Or it could be Knox knew what he was talking about.

Hannah chose a tomato sandwich from the selection Knox offered her while he plated up servings of potato pie—delicious wedges of creamy, cheesy mashed potatoes baked in a bacon shell. They ate, quiet and contented as they basked in the surroundings and each other's company. Hannah was certain she had never been as happy as she was at that moment.

When they had finished their meal and Hannah had helped Knox put the food and other provisions back in his pack, he sat down again on the blanket. He splayed his long legs in front of him, taking up the entire length of the fabric. He took her hand, drawing her closer. "Take your hair out," he said, "and lie here on my lap."

Freeing her ponytail from the elastic holding it in place, Hannah laid down, her head resting on Knox's legs.

"I like your long hair," he said, admiring it and running his fingers through her wavy locks.

"It's too thick and wild," she protested, loving the way he stroked her hair.

"Your hair is sexy—like the rest of you." His hand moved to rub her breasts. "I'm obsessed with yir tits."

Hannah sighed. "Obsess away." Knox's hands on her had already become her favorite thing in the world.

After a moment he went back to stroking her hair. "Last night you said you're not going to have a job in New York. You'll be busy with your daughter ... not working, though, will you have more free time to travel to Scotland, or spend time with a wayward Brit when he comes to New York?"

It took all of Hannah's will to keep her breath from catching. He wanted to continue seeing her as much as she wanted it? There was always a chance it was all about continuing sex with her more than building a relation- ship. At the moment, however, she didn't see a thing wrong with that scenario.

"Yes, I'd like that," she said, managing to sound nonchalant.

"So I haven't overwhelmed you?"

"Not at all. I'm comfortable with you," Hannah admit- ted, sitting up and turning to kneel before him. "And you must know you're a smart, handsome and sexy beast." She leaned into Knox's hard body and pressed a kiss to his lips. When she turned and sat on his lap, leaning back against his chest, she could feel him growing hard.

He gripped her legs and spread them out, then he began caressing her arms and stroking her sides. When he moved her around, positioning her the way he wanted, it made her feel like a doll with moveable parts.

She couldn't say why, but it turned her on when he man-handled her.

"Pull your zipper down," he whispered into her ear, sending gooseflesh rippling across her body. "I want to put my hand inside yir knickers."

The uneasy feeling was back in an instant. "This is an open area," Hannah demurred. "What if someone comes walking along the shoreline? It's a long way away, but still. It's indecent."

Knox wouldn't be deterred. "I want satisfaction, sweetheart," he insisted, his hand dipping between her legs outside of her jeans. "And that includes hearing you quietly come against my fingers out here in the open air." He kissed her temple and worked his way down, pulling her hair back to nip at her neck.

A low moan of ecstasy rose in Hannah's throat and Knox pulled back, the look he gave her saying, *Ah, see? You want it too.*

Mischief glinted in his eyes when he told her, "Lean against me on your side. I can put can my hand in without anybody seeing us."

Grinning, she adjusted her position and pulled her jacket over her legs, as if covering herself from a chill in the air.

"Knock yourself out, Mr. Neanderthal," she dared him once she had undone the zipper on her pants.

Although his eyebrows went up, his look telling her he accepted her challenge, he didn't move right away. He stroked her hair, then the sides of her breasts. After an eternity, he moved to fondle her nipples with his thumbs for what felt like ages. He took his time, driving her wild with his touch.

Hannah's breathing grew deep and ragged. She wanted to beg him to give her the orgasm he had promised and at the same time rebelled against the urge. It wasn't like she wasn't enjoying herself, and she suspected begging was exactly what he wanted her to do. Her brain and her body were at odds on who should be calling the shots. Still, she had to admit she had a new appreciation for why those crazy BDSM chicks got off on calling men "Master." No question—Knox was a master in the foreplay and sex department.

When Hannah was on the brink of giving into her body's needs, Knox leisurely slid his hand down beneath her jacket. "Don't talk and don't make a sound," he instructed, his voice a low rumble in her ear.

All but bursting with anticipation, Hannah stifled a whimper.

"I've decided you can't make any sounds when ya come," he went on, his hand snaking down, taking an excruciating amount of time to make its way to her trembling vagina. "And I'm going to take my time with yir pussy. It's your punishment for using your tongue like a sharp weapon. If I hear you make any noise, even if I hear you purring with pleasure, I'll stop."

His words in her ear were almost enough to do Hannah in. She knew he would find her drenched when he finally got down to business.

He continued teasing her, caressing her stomach, then palming her entire, heated mound roughly. When at last he moved to lightly finger her pussy over and over, he chuckled. "You're pretty soaked for a prude who doesn't want to be indecent in the outdoors."

Hannah pinched her lips together between her teeth. Knox was a devil, maybe *the* Devil, and he was going to kill her with anticipation. Though she was making a valiant effort to stay quiet, her body began twitching with need for release.

"Don't move," he coaxed, his quiet tone loaded with warning.

Her breath catching, she reached across her own body and found Knox's hard shaft. When he removed her hand, she clenched it in frustration.

Right about then, Knox started tapping her clit in a light rhythm. After he did it about the twenty-fifth time, Hannah wanted to scream for him to press harder and let her orgasm. Her entire body was straining with desperation and desire.

"Look at me," Knox directed, only the slightest hint of a tremor in his voice. "I want to see your face when you come."

She turned her head, looking up at him. When their eyes locked, he drove his fingers over her clitoris, giving her the release she had so badly wanted. A shriek rose in her throat, but she was determined to follow Knox's instructions. However, she couldn't keep her face from contorting, or stop her body from convulsing in relief.

Spent and satiated, Hannah lay against Knox without moving or adjusting her clothes. "Damn, you are really good in the sack—or on a picnic blanket. Can I help you out now?" She rubbed his erection.

"As much as I'd like nothing better than ya milking my cock with yir hands, tits, mouth, or cunt right now," he said, touching or kissing each body part as he mentioned it, "that much of a public display of affection is not acceptable. Besides, I've had my satisfaction for now."

"Are you sure?" Hannah cast a skeptical glance at the shaft of granite inside Knox's pants.

"Maybe not physically." He smiled. "But emotionally, I'm there."

Although Hannah was still unconvinced, she had to let the issue drop when Knox stood and pulled her to her feet.

"I've got to get back to the hotel," he told her, drawing her in close for one more embrace. "I'm meeting with Thomas and a new architect this evening, and I've got some loose ends to tie up before tomorrow, so we should get going." He brought his hands up to frame her face and gave her a lingering kiss, leaving her wanting more.

And that was the problem, she thought as they gathered up the debris from their picnic, tucking everything away in Knox's pack with the blanket. All interaction with him seemed to entail an unrelenting state of wetness for her and hardness for him. Thank God it all culminated in orgasms a good amount of time. Otherwise, Hannah knew she would go mad from the frustration. It occurred to her the uneasiness she felt earlier was the combination of being alone with him in this idyllic, secluded area and the strong physical chemistry between them. Now that Knox had satisfied her, she was far more relaxed. And she still couldn't believe she had three orgasms the night before. Knox had the ability to pull her into a state of hedonism she never contemplated was possible. It was as if he had the proficiency to push all her carnal buttons just the right way, both giving and taking.

On the walk back to his SUV, Knox said, "You're leaving the day after tomorrow for a few days. I'll have a late night tonight, and you have a hike scheduled for tomorrow. Tomorrow night will be our last night together until I see you again in Edinburgh before you leave for home."

Hannah's wrinkled her brow. "Yes?" What was he getting at?

"I was going to ask you to have dinner at my parent's house. It will be a family thing. Sam and Stuart and his girlfriend will be there. You'll get to meet everyone in one shot." His expression and his tone were unreadable.

"You *were* going to ask me? Has something changed?"

They were already holding hands, and Knox gave hers a squeeze. "I want you to myself," he said with a roguish grin. "I don 't want to share you with the pesky relatives, but my mam's planning on it, and I'm sure she's been all a twitter about it all day. She'll never forgive me if I cancel."

They had reached the parking lot and Knox stopped near his Range Rover and turned to face her. "Do you want to have dinner at my parent's house tomorrow night? It's alright if you don't."

Hannah couldn't control the huge grin spreading across her face. Knox sounded as if he were only extending the invitation out of duty, and she could imagine what he would rather be doing with her for their last evening together in Glasgow. Even so, she beamed her biggest, brightest smile and said, "I'd love to."

Knox rolled his eyes as he thumbed his key fob to unlock the SUV. "Of course you would."

Chapter 13

Hannah was still smiling the following evening as she and Knox were making their way up his parents' walkway to the front door. At the moment, however, her elation over meeting Knox's family was tinged with nerves.

"What have I gotten myself into?" she fretted, smoothing her damp palms down the sides of her dress. "I feel like I'm a teenager again."

Knox clasped her hand, calming her down. "Me too. I've haven't brought a girl home since Jayne."

Hannah peered up at him and blinked. "Honestly?"

Nodding, he smiled. "We can handle this together, sweetheart. We'll be strong." He gave her hand a squeeze, his feigned solemnity putting her even more at ease.

As they walked toward the door, Hannah took in the lovely home. It was a traditional stone house too big to call a cottage, but it had the inviting allure of a quaint country home, with black shutters and a red door. A pretty English garden encompassed every available inch of ground, and additional plants and flowers flourished in window boxes and pots arranged on the porch.

"My mam's a gardening buff, as ya can tell," Knox remarked, seeing Hannah admiring the foliage. "She's also a great cook. Italian, of course. She's got a vegetable garden and a greenhouse in the back, and she grows most of the food she cooks." He chuckled. "Her garden gets bigger every time I come over. It won't surprise me when her precious *le verdure* and *erbe aromatiche* take over and edge out all the flowers in the front."

Hannah surveyed the flora in the beautifully land-scaped garden. "I can see she has a knack for it. Maybe she should open a greenhouse business or sell her produce and herbs."

"She already sources some for the hotel's restaurant," Knox confirmed. "The chef from the Francesca comes over here all the time to snip herbs for his kitchen. He says my mam's Italian basil is the best he's ever had."

Although they had reached the front door, Knox hadn't made a move to open it or knock. They were stalling, and both of them knew it.

"Your accent was perfect when you spoke Italian a moment ago," Hannah said, taken with it, drawing out this last moment as long as possible. "I'd love to hear you speak it with your mother."

Knox shook his head. "She won't. Not in front of company."

"I bet you could get her to do it," Hannah pleaded, then gave him a sly look. "It would be very sexy, if it were possible for you to be any sexier."

As she spoke the last words, the front door opened, and her face flushed hot as she gaped up at a younger version of Knox. It had to be one of his sons, and she hoped he hadn't heard her remark. But the knowing grin he gave them both said he had.

"Da!" the young man said with obvious delight. "Are you coming inside, or are you planning on staying out here all night?"

"We only just arrived, Sam," Knox protested. "I was reaching for the door when you opened it."

Sam's eyebrows twitched as he gave Knox a skeptical look. Then his eyes shifted to Hannah. "And are you going to introduce me to your friend?"

Obviously used to his son's joking, Knox rolled with it. "This is Hannah," he said, placing his hand on the small of her back. "Hannah, this is my son, Samuel."

Hannah put out a hand, but before she could respond, Sam grasped it and gave it a warm shake. "Nice to meet you, Hannah. You're, well, pretty. I can see why my da wants to keep you to himself out here." He glanced at Knox and gave him a crooked grin. "And no wonder he has a goofy look on his face."

Hannah blushed, although she couldn't help laughing. "Nice to meet you too, Sam," she said.

"Well, now you've interrupted us," Knox insisted, grasping Sam by the shoulders and moving him aside, "let us in."

The rest of the family poured into the living room as Hannah and Knox stepped inside. There was a flurry of introductions and kisses. Hannah met Stuart and his girlfriend, Violet, Knox's mom, Francesca, and his dad, Bruce.

Francesca was everything Hannah expected, warm and inviting and yet very elegant in a Roberto Cavalli dress. When Knox took Hannah's coat, she smiled and said, "I see you got your good taste in clothes from your mother."

"It certainly wasn't from my father," Knox retorted. "You can be sure my mam made him wear those Nicola Trussardi trousers. If she left him to dress himself, he'd be wearing something ugly and threadbare he's had in his closet for thirty years or more." He leaned down to peck Hannah's cheek. "My mam's from Milan—fashion is in our blood, and my boys are worse clothes horses than I am."

"Da, are you already telling all the Munro family secrets?" Stuart teased, coming to stand beside Knox. He was shorter and not quite as muscular as Knox and Sam, but he was trim and toned. "Wait until she's known us a little longer before you try to scare her off."

Hannah loved seeing Knox with his sons and couldn't help comparing the two boys to their father. Sam seemed to have been made from the same mold as Knox, although his coloring was a bit lighter. He and Stuart had dark-blond hair, which they must have gotten from their mother, and Stuart's skin was lighter and freckled, too; another feature Hannah assumed he had inherited from Jayne.

It soon became apparent that Stuart and the pretty, dark-haired Violet, seemed to be joined at the hip. Hannah noticed they took every opportunity to cast longing looks at each other and steal touches and kisses, and it made her wonder if she and Knox looked like them. She certainly wanted to touch him everywhere, all the time.

Francesca bustled in with a tray of cocktails and appetizers. "Hannah, we've got Old Fashioned's in your honor, made with the best whiskey, of course," she said with a gleam in her eye, referring to their family's whiskey.

"Of course!" the family chorused, then lifted their glasses and added, "Cheers!"

After taking the first drink, Bruce held his glass up again and offered another toast. "And here's to my son and the lovely Hannah. We are so pleased Knox brought his girl to meet the family."

His girl? Hannah liked the sound of that. Her eyes found Knox's and she lifted a brow. His cheeks colored and he shook his head as he took her hand and drew her to sit beside him on the sofa.

"Mam," he started when his mother sat in the chair next to him, "Hannah would like us to speak Italian tonight."

"Oh—do you *parlare Italiano?*" Francesca asked Hannah.

"Um, no." Hannah shook her head. "I just thought it would be interesting to hear you two speaking it."

"It wouldn't be polite, then," Francesca told Hannah. "Because you don't speak it."

Knox looked at Hannah and smirked. *"Conosco i miei polli."*

In response, Francesca spewed a rant in Italian. Knox laughed and responded back, and whatever he said made his mother purse her lips.

"See?" Francesca raised her eyebrows. "That was very rude. Hannah didn't understand anything we said." She tried and failed to put on a serious face.

"My wife's very proper about everything," Bruce told Hannah. "Including not speaking Italian in front of non-speakers, unless it's me. She and Knox and the boys have a fine time in their Italian world whenever I'm around."

Francesca got up and went to her husband. She gave him a peck on the mouth. "Ah yes, you are very neglected. I'll have to make it up to you later."

Bruce smiled wide at the boys and waggled his eyebrows.

"Ugh! Make them stop, Da!" Sam complained.

Knox ignored him. "Can I help you with anything, mam?" he asked his mother.

"No, thank you. Wanate came earlier and helped me with the preparations. She's helping in the kitchen tonight with the food and clean up." She beamed at Stuart's girlfriend. "And Violet did the beautiful table setting and flower arrangements."

"Well, then. What are we waiting for?" Bruce said with enthusiasm, rising from his chair and shepherding everyone into the dining room.

As they were taking their seats, Hannah leaned over and asked Knox, "What did you say to your mom in Italian?"

"The literal translation is 'I know my chickens.'" He smiled when Hannah knit her brow. "It means 'I know what I'm talking about.'"

"Oh," Hannah said, a bit disappointed. Hearing the foreign words coming from his lips so effortlessly had turned her on. She supposed he could make her hot by saying anything to her in Italian. Then again, he didn't have to say anything at all.

Leaning closer, Knox put his lips near Hannah's ear and murmured, "Don't worry, sweetheart, I'll speak Italian for you tonight."

A shiver of excitement pulsed through Hannah, and she ducked her head to hide the giddy grin on her lips.

They sat down and enjoyed an incredible home-made feast. Everyone ate and drank and laughed and talked. As she dined on antipasto salad and savored the fusilli pasta and smoked turkey with Italian basil, Hannah marveled at the meal. It could have competed well with the seven-course taster Knox had ordered at the hotel.

"Hannah," Sam said, pulling out his cell phone, "Did my da tell you I like to skydive?" He swiped and poked at his phone's screen to call up his Facebook page. Once he had found videos of himself and his friends BASE jumping and wingsuit flying, he turned the phone over to Hannah.

She watched a few clips, her heart in her throat as the boys threw themselves out of airplanes and off bridges and cliffs.

Knox scowled, stealing glances at the phone over Hannah's shoulder. "I keep hoping he'll grow out of this fascination in these dangerous activities." He turned to Sam. "What if you collide into another parachuter or if someone doesn't jump out of the plane or pull up correctly? What if your chute doesn't open?"

Sam gave a weary sigh, as if tired of explaining something simple. "The risk in parachuting isn't that the chute won't open. It's only dangerous if the jumper doesn't have the skill to control his body and the parachute. And you don't need to worry about that with me." He lifted the bottom of his shirt to his neck to show his rock-hard, twelve-pack abs.

Hannah passed Sam's phone back to him with an uneasy smile.

"Very classy, Sam," Stuart jeered. "Da, you think it's alright for him to do that at the dinner table in front of Violet and Hannah?"

Looking harassed, Knox turned to Hannah. "Welcome to my world. You're lucky you only have one—otherwise you're always playing referee."

Looking back to Sam, Knox said with a touch of exasperation, "Can't you at least stop doing the wing suiting or BASE jumping? Isn't the skydiving enough of an adrenaline high?"

"Let's change the subject," Sam said, avoiding his father's gaze.

"I've got something we can talk about," Stuart interjected, breaking the tension.

Everyone consented with relief.

"It's more of an announcement," Stuart hesitated, color rising in his cheeks as he stood and held up his glass. He paused for a moment, glancing down at Violet, who was looking down, trying to hide a smile.

"I'd like you all to know I've asked this enchanting woman to be my wife. And she has said yes."

There was a beat of silence before the family overwhelmed the happy couple with cheers and congratulations. Knox rose from his seat and went around the table to give Violet a peck on the cheek and clap Stuart on the back. "I'm so happy for ya, son. Best wishes. She's a wonderful lass."

Sam raised his glass to the happy couple. "Congratulations Violet, you have now found that one special person who will annoy you for the rest of your life."

Stuart gave Sam a dirty look and put his arm around Violet. "You're just jealous because I've got the best girl in the Kingdom."

"Boys, please," Francesca purported to scold them, "This should be a happy occasion."

"It is, mam," Knox agreed, pinning a stern gaze on his sons, warning them with a look to stop their bickering. He took his seat again, next to Hannah.

"Where's the ring?" Francesca asked, redirecting the conversation.

"We wanted to wait to tell everyone," Stuart smiled, drawing a box from his pocket with pride. He got down on one knee in front of Violet. "I'll ask you again in front of my family. Will you marry me?"

"Yes." She gave an enthusiastic nod as Stuart slid the ring onto her finger. "Oh, yes!"

"How beautiful." Teary-eyed, Francesca clasped her hands to her chest.

"Have you set a date yet?" Hannah asked.

Smiling, Violet bit her lip and looked to Stuart. The corners of his lips tugged up and he raised his brows. When she nodded, Stuart turned to his family and revealed, "We've been talking about getting married for months, and we'd already decided on it when—" Stuart paused when Violet reached for his hand. He gave it a squeeze and went on. "—when Violet found out about the baby."

After a beat of stunned silence, Francesca whispered, "Oh … does that mean …?"

"It means you'll have another grandchild to spoil by the end of the year." Stuart grinned at his grandmother and the family erupted into more pleased and happy well-wishes.

With the meal finished and Stuart and Violet's news announced, the party seemed to be winding down. Wanate appeared bearing a tray of fruits, cheese tarts, and an elegant silver coffee service, and began clearing the dinner plates from the table.

Pressing her hand to her stomach, Hannah tipped toward Knox and groaned. "Ugh," she said in a low tone meant only for him. "Between you and your mother, I'll weigh a ton before this trip is over."

Knox placed his hand over hers and cocked an eyebrow. "Actually, I have other plans for dessert, if you're up for it."

A thrill fizzled through her as she tried to bite back a smile. "Yes, please." She beamed with anticipation.

Standing, Knox drew Hannah up with him. "We can't stay for coffee," he announced. "I have to get Hannah back. She's leaving early in the morning for Inverness."

Francesca fussed and gave a weak protest but didn't insist they stay. Everyone hugged Hannah in turn, exclaiming how nice it was to meet her. After the pleasant goodbyes, they were back in Knox's Range Rover and on their way to the hotel.

On the drive back, Knox seemed to be in a contemplative mood, so Hannah didn't interrupt his thoughts. When they were back in his suite, she finally broke the silence. "It was a special evening," she said, removing her earrings and setting them on the nightstand.

"It was," Knox agreed, coming to her and taking her shoulders in his hands. He slowly slid them down to her elbows and back up. "And at the same time, it was agonizing. I couldn't keep my mind off getting you alone." He bent and kissed her lips. "The entire time, I was imagining what I'd do to you when I did." He moved to kiss her ear and tugged at the lobe with his teeth before planting kisses down her neck.

Unable and unwilling to fight him off, Hannah gave a low moan. "Oh? And what did you imagine?"

He growled and nipped at her collar bone. "I imagined taking you quickly. Now we're here, though. I'm going to force myself to take it slow." He came back to her ear and placed a kiss on it, then whispered, "*Spogliati lentamente per me, amore mio.*"

For all Hannah knew, he was talking about chickens again, but her knees still buckled at the words.

"Oh God. What did you say?" She felt hot wet heat between her legs and wondered if she could talk him back into his initial plan of taking her quickly.

"I said—" He broke off to kiss his way to her other ear, where he murmured, "Undress slowly for me, my love."

Goosebumps prickled up Hannah's arms and her heart seemed to skip a beat. *My love?*

She had thought about where this was going with Knox. Before she met him, she wouldn't have thought it was possible to have such crazy, dirty sex and still have strong feelings for someone. She had somehow thought the two must be compartmentalized. But here she was. Everything he did and said made her wet. He was sex on a stick, and he could just about make her climax with only a touch. She knew she was falling for him and had been afraid to hope he felt the same way.

In the moment, at a loss for words, Hannah responded the only way she could. She stepped back and, as Knox sat down in an armchair, began undressing, the anticipation of the pleasure to come, as he had said, sending pleasure sizzling through her.

Chapter 14

She had barely fallen asleep, Hannah was certain, when she felt Knox gently nudging her awake.

"Hannah, sweetheart. I'm sorry to wake you," he said with trepidation, giving her shoulder a soft shake. "Stuart's been in an accident. I have to go to the hospital."

Blinking herself awake, Hannah tried to sit up. "Is he okay?"

Knox pressed her down and pulled the comforter to her shoulders. He was dressed in jeans and a cashmere pullover and looked ready to go. "Not sure. Apparently, it was bad, though. He and Violet were taken to emergency care at Glasgow Royal Infirmary."

"Oh my God." Hannah sat up, the news shocking her into full wakefulness. "What about the baby?"

"I don't know anything else."

"I can get ready quickly and go with you," she offered, moving to get out of bed.

He stopped her again. "No. Sweetheart, it's not necessary but thank you." He settled her under the covers once more. "Please, keep your plans for today. Go on with your trip. I've got to go." He leaned in to kiss her on the forehead, then was up and walking toward the door before she could respond.

"Are you sure?" Hannah called out, feeling the need to do something useful. "I can stay here today and wait for you."

Knox seemed distracted and concerned, although not overly worried. "No. I'm sure everything will be fine. I don't want anything to interfere with your holiday." He grabbed his cell phone and duffel bag and checked the phone before tucking it into his back pocket.

"Will you let me know how they are?" Hannah asked.

He turned before stepping from the room and gave her a tender smile. "Of course."

Hannah only stayed in bed for another half an hour. She tried to get back to sleep, but her mind wouldn't let her. She laid there wondering how Stuart and Violet were. Should she have insisted on going with Knox? If Stuart was in critical condition, if something horrible had happened to Violet or the baby, she wanted to be there to support Knox.

In the end, she got up and got ready for her hike to keep her thoughts from going round and round. Then she got herself packed and went down to the hotel's coffee shop to have breakfast and wait for Henry.

He arrived right on time and kept up a stream of cheery chatter as he bundled her luggage in the car and drove her to the train station.

"The train will arrive in Inverness at fourteen-eleven," he confirmed, then added, "Uh, that's two-eleven, p.m. Caesar will meet you at the station and take you to the hotel. He can confirm your itinerary for your afternoon hike today and the plans for tomorrow, too."

"Sounds good." Distracted, Hannah wasn't contributing much to the conversation. She checked her phone for a text from Knox. Nothing.

On the train, she continued to struggle with her thoughts, wondering if something horrible had happened with Stuart, then convincing herself no news was good news. When she alighted from the train car, Caesar was there to greet her. His friendly face was a welcome sight. Somehow, it reassured Hannah she was worried about nothing.

On the drive to the hotel, Caesar pointed out historic landmarks and sites he thought would be of interest.

"We emailed this to you, but I thought you might want a hard copy," he mentioned, handing her a print-out of the itinerary for the next few days.

Hannah took it and gave a surreptitious glance at her phone before studying the paper in earnest. No word from Knox yet.

"After you check in," Caesar was telling her, having launched right into the schedule, "I'm going to drop you at the Old High Church. You 'll join the four-p.m. tour there. It will be finished at six. I'll meet you there, and we'll have a quick walking tour of the city. We have reservations at the 'Ole Scottish Gaelic House at eight o'clock with a larger group. Annie will be joining us, too. She's guiding the group around the Isle of Skye tomorrow."

"That's wonderful," Hannah perked up at the mention of Annie's name. "I can't wait to see her."

With a smile, Caesar continued. "It's a short walk from the restaurant back to your hotel. Annie and I will walk you back. Then tomorrow, you'll be picked up at your hotel at seven a.m. to join a tour of Culloden Moor and the countryside surrounding Inverness. And you'll tour Inverness Castle in the afternoon."

After a brief silence, Hannah remembered a particular place she had wanted to see. "Were you able to schedule a tour of Fort William for me?"

Caesar nodded, looking pleased. "Since you wanted to add in the Fort William tour without giving up the other scheduled hikes, we put it on your last day. You'll go on the twenty-five kilometer hike in the morning, tour the fort in the afternoon, and then have dinner on your own in Inverness. I'll have to pick you up at four-thirty a.m. to squeeze it all in. Are you still up for it?"

Hannah tried to sound certain. "Absolutely." Suddenly, three days away from Knox seemed like a lifetime. She started to glance at her phone, then forced herself to put it away without checking it for calls, emails or text messages from Knox.

While touring Inverness Castle the next morning, Hannah was determined to concentrate on everything the docent said. She was doing a good job of it, too, until the woman said something about Mary, Queen of Scots, being denied admittance, and the Clans Munro and Fraser taking the castle back for her.

Although Hannah found it interesting to learn the Munros were a famous Highland Clan in 1562, her thoughts went to Knox.

I wonder what he's doing right now.

Hannah had called him the previous night before she went to bed. The call had gone straight to voicemail without even ringing. Although she had managed to keep herself from leaving a rambling, needy message, she had given in and texted him that morning before catching her ride for the Culloden Moor tour.

Hi Knox. Don't want to b a bother. Just wondering how Stuart is doing. xoxo, Hannah

When she couldn't keep her mind on the tour, she slipped away to check her phone. Still no response from Knox. Hannah wandered outside, to the Gaelic gardens surrounding the castle. She saw their rustic elegance, the old-world stonework and lush greenery as if through a veil. Her attention was focused on second-guessing herself for falling for Knox so completely, so quickly. Maybe her insecurities had been there for a reason. She had never been good at figuring out men's motives. Her failings with Lawrence were proof enough of that.

Make it all about you, Hannah. Knox's son and soon-to-be-daughter-in-law are in the hospital, a voice inside her head chided. *The poor guy is dealing with Stuart's accident. It could be bad.*

On the other hand, it would take all of two minutes to send a text and let her know whether things were bad or not. If he would just do that, she wouldn't be wavering, going back and forth over whether she should go back to Glasgow to support him. He had told her not to. She wanted to respect his wishes, not overstep boundaries. At the same time, she didn't want to appear not to care. Without word from Knox, it seemed like a no-win situation.

Later, when Caesar picked her up for dinner, she was still wrestling with what to do. She was quiet, lost in her thoughts, not giving actual verbal responses to her friend's attempt at conversation.

After strolling in silence for a block, Caesar asked, "Didn't you mention you met the owner of the Prestige Hotel when you were in Edinburgh?"

That got Hannah's attention. "Yes ..." she replied hesitantly.

"Did you see the news? His son died in a car accident. Horrible. A lorry went across the divider and struck the driver's side of the car. They believe he died on impact. There was a passenger in the car as well, and she's in the hospital."

It seemed Hannah's heart had stopped. She couldn't have heard correctly. "I'm sorry, Caesar. Could you repeat that, please?"

Caesar cocked his head, giving Hannah a curious sideways glance as he continued to walk along. "The owner of the Prestige Hotel, Knox Munro. His son died in a car accident a day or two ago," he repeated.

Hannah stopped walking, and grabbed Caesar's sleeve, tugging him to a halt. "You're sure he's dead?" A ringing had started up in Hannah's ears. She studied his face and tried to focus on his words.

"I believe so. It's what all the news channels are reporting." He looked bewildered at her reaction.

Hannah scrabbled in her purse and pulled out her phone. She Googled Stuart's name and stared in shock at the first headline to pop up. Her fingers pressed to her lips, she began to cry.

"Hannah ...?" Seeming to be at a loss for words, Caesar put a hand on her shoulder.

She looked up at him through her tears. "I need to get back to Glasgow as soon as possible. Is it possible for me to leave now?" Her mind going in a million different directions, she turned and started back for the hotel, frantically scrolling through every bit of information she could find about Stuart's accident. "There's a mention of donations to the Glasgow Vegetable Garden Society for Primary Student Education in lieu of flowers, but I can't find anything about funeral arrangements." She shot a helpless look at Caesar as he caught up with her.

"I can try to find out where the funeral will be and when," he offered, still looking as if he wasn't sure why Hannah was concerned.

"Thank you." Grateful, Hannah clutched his arm and let him lead her back to the hotel. "And can you get me train and hotel reservations? I've gotten to know Mr.

Munro quite well. Met his family, too. I want to be there for the funeral."

"It might be easier if I drive you to Glasgow," Caesar offered, understanding at last. "You can sleep in the back of the van, and you'll be in Glasgow by the morning. It won't be as comfortable as a bed, but I don't like the idea of you being alone right now."

Hannah's tears started up again. "Thank you."

Four days later, Hannah arrived early to the Anglican church. She hadn't heard a word from Knox at all and had been grateful Caesar had been able to find out the location and time for the funeral service. It seemed like she had picked up her phone a million times to call Knox or text him, but what would she say? What *could* she say? He had ghosted her. A tiny part of her allowed that he could have his reasons. She recognized he might need space during a difficult time like this. Still, she wanted him to know she was there for him. In whatever way he needed her to be.

As she made her way through the crowd of mourners, Hannah recognized some of the staff from the hotel. She kept her eyes peeled for Knox, and it wasn't long before she saw him come in with his parents and Sam. His arm was around Francesca, who was crying into a handkerchief. Violet wasn't there. Hannah hadn't been able to find any news online about her condition or whether she had lost the baby, and she supposed Violet would still be in the hospital.

Hannah watched the family make their way into the sanctuary and up to the front pew. She took a seat a few rows back and on the opposite side of the church where she could see Knox. His serene, unemotional expression seemed unreal, like a wax figure in Madame Tussauds Wax Museum. He stared straight ahead throughout the service, not reacting to any of the minister's words or singing any of the hymns.

At the end of the service, Hannah stood and edged toward the aisle, her gazed pinned on the Munro family. Her heart fluttered when she caught Knox's eye. There was a flicker of surprise on his face when he recognized her before the placid mask he had worn throughout the service replaced it and he looked away.

Instead of going after him, as she had planned, Hannah filed out of the church with the rest of the mourners and took the car she had hired back to the hotel. The minister had said the service at the cemetery was going to be private. He also informed everyone there would be a reception at the Madison Row Restaurant and Bar in Glasgow all day and into the evening. Hannah decided it would be the better place to pull Knox aside and express her condolences. There was no way she could comprehend what he was going through. She hoped, however, once he had gotten through the hardest part of this horrible day, he might be happy to see her.

When it came time for the reception, nausea washed over Hannah as she forced herself to walk into the Madison Row Restaurant. She tried to pick out Knox or his parents or even Sam in the groups of people milling around but didn't see any of them. Unsure where to go or what to do, she looked for a powder room. She thought it would be a good place to try to compose herself and choose the words she would say to Knox when she found him. However, as she headed toward a hallway she was certain would lead her to the restrooms, she saw him standing with a group of people. She froze, not knowing whether she should go to him. In the end, he saved her from having to decide.

"Hannah. Thank you for coming," he said cordially as he came toward her. "I'm sorry I didn't contact you earlier. It's been a ... difficult time."

"Of course it has. There's nothing to apologize for." Hannah reached out to take his hands in hers. She searched his face, noting the dark shadows smudged beneath his glassy eyes. Her heart broke at the grief and shock etched across his handsome features. "I'm sorry for your loss," she said, her voice catching when tears began pooling in her eyes. So much for not getting weepy.

Knox gave a small grateful nod. He had probably heard the same inadequate sentiment from everyone in the room.

Dabbing a tear from the corner of her eye, Hannah asked, "How is Violet? And the baby ... did she ...?" She stopped short of asking whether Knox had lost his first grandchild in addition to his son.

"She didn't lose the baby. Thank God," Knox affirmed in an oddly flat tone. He was going through such a hard time, and Hannah didn't know how to reach him through his shroud of grief and shock.

"May I introduce you to some people here?" Knox asked, seeming to need to steer the conversation toward a less painful topic.

"Yes. Of course," Hannah accepted his offer. At least he wasn't dismissing her.

Knox took her to the group of people he had been chatting with and began the introductions. "Hannah I 'd like you to meet my partner, Thomas Holiday. Tom, this is my friend, Hannah Vander Dussen. And you know my father and mother."

Hannah hugged Francesca. After an awkward silence, two more people walked up to the small group to express their condolences, and Knox introduced Hannah to them. Sam wandered over, too, his eyes bloodshot and his face pale. Hannah tried to talk with him. He only managed a few distracted nods of his head in response to her questions.

As the small cluster of people gradually drifted off, Knox turned to Hannah. "Would you like anything to eat? Can I get you a drink?"

"No, thank you." What she really wanted was to get him alone, put her arms around him, and try to convey how horrible she felt for him. More than anything, she wanted him to know she was there for him, whatever he needed.

"I saw you at the church," he said, his voice stilted and unnatural. "It was very kind of you to attend. I'm sorry you had to postpone your return to the States."

"It's not a problem." Hannah tried to catch his eye. This was all wrong. He wasn't looking at her and, when he did, it was as if he were looking through her. And when he spoke, he talked to her as if she were any other person in the room. "I don't know what to say. It's so horrible."

"There's nothing to say because it is horrible." He looked down and swallowed hard before bringing his eyes to hers. There was a wall there, erected to keep everyone out, including her. "I should return to my mam. She hasn't taken this well."

"Of course she hasn't. I can't even im—" Hannah started to say. Knox continued, cutting her off.

"You're probably wanting to get back home. Were you able to rebook your flight?"

Stunned, Hannah faltered. She might not be the best at reading people, but this was an obvious brush-off. She composed herself after a moment and replied, "I'd like to say goodbye to Francesca before I go. If it's okay."

"Yes. I'm sure she'd like that," Knox said in his empty monotone, his expression unreadable. He looked around the crowded room, then put a hand to the small of Hannah's back. "I think she's gone with my da to have a drink," he noticed, propelling her toward the bar area.

They found Francesca and Bruce standing near a high-top table, short, thick crystal glasses half-filled with whiskey sitting untouched in front of them. Hannah hugged Bruce, then Francesca, expressing her sympathy once more and telling them she wanted to say goodbye before she left.

"You're leaving?" Francesca asked, alarmed.

"Yes. I have to get back ..." she hesitated, her eyes going to Knox, searching for the smallest hint he wanted her to stay. He was looking away, though, seeming pre-occupied with scanning the crowd around them. Hannah cleared her throat and refocused on Francesca, leaning in for another hug. "I'm sorry. I have to get back to my daughter. But please let me know if I can do anything for you. Knox has my information if you need to get in touch with me."

Francesca squeezed her tight. "Please don't give up on him," she whispered in Hannah's ear before pulling back and giving Hannah a teary half-smile. Then she tugged on the arm of her son's suit jacket and directed, "Knox, see Hannah outside, will ya?"

Knox gave his mother a tight smile and walked Hannah out of the bar and through the reception area.

Hannah texted her driver as they walked, then slipped her phone back into her bag. When they reached the restaurant's front door, she turned to Knox, unsure what to say. There were a million things she wanted to tell him, and she had just as many questions to ask. This wasn't the place or the time, though, and her heart ached with panic and anguish at the thought she would never have a chance to say any of it.

Before she could come up with something meaningful to say, Knox turned to her. "Thank you again for coming," he said in the wooden tone he had adopted. "Have a pleasant flight home." He leaned forward and for one brief, hopeful moment, Hannah anticipated a kiss. However, his lips went first to one cheek, then to the other. The contact was brief and light and carried no warmth or meaning. It happened so quickly, she couldn't have said for certain it had.

She mumbled a "thank you," noticing her car pull up outside the door. As the driver stepped from the car, Knox walked away, not looking back.

"I guess it didn't take as long as you expected," the driver remarked, as he held the car door open for Hannah.

If she hadn't been numb from the old shock of Stuart's death, and the new shock of Knox's brush off, she would have responded.

Now, she only wanted to get back home to Charli.

Chapter 15

When Hannah walked into the Vine Restaurant in Beverly Hills three months later, it was like coming home. Marcie, the hostess, greeted her warmly and asked why she hadn't been in for Friday night cocktail hour and dinner with Grace. Hannah explained that she had retired from her job with the City Attorney's Office and had moved to New York.

With a disappointed frown, Marcie lamented, "It's always sad to see our regular customers move from the area. Good to see you back, though. Is it temporary or permanent?"

"Temporary, I'm afraid." A regretful expression scrunched Hannah's face. "My mom lives in the South Bay, and I've finally convinced her to move to New York with me, so I'm here to help her with the move."

"And she's also here to see friends," Grace put in, her arm coming around Hannah's shoulder. "What am I, chopped liver?" Grace challenged, her free hand going to her hip.

"Hey, you." Hannah laughed and kissed Grace's cheek. "It's about time you got here."

"It's nice to see you again, Ms. Klum," Marcie greeted Grace. "Have you moved to New York, too?"

Grace made a face of exaggerated relief. "God no, Marcie. You haven 't seen me around because I can't afford this place. My best friend, here, always insisted on fine dining and always insisted on paying. It's hard to have friends like this, but I suffer through it."

Hannah regarded her with amusement. "You always did know how to make the best of a good situation."

Marcie laughed. "Why don't I show you to your table?"

In a fit of nostalgia, Grace and Hannah placed their "usual" order, and had to fill in the new waitress on what those were. Once their watermelon martinis had been delivered and their meal of assorted appetizers was on its way, Hannah asked Grace for the latest work gossip. Grace was a paralegal and investigator who worked with Hannah before she had retired from the City Attorney's office. They had hit it off from the start and, after working together only a few times, Hannah was soon requesting Grace on a regular basis.

"Eh—it's the same shit, different day down there." Grace waved off the question and took a sip of her drink.

Hannah's lips crimped on one side. "I can imagine. Is Mason still brown-nosing everyone at the D.A.'s office?"

"Oh yes." Grace nodded. "He still wants to make the move and couldn't be more obvious." She rolled her eyes.

"You know I've always said you're the best investigator and computer whiz at the City Attorney 's office." Hannah snatched up a jalapeno popper as the waitress delivered their food. "My offer is still on the table—I'll help you if you want to go to law school. We both know you'd make a great lawyer. You're smarter than any of the attorneys at the office."

"I am hands-down smarter than most of those schmoes," Grace agreed. "You should see the new crop of entitled ass-wipes they just got in. All bookish and zero personality. And remember when you started and you got all that training? There's no training now. They just throw them in the deep end and tell them to swim. One of the new lawyers asked me this week what *voir dire* means."

Hannah put a hand to her mouth as she laughed, trying to keep from doing a spit-take with her martini. "I thought talking with you would make me miss the office," she spluttered, once she managed to swallow, "but you're making me glad I left."

"Don't get me started on the new computer system that doesn't work, and the continual layoffs. And the top dogs keep wondering why everyone's work is back-logged, and why so many trials are ending in acquittals." Grace picked at a stuffed potato skin. "Seriously, though, I thought about going to law school." She shrugged. "It's not for me. Not sure what I do want, but not that."

"Well, fill me in on your love life, then," Hannah indulged, switching topics.

"Ha," Grace snorted. "Or my lack thereof, you mean."

"You have to be kidding." Hannah shook her head. "Look at you—blonde hair, big blue eyes, a body to die for, and legs that go on forever. You could get any guy you want. I don't know why you haven't found Mr. Right."

"I've come close." Wistfulness colored Grace's tone. "I thought Jeremy was Mr. Right—until his wife burst into Giuseppe's Restaurant and announced Jeremy was most definitely Mr. Wrong." She sighed. "I just wish she hadn't assumed I knew he was married. It was embarrassing, and as you know, I'm not easy to embarrass."

Hannah gave a sympathetic nod. "I thought he might be the one, too, honey. He seemed perfect for you—too bad you can't ask a guy for a C.V. on the first date."

"Hey—not a bad idea," Grace chortled, her brows rising in optimistic arches. "There's this guy at the jiu-jitsu studio who's a retired LAPD officer. He's a P.I. now. I could hire him to investigate everyone I consider dating."

Stifling a chuckle, Hannah jested, "Too bad you can't use the computers at work for personal investigation to do it yourself."

"Don't I know it, sister," Grace responded, holding her glass up to toast Hannah. "You and I have always been the rule followers, though, so there's no chance of that." She took a long draw on the straw, then stirred it around in the glass as her expression changed to thoughtful. "So ... no news from the tragic, bossy Scot?" she asked.

"Not a peep." Hannah shook her head. "The only communication I've received from anyone or anything

Scottish-related was a postcard from the Glasgow Vegetable Gardens Society for Primary Student Education thanking me for my donation in honor of Stuart Gregorio Munro."

"That's tough," Grace commiserated. "I can't start to imagine what it would be like to lose a child, let alone know what to say to someone who has."

Hannah shook her head. "I've almost called or texted him a hundred times, but how do I even start a conversation? He couldn't wait to get away from me the last time we saw each other. He may not want to talk to me. I keep hoping he'll come around and realize how good we were together."

"You haven't made any moves either," Grace pointed out. "Don't you think enough time has passed? Maybe you should give it a try. You're still in love with him, right?"

"Yes," Hannah admitted. "I don't think I'll ever get over him. It's crazy. I'll be eighty-five years old and still pining for him."

"You don't have anything to lose by contacting him," Grace encouraged. "He'll either want to start up again, or he'll reject you and you'll be in exactly the same position you're in now."

"I'm trying to give him time to grieve in his own way." Hannah twisted her empty martini glass around and around. She had been using the same excuse with herself over the last months, and it sounded even weaker out loud. "Stuart's passing was such a horrific thing. I've been hoping he'll contact me when he comes around, but the longer time goes on, the less it seems likely we'll reconnect." She blew out a despondent sigh. "For all I know, he may have already found someone else, and remarried."

Grace leveled her with a no-nonsense gaze. "Doubtful." Then, cocking her head, she teased, "So you're really hung up on this guy who was demanding in bed? I can't believe you're this far gone over someone who tells you when to come."

"Jeez, Gracie!" Hannah's cheeks flared and she cast around, looking to make sure no one had heard her friend's remark. "I guess that's what I get for telling you my dirty secrets." Leaning closer, she lowered her voice. "Actually, even though he was bossy, Knox was a selfless and giving lover."

"Mmm!" Grace gave an appreciative nod. "No wonder you're hooked."

"I am!" Hannah's hushed tone took on a desperate edge. "When I masturbate, I can't get off unless I fantasize he's telling me to come, or that he's going down on me and I'm following his instructions about coming." Hannah sat back and pinned Grace with a helpless stare. "Am I the most pathetic person you've ever met?"

"No, sweetie, you're not. You're the best person I know." She clasped Hannah's hand. "I'd just love to see you happy. Either with him in your life in some capacity, or over him and finding someone else who deserves you. Or, hell, even moving on and being happily single."

Hannah considered her friend's words. "I'll think about contacting him," she acquiesced at last. "It scares me, though."

"Ah, but what doesn't kill us, makes us stronger," Grace said sagely.

"Ha. Way to kill a pep talk," Hannah chuckled.

Grace brightened. "Since I'm free and easy and single right now, I'd love to have some crazy adventures like you had in Scotland. Unfortunately, I can only afford a vacation to El Cajon to visit my foster parents."

"I keep telling you to come visit me in New York." Hannah coaxed, handing her empty glass to the waitress, exchanging it for a fresh martini. "I'm only working part-time, and the Legal Aid Clinic allows me flexibility to work around Charli's school schedule. I can take time off whenever you want to visit."

"A trip to New York *would* be less expensive than a Scottish excursion." Although Grace looked like she was considering it, it seemed she needed some convincing. "It's still more expensive than El Cajon, though."

Hannah gave her friend a fond smile. "Put your pride in your pocket, my love, and let me pay for you to come to New York. Heck, I'd love for you to come live with me. I'm desperately lonely for your company."

"I miss you too," Grace replied in earnest. "More than you know. We still FaceTime a lot."

"Don't get me wrong. I love to FaceTime with you, but I prefer face-to-face time."

When Grace looked down and a small smile started creeping across her lips, Hannah knew she was on the verge of crumbling.

"I do have a lot of vacation time accumulated. I was told to use it or lose it," Grace admitted, speaking as if she were thinking out loud. Bringing her eyes to meet Hannah's, she asked, "You'll be here for another week helping your mom, right?"

Hannah nodded.

"That would give me enough time to fix my schedule at work." While enthusiasm seemed to be ramping up, she was biting her lip and the look she was giving Hannah said, *This is crazy, right?*

Eyes wide with excitement, Hannah was practically trembling. "Are you serious? Don't lead me on here, Grace. I've had enough heartbreak for one lifetime."

Grace had her lips pinned between her teeth, but she nodded. "Yeah. I think I'm serious." She feigned putting more thought into the notion, then nodded again. "Yes. I'm serious. Let's do this."

Throwing her arms around Grace, Hannah let out a squeal. "Gracie! Thank you, thank you, thank you! Oh, you made my day." Pulling back, she started planning. "I'll book the flight for you as soon as I get to mom's townhouse. It's going to be perfect timing because we just finished construction on the separate suite for my mom, so the guest room will be available. In fact, Charli and I call the guest room 'Gracie's room.'"

Touched, Grace put a hand to her heart. "That is so sweet. I really miss Charli. I can't wait to see her."

"She'll be happy to see you, too."

Hannah held up her glass and Grace followed her lead.

"Here's to best friends," Hannah declared, clinking her glass against Grace's.

"To all the laughter and the tears," Grace said, adding to the toast, "and being there for each other no matter what."

Chapter 16

On a bright early autumn morning, Hannah and her driver, Jonnie, walked into Hannah's spacious co-op after dropping Charli off at her Upper East Side school and running a few errands.

"You can put the grocery bags there, Jonnie." Hannah gestured toward the kitchen island as she hung the plastic-encased dry cleaning on a hook inside the laundry room door. Turning to Jonnie, she pointed out, "I think Grace is still asleep and Mom has probably been up for hours puttering around in her suite. Would you like to join me for a cup coffee?"

"No thank you, Mrs. Vander Dussen. I've got an appointment to have your oil changed. I need to get going," Jonnie replied.

Hannah smiled. "Alright, but I keep telling you—please call me Hannah."

Jonnie's cheeks colored and he ducked his head, hiding a self-conscious smile. "Sure thing, Mrs.—uh, Hannah."

With an affectionate shake of her head, she watched him go before pouring herself a cup of coffee. Then, she settled down at the table in the breakfast nook with her phone.

Ever since their talk over drinks the month before, Hannah had been mulling over Gracie's advice to contact Knox. Although it was a scary prospect, the more she had thought about it, the more she wanted to do it. She missed him and every day she wondered how he was doing. He was still grieving, she was certain. However, maybe enough time had gone by. He might welcome a friendly shoulder to lean on. And, if she did contact him now, it might awaken the possibility of a new beginning. Pulling up his name in her phone's contact list, Hannah tapped the message icon and began typing a text. It took more than one round of edits before she came up with something that didn't make her cringe.

Hi Knox, I hope u r doing well. U and ur lovely family remain in my thoughts. Love, Hannah

Heart racing, she hit send before she could chicken out. She held her breath as she watched for the telltale pulsing dots indicating he was responding. When the screen remained static, she exhaled a sigh. Maybe enough time hadn't passed, she thought, setting the phone aside and heading off to check on her mother, and maybe it never would.

A couple of days later, however, her phone pinged with Knox's response. Hannah did a double-take when she saw his name next to the text notification. Her heart skipped an actual beat, and with a trembling finger, she tapped on the message and read it.

Hi Hannah. Thnk u for ur text. I hope u and Charil r doing well. Everyone here is doing as well as can be xpected. I'm going to b in NY in a few days. Would u have time to get together for a cup of coffee? Hugs, Knox

Her mind was in a whirl, analyzing every word. She ran to find Grace. Hannah needed her to help pick the message apart.

Grace was lying on the bed in the guest room reading a book when Hannah rushed in through the open door. She set her book aside as Hannah, without preamble, began reading the text in an excited, anxious voice.

"He didn't say 'love' back to me," Hannah fretted once she had shared Knox's words with Grace. "Why did I say 'love' in my text? It was too much, wasn't it? Why didn't I think to put hugs?"

It took Grace a moment to catch up with what Hannah was talking about before she put it all together. "Honey, this isn't like you." Grace pulled her friend to sit beside her on the bed. "With Lawrence, you always acted with purpose and direction and confidence. Even once things went sideways and you figured out what a schmuck he is." She took Hannah's phone from her and held it out so they could both see Knox's text. "Look, he wrote back. And he asked you for coffee. That's a big step. You have an opportunity to meet with him. Focus on the positive."

Hannah nodded. Grace always made her see things in a realistic light. "You're right. I'm going to answer him back right away."

"Good." Grace gave her a side hug, tilting her head to rest against Hannah's. "And remember, you're an awesome person. That has nothing to do with anybody but you."

Back in the privacy of her room, Hannah carefully constructed her reply to Knox.

Hi there! Charli and I r doing well, thnk u.

Yes, I'd like to c u. xoxo, H

Considering Knox hadn't responded to her initial text right away, she tried not to let it bother her when an immediate answer didn't come to her latest message. She talked herself into focusing on the positive, as Grace had counseled her, even though she was battling feeling like a bit of a stalker. She had had her moment in the spotlight of his attention and affection and had never wanted it to end. At the same time, she had a nagging suspicion they weren't on the same page with each other. His feelings for her had probably never progressed as much as hers for him. Although she had resolved not to hound him, it was hard not to obsess over him, over what she could have said and done differently.

At last, a few days later, Hannah received a text:

Hi Hannah, I'm in NY. Would u b able to meet for a coffee tomorrow? Knox

Like last time, no love. No hugs or kisses, either, Hannah noted with a sinking feeling.

He wants to see you. Focus on the positive, Hannah told herself as she typed out her simple reply:

Yes, I can meet u. H

This time, Knox's reply came right away.

There's a Starbucks at 58th and 8th at 4 Columbus Circle. Can u meet me there around 9 am?

Hannah typed a response:

Yes I'll b there. C u tomorrow.

On impulse, she added "xoxo" to the end of her text and sent it, then put it out of her mind. She would know soon enough if he had any lingering feelings for her.

The next morning, Hannah fussed over her wardrobe, and settled on a casual fall outfit in neutral browns and beiges. Looking at herself in the mirror, she wondered if she should go with a cardigan instead of the over-sized linen blazer over the cropped knit tank top and pinched waist jeans she was wearing. She had lost a little weight, and the blazer seemed to accentuate it. Glancing at her phone, Hannah decided she didn't have time to switch outfits yet again, and hoped Knox wouldn't scrutinize her too closely for changes.

As Hannah was slipping on her shoes, Grace walked into the room.

"My God, woman, you are beautiful—and so hot!" Grace exclaimed. "You look like Natalie Portman—if Natalie had blue eyes and wore a size D cup."

Hannah laughed. "Just the ego boost I needed right now."

"You'll knock him dead," Grace encouraged, then faked a look of remorse. "Oops. Wrong thing to say. Too soon?"

Snatching up her pocketbook, Hannah gave her friend a mildly scolding look. "Honey, your gallows humor is tacky, and I'll have to punch you if you say anything like that again."

"Noted," Grace pouted, struggling to pull off the penitent look she was trying for. "So are you ready for this? How do you feel?"

"I feel sick, but I'm going anyway." She kissed Grace on the cheek. "Wish me luck. Love you."

Deciding the fresh air might calm her nerves, Hannah decided to walk the two miles from the Upper East Side to Columbus Circle. When she arrived at the coffeehouse, Knox was already there, sipping a coffee. All her pent-up emotions came flooding to the surface as she saw his handsome face in profile. Like her, it seemed he had lost some weight. Even so, he was still gorgeous. She almost couldn't believe he was there in person. Over the months since she had returned from Scotland, it sometimes felt like she had dreamed her time with Knox. She had only taken one selfie with him, during their picnic at Loch Lomond and had taken to looking at it occasionally to remind herself it had all been real. That he was real.

And now he was there, across the room.

As if feeling her eyes on him, Knox turned and looked at her. An unreadable emotion passed over his face, there and then gone. He got up and came to greet her, kissing both her cheeks in turn. "I got here early and grabbed a coffee. I have one for you, too. Do you still take it with a little milk?"

Hannah nodded, overwhelmed with having Knox right there, close enough to touch, and that he had remembered such a little detail like how she took her coffee.

"Please, let's sit." Knox guided her to the little bistro table he had been sitting at and pulled a chair out for her. He slid the extra coffee toward her before taking the seat across from her.

"Ya look beautiful." Knox's gaze was serious, and he spoke with an even tone. It seemed sincere but told her nothing about what, if anything, he felt for her.

"Thank you," she said, ignoring the troupe of circus performers tumbling through her stomach.

"How's Charli?"

"She's doing well." Hannah took a sip of coffee, and hoped Knox didn't see her hand shaking as she placed the cardboard cup back on the table.

"And are ya working?" Knox asked.

"A little. I'm working part-time for a legal aid clinic."

"Sounds interesting. What type of cases are ya handling?"

Hannah couldn't decide if the neutral territory this conversation was in was soothing or if it was driving her crazy. On the one hand, they were talking about banal, safe things. On the other hand, she wanted to scream and beg him to kiss her.

"A little bit of everything," she answered. "It's attached to a women's shelter, so cases principally relating to domestic violence."

"Are ya working as an attorney, like ya were in California?" Knox seemed happy to stick with the polite conversation. "I thought in the U.S., lawyers had to pass the Bar in each state to practice law in that particular state."

"They do. Lawrence went to law school here, and he wasn't sure if he was going to practice in California or New York," Hannah explained. "So, we sat for both the California and New York state Bars. I'm glad I did, because I don 't think I'd have the fortitude to go through the preparation process again."

Does he even want to be here? Hannah wondered. If this was the game they were playing, she could make small talk, too.

"How's your family? Francesca and Bruce? Sam?"

"As I said—as well as can be expected under the circumstances. Sam has taken it all really hard. He feels guilty about his relationship with Stuart. We all feel guilty. It's been a difficult time."

Hannah nodded, eager for him to go on. Maybe Knox would open up if she could keep him talking.

"Sam's given up his interest in extreme sports," he continued, putting fuel on the little fire of hope burning inside Hannah. "He's working a lot more hours, too. It's ironic – he was the one I was always worried about. Stuart was predictably stable." He gave a small, rueful chuckle.

"And Violet? How is she?"

"The doctors erred on the side of caution and kept her in hospital for a few weeks. She's been released now. She didn't suffer any permanent injuries. And the baby is fine, thank God." Knox paused and looked down at the table, and Hannah could see he was struggling. They had all been so happy when Stuart had told them about the baby. Now, with Stuart gone, though a part of him would live on, a baby wasn't a consolation to Knox for losing his son.

"Goodness. Well. What a relief, right?" *What else could I say?*

"Yes." Knox met Hannah's eye again and gave her a tight smile. "We've been trying to find the silver linings where we can."

Hannah was trying to formulate a helpful reply, but Knox continued speaking.

"There has been a recent, strange turn of events. It's really the reason I wanted to meet with ya."

Brow creased, Hannah inclined her head, inviting him to go on.

"Violet is from Edinburgh," he began, heading in a direction that had Hannah completely lost. "She started coming into the hotel to visit with me, and to discuss her future with the baby. She met a man during one of the visits when I was tending bar, and they are seeing each other seriously now."

"Does he know about the baby?" Hannah asked, still unsure what this had to do with her.

"He knows and is very excited and supportive about the baby—or so Violet maintains. They are planning on living together and raising the child together." Knox gave a grave shake of his head. "I have to admit ... the whole thing bothers me because it's too soon after Stuart's death. How could anyone truly love someone, then move on so quickly?"

"It doesn't make sense," Hannah agreed. She had been asking herself the same question about Knox's ability to let her go so easily.

"None of it is the worst or at least the strangest part." He paused to take a drink from his coffee, fixing his gaze on a spot in the middle of the table. "The man Violet has fallen in love with is Eric McGregor."

Hannah had put Eric out of her mind. Hearing his name now had the same effect as getting doused with a bucket of ice water. "Wh-what? No. How can that be?"

"It stunned me, too." Knox's shoulder came up in a helpless shrug. "I don't think it's a coincidence. He was obsessed with ya. Have ya seen or heard from him since the night in the bar?"

"No. Not at all." Hannah shook her head.

Knox thought for a moment, then nodded. "Good. I asked Eric about it. Interrogated him and he didn't appreciate it. He claimed Violet never mentioned anything about ya, and claimed he didn't know you and I were together when you were in Scotland. So, if that's true, it was coincidence, and he didn't plan it. He'd have to be a sociopath if he did. It's too bizarre, though. I've asked him not to mention it to Violet, or to my family, and he agreed."

As Hannah processed the news, Knox's phone chimed and he glanced at the screen. "I have a meeting I need to get to. Ya have my information. If Eric McGregor contacts ya for any reason, will ya let me know?" Knox stood and tossed his coffee cup in a nearby trash can.

"Wait," Hannah reached out and caught his wrist. "Is that it? You don't want to ...?" Hannah couldn't finish her question as she sat blinking, unable to believe talking about Eric was the only reason he wanted to meet with her.

"Hannah ... I ..." Knox started, then sighed and sat down again. He almost reached for Hannah's hand, then drew back. "You know, I did this same thing when Jayne died. I pulled away from everyone and poured myself into work. It's how I deal. I've been a walking zombie trying to get through the days."

"You don't have to go through this alone." Hannah scooted her chair closer and placed her hand over his. If she could just get through to him, make him see how much she cared.

"I've started seeing a grief counselor. It's been in the back of my mind if I can get through this somehow, if I can get myself sorted, I'd be in a better place to ..." he trailed off, grimacing, and slid his hand away from hers. Weary helplessness filled his eyes when he looked at her. "I don't know, Hannah. What do ya want me to say?"

"I don't want you to say anything." Hannah hesitated, her heart pounding. Did she dare tell him she still had feelings for him? If she didn't, she might never have the chance again. "I'm still in love with you, Knox," she gushed, terrified and elated at the same time. "I want you to say you still have feelings for me, too. What I want is for you to kiss me and say you don't want to spend another day apart."

Knox gazed at her for a moment, a string of emotions passing through his eyes so fast, Hannah couldn't guess what he was thinking. At last, he leaned forward and kissed her, a soft, gentle kiss that took her breath away and broke her heart with its tenderness.

A lump rose in Hannah's throat as he deepened the kiss, bringing his hand up to cup her cheek. His tongue slipped through her lips, lapping soft strokes, sensual and undemanding. This was nothing like the insistent, challenging Knox who had seemed to need her like he needed the air he breathed.

Too soon, he broke the kiss and stood again, not meeting her eyes.

"Where are you going?" Hannah asked, incredulous. "You can't just kiss me and leave without saying a word. I just told you I still love you. If you don't have feelings for me, you at least owe it to me to say so."

"God, Hannah, how can you say that?" Knox raked his fingers through his hair. Seeing his reaction had caught the attention of the other patrons in the coffee shop, he lowered his voice. "Of course, I love you. I've been in love with you since I first met you. Wasn't it obvious?"

"You never told me." The entire scene had Hannah stunned. She had finally heard the words from him she had longed to hear for months, but his tone and actions were all wrong.

"Look, Hannah. Guilt is eating me alive. I feel guilty about telling ya the night before Stuart died that you were lucky to have only one child. I feel guilty about almost every parenting decision I made with Stuart. I feel guilty I was having sex while my son was dying. And I particularly feel guilty for missing you more than my own son." He looked away, and when he looked back, tears glimmered in his beautiful dark eyes. "What kind of a monster does that make me?"

"Of course you miss Stuart more than me," Hannah consoled him, aching to reach out and touch him again, afraid he would pull away. "The loss of your son is permanent and horrendous. I can't begin to understand what it's like, but you living in a black hole won't solve anything. You don't deserve to keep punishing yourself."

Knox shook his head. "I'm sorry I dragged you into my wretched life. Seeing ya suffering as a result of our meeting—it's just one more regret I have." He chuckled, but there was no humor in it. "I don't have anything left to give. Not to you, not to anyone."

When he turned and started walking away, Hannah jumped up and went after him. She followed him out onto the sidewalk so she could say her peace without everyone in the coffee shop eavesdropping.

As they stepped through the door, she grabbed his arm and pulled him around to face her.

"Listen, you big jerk, I understand your feelings are all in a jumble, but before you walk away, probably forever, I want you to know—" The words stopped coming and Hannah had to ask herself, *What else can I say?* She had done everything except get down on her knees and beg him to take her back.

Knox's eyes darted to her hand, still holding onto his arm.

Hannah let go and took a step back. She looked around, feeling as if she was on display, being watched. While she wouldn't get on her knees right here in this too public place, neither would she let him burn his bridge with her.

"When you decide to get yourself together, I'll be waiting for you," she told him, taking another step back and standing taller. "I'll take anything you're willing or able to give to me. A phone call, a text, a date." She paused and swallowed, trying to speak strong and steady. "I'll take marriage, a kiss, sex—anything you're willing to give. But I'm not contacting you again. The ball's in your court now."

Chapter 17

On a sunny afternoon three weeks later, Hannah sat on her bed, looking out the window at the stunning view of Manhattan's Upper East Side, the satellite radio tuned to her favorite alternative rock station. The spacious suite she had designed and decorated herself was her haven. Awash in a serene palette of pale blues, periwinkle, and violet, surrounded by a mix of antiques and modern furniture and artwork she had brought from California, it was more than comfortable. It was completely hers, and it also gave her privacy when she wanted it. And it was roomy enough for her to work from home when she wanted to or for her daughter to join her, whenever Charli needed help with her homework.

While the suite was her refuge, lately it hadn't offered the comfort Hannah needed. To be honest, since she had met Knox for coffee, nothing seemed to feel good. Sitting alone in the middle of her king-sized bed, she had never felt more alone or heartsick, and it frustrated her. Sure, she had had a wonderful time with Knox in Scotland.

And, no, she hadn't dived into the relationship expecting it to last beyond her vacation.

Well, not at first, anyway. But as she let herself fall for Knox, she had been certain he was falling for her, too. Although he hadn't actually said he loved her, he had called her "my love." Why had she read so much into it? And why, after he had told her he didn't have anything left to give her, did she keep dwelling on thoughts of him? At least when Grace was still in town, she had been a source of support as well as a distraction. When they were shopping or walking through Central Park or kicking back with a glass of wine, Grace had kept Hannah's mind occupied. Kept it off its endless circling around what had happened with Knox and what she could have done differently. And, on those occasions when Hannah couldn't help thinking of him, Grace gave Hannah a shoulder to lean on. Better yet, she lent her ear to listen, and offered her brand of support laced with wry humor.

Now, Hannah exhaled a heavy sigh. Anymore, it seemed as if she was always missing someone, either Knox or Grace. She reached for her phone. Hannah had left the ball in Knox's court and the message his silence sent was loud and clear, but she knew she could always count on Grace. Before she had a chance to bring up her friend's number, her phone chimed with a text. Hannah's breath caught when she saw Knox's name pop onto the screen.

Hello Hannah. It's Knox. How have u been?

Heart pounding, Hannah could only stare at her phone. Her thoughts were swirling so fast, she couldn't follow any of them. At last, she tapped out a reply.

Hi. Of course I know it's u. I've been ...

Fine? Good? Miserable without you? What was the best answer to that question? The typical response touched nowhere near her reality, and the truth might be more than he could handle. Deciding she needed to know why he was contacting her now after almost a month, she opted for the safe choice of words.

Hannah: ...I've been busy, doing well. How r you?

Knox: Busy, as well, and doing better— not great.

Leaving Hannah no chance to dissect his message, another text popped onto the screen:

Knox: I miss u.

Too many emotions hit her at once with those three words. Though tears prickled in her eyes, she couldn't stop the huge smile from spreading across her face.

Hannah: I miss u 2.

Knox: Can I call u 2nite 2 chat?

As she began typing out an excited "yes," Hannah stopped herself. What did he need to say on the phone he couldn't say in a text? Was it more bad news about Eric? Or could she even let herself hope he wanted to reconnect with her? Erasing her initial response, she typed:

Hannah: I think that would b ok. Is everything alrite?

Knox: Everythings fine

Hannah frowned at the simple two-word message as three dots pulsed, indicating Knox was still typing. At last, another message appeared.

Knox: I'd just like to talk for a bit. It would be good to hear your voice, and if I haven't completely cocked

things up between us, I was wondering if you mite give me another shot.

She bit back a smile. Knox wanted her back. The lonely ache she had been indulging in only minutes before gave way to a surge of joy.

Hannah: Well…I'm open to possibilities.

She punctuated her message with a pink sparkling heart emoji.

Knox: More than I hoped for. (smiling emoji) I don't know what I did to deserve a second chance with you, but I promise I'll make it worth it. (winking kiss emoji)

Hannah: I was going to say you can thank my questionable judgment and poor taste, but I like the sound of that promise. I'm going to hold you to it, you know.

Knox: You'd better—I'm counting on it.

Grinning, Hannah pressed her phone to her heart. They had slipped back into their playful groove. She felt like a teenager flirting with her crush. When her phone pinged with another text from Knox, she held it up and read:

Knox: So, I'll call you around 9 pm?

Hannah: Ok—can't wait

Knox: Me 2. xx

Hannah stared at the two kisses Knox had signed off with, ecstatic joy flooding her heart until it felt like she would burst. When "Viva la Vida" started playing on the radio, she jumped up, cranked the volume and began singing along.

"I used to rule the world …"

Pumped with elated energy, her body wouldn't keep still. She started swaying to the music, then progressed to full-on dancing, her feet carrying her across the room. Hannah threw open the French doors and burst out onto the patio. She danced while singing to the colorful flowers in the large and small pots scattered among the comfortable chairs and bistro table.

"... Roman Cavalry choirs are singing ..."

"Mom?" Charli popped her head inside Hannah's bedroom door and pounded a loud rap on the door jamb. "Mom, what are you doing?"

Hannah whirled around, unable to stop celebrating. Wearing a broad smile that wouldn't quit, she waved Charli over while she continued to sing.

Looking bemused, Charli joined her for the final chorus, although not quite putting in the dance effort Hannah was.

When the song was over, Charli snatched up the remote control and dialed the volume down to single digits.

"Wow," she declared, giving Hannah a careful look. "What's up with the excitement? Are we going to a Coldplay concert?"

With a laugh, Hannah drew her daughter in for a hug. "No, sweetie. I just got some good news. I reconnected with a friend I met in Scotland."

"Ugh," Charlie groused, squirming in Hannah's tight embrace. "Mom! I can't breathe!"

Hannah giggled and let Charli loose. "Sorry, honey. I'm just ... it was good to hear from him."

At 8:55, Hannah's phone lit up and Knox's name flashed on the screen. She pushed excited anticipation aside and forced herself to let it ring a few times while she settled in on the plush sofa in her bedroom suite.

"Hello?" She wove uncertainty into her tone, as if she didn't know for a fact who was calling.

"Hello, sweetheart." Knox's smooth brogue sent her heart racing. "How are ya?"

"Better," Hannah responded, "now I'm talking to you. Where are you?"

"I'm in London."

Hannah did a quick calculation in her head. "So, eight hours ahead. It must be early morning for you."

"It is. I set my alarm so we could chat a bit before I head out." When he paused, Hannah wondered if he was as nervous as she was. Before she could come up with something to say, he cleared his throat and said, "I didn't mean to apologize in a text. I wanted to say all those things to you in person. That's why I asked about phoning you."

"Then why didn't you go ahead and call?" Hannah chided him gently, her smile warming her words.

"I wasn't sure you wanted to hear from me," he admitted. "It wasn't exactly the brave way to go about it, but I thought it would be easier to handle rejection through a text than have ya hang up on me if I called out of the blue."

"I wouldn't hang up on you!" Hannah replied through an incredulous laugh. "I've been thinking about you almost non-stop. The only reason I didn't call you first was because I left the ball in your court. Remember?"

"Yes, I remember." Knox chuckled. "Yir stronger than I am, sweetheart. I thought the best thing I could do for ya was to stay away. I'm a selfish bastard, though, because it turns out it was the worst thing for me, and I couldn't go one more day without talking to ya."

Tears welled in Hannah's eyes. "I'm glad you're a selfish bastard," she responded through a wobbly smile. "It saved me from breaking down and begging you to take me back."

Knox laughed. "Oh, Hannah...I've missed you. Talk to me, please, sweetheart. Tell me about yir day. Tell me what ya've been up to."

That was easy enough. She told him about her work, about Charli, and about living in New York. After going on for several minutes, it started to feel like she was monopolizing the conversation. She stopped her monologue and asked, "What have you been up to?"

"I promise to catch ya up soon, but will you indulge me and keep talking? I've missed hearing yir voice."

"Ha—I've talked your ear off. You'll be sick of the sound of me soon."

"Never," Knox assured. "In fact, if I'm out of the dog-house now, will ya contact me sometimes, rather than waiting for me to initiate?"

"Yes. Of course," Hannah agreed.

Knox sighed. "I'd like to talk to ya all day, but I've got to get to work. Can I call ya tomorrow at the same time?"

Although he couldn't see her, Hannah nodded. "I'll be waiting to hear from you at nine o'clock tomorrow night."

"Sweet dreams, then, sweetheart." His low voice tingled into her ear and sent heat pulsing through her body.

"You've pretty much guaranteed that, Mr. Monro," she teased.

For the next few weeks, Hannah and Knox got reacquainted, talking or texting almost every day—and sometimes both. One afternoon, as Hannah was wondering whether she would hear from him or if she should stay up to call him later, he texted her.

Knox: Hannah, my schedule's changed, and I'm going to b in NY next week. Can I see you? xx

Hannah: Yes, of course. It will b Thnxgiving week here. xx

Knox: It's the only time one of our important vendors will be able to meet, the Wednesday before your holiday. It's just another day for those of us across the pond. (winking emoji)

After weeks of flirtatious texts and long phone conversations, the prospect of seeing Knox again in person was more than exciting. Hannah bit her lip as she debated whether to ask the question she wanted to ask.

Hannah: Since u'll b in town, do u want to come over for Thnxgiving and meet mom and Charli?

Was asking him to meet her family too much, too soon? She had her answer before she had time to wish she hadn't put the invitation out there.

Knox: Don't bite your lip, sweetheart. That's my job.

Hannah smiled. He knew her too well.

Knox: Yes, I'd love to.

Yippee!! She did a little victory dance in her seat.

Knox: What time do you want me to be there?

Hannah: We eat early. It's my mom's thing. Around 3 for cocktails and 4 for dinner?

Knox: That's fine.

Hannah: Do u want to spend the night?

Heat prickled up Hannah's neck as she watched her screen for Knox's reply. At last, it came:

Knox: Would it b ok? I mean, with your family there...

Hannah: Chari is going to her dad's after dinner to spend the weekend w/him. Mom has a suite here— she's in her own separate world. We probably won't see her the whole weekend, but if she asks—and don't freak out!—I'll tell her you'll b staying over b/c ur my boyfriend. It will be fine w/her.

Another interminable beat went by before Knox replied.

Knox: I'm your boyfriend?

Hannah: Is that ok?

Knox: Yes, I'm your boyfriend—and you're my girl, amore mio.

Hannah: So, u'll stay at my place, then?

Knox: It's a sacrifice, of course.

Hannah: Yes. Ur such a martyr. Bring lots of wine, you wine snob!

Knox: Will do. Xx

Chapter 18

At 2:55 p.m. on Thanksgiving Day, the intercom of Hannah's co-op buzzed, and the doorman announced Hannah's guest had arrived and was on his way up. When she opened her door, she found Knox standing there holding several carrier bags filled with bottles in one hand, a small Italian duffel bag dangling from the other. As handsome as ever, he was wearing a nervous smile, along with tailored Armani slate gray slacks and jacket over a silver sand button down shirt. Hannah had been battling disbelief, unable to trust she would actually see Knox in the flesh again. Even with him there at her door, it still didn't feel quite real. She rose up on her toes and kissed him on each cheek. Then she drew him inside and stashed his duffel in the hall closet before taking him to meet her mother and Charli.

"Charli's a nickname," she explained as she guided Knox toward the kitchen. "She's named after my mom, Charlotte, so we call my daughter 'Charli' to keep things from getting too confusing."

Grandmother and granddaughter looked up from their food preparations when Hannah and Knox came into the kitchen. As Hannah made the introductions, she noted the bashful smile her daughter gave Knox along with a mumbled greeting and hoped Charli would come out of her shell before long. Knox would only have the afternoon to get to know her before she left to spend the rest of the holiday with Lawrence; Hannah wanted to see how they would get along.

"Charli put together the trays of appetizers," Hannah told Knox as she took two of the carrier bags from him and set them on the countertop.

"Very nice." Knox complimented Charli. "I like how ya've arranged it all. Presentation is everything."

Color pinked Charli's cheeks. She dropped her gaze and murmured a shy, "Thanks."

"I don't have a fancy wine thingy like the one you use at the restaurant." Hannah held up a corkscrew. "But I have this, if you would like to open a bottle of wine."

Knox produced a double-lever waiter's corkscrew from the bag he still held. "I came prepared," he said, pulling out a bottle, along with the corkscrew. "And, if ya don't mind, why don't we start with champagne? I brought sparkling apple cider for Charli." He turned his smiling eyes on Hannah's daughter, who grinned back at him this time.

"Wonderful idea," Hannah concurred, going to the cupboard for the champagne flutes while Knox popped the cork. "Mom, would you mind making the toast?"

Charlotte looked up in surprise from slicing vegetables. "Oh, dear ... I'm not sure." She set down the knife and wiped her hands on her apron. "But I suppose I could give it a shot." She accepted the glass Hannah held out to her as Knox poured fizzing cider into a flute for Charli. When everyone had a drink in their hands, Charlotte raised hers high.

"I'm thankful to be here today with my wonderful daughter and my wonderful granddaughter," Charlotte shared, "and I'm thankful Knox could join us all the way from Scotland."

Glasses clinked and everyone exclaimed, "Cheers!"

After a few sips of champagne, Charlotte said she and Charli needed to get back to work if dinner was to be served on time.

"We all pitched in and made different parts of the meal today." Charli had been quiet up to that point and even though she offered the information for Knox's benefit, she didn't look directly at him when she spoke. "Grandma is doing the turkey and dressing, and Mom made the pumpkin and pecan pies and the rolls. And Grandma and I walked to the grocery store to buy the appetizers."

When everyone laughed, Charli grinned. "What? It counts."

Knox put a fond hand on her shoulder. "Yes, it definitely counts. And not only are the appetizers delicious, you arranged them very artistically."

The compliment did the trick of chipping away a bit more of Charli's shyness. Pleased, she beamed at Knox before turning to help Charlotte with the salad.

As Charli and Charlotte got busy, Hannah and Knox exchanged a longing look.

"Is there anything I can do to help?" Knox asked.

Hannah thought for a moment. "Well, you could help me get the table and chairs situated, and then we could get the serving platters out of the cupboard and wash them."

He nodded, and followed her direction in moving things around, then trailed Hannah to the cupboards by the sink. When she went up on tiptoe, trying to reach the platters on the highest shelf, he came up and reached over her from behind to bring them down. After an eternity apart, her body responded to the contact, rippling with a warm, pleasant sensation, a heated flush coloring her cheeks. She bit her lip, thankful neither her daughter nor her mother could read her mind.

While Hannah washed the platters, Knox dried them and put them in a stack on the counter. When they had finished, Hannah sneaked a glance at Charli and Charlotte. Their heads were together over a simmering pot as the older woman schooled the young girl on the secrets to a silken gravy. Hannah edged toward the door and motioned Knox to follow her.

She led him to her bedroom and, once inside, she locked the door behind them. Without a word, Knox lifted her up and started kissing her. Hannah wrapped her legs around him as he walked her across the room and pressed her against the wall. The kiss was passionate, more than Hannah had experienced with Knox in the past. The kiss told her, with no need for words, that he loved her and was as happy as she was they had found their way back to each other.

As Hannah felt her own excitement rising, Knox reluctantly drew away. Resting his forehead against hers, he asked, "Should we get back out there before yir family comes looking for us?"

Hannah released her legs from Knox's waist and let him set her on her feet. "I guess we should," she agreed without conviction, pressing herself against his erection.

Knox moaned, pleasure and misery chasing across his face. "I've missed you, Hannah. Every inch of you and everything about you."

"Not more than I've missed you." She pulled him down for another kiss, nipping at his lip before she released him.

Back in the kitchen, Charlotte looked up from supervising Charli. "There you two are, just in time. Dinner is ready."

Knox picked up the platter holding the turkey and took it to the dining table. While Hannah, Charli and Charlotte ferried the rest of the food to the table, he asked Charlotte about her wine preferences. Then he opened bottles of wine and poured and distributed wine glasses to everyone seated around the table. He filled Charli's champagne flute with more sparkling cider and brought it to her before taking a seat next to Hannah.

"Everything looks delectable," he praised, raising his glass. "To the beautiful cooks of this wonderful meal."

The ladies raised their glasses to his toast. However, after taking a sip of wine, Hannah confessed, "While the three of us have been cooking and baking up a storm all week long, I have to admit, I didn't contribute much to the meal. I'm not much of a cook, but I do like to bake."

"That's why Mom made the rolls and pies," Charli explained to Knox. "Her pies are awesome, but Grandma did everything else. Well, except for the green bean casserole, the yam mousse, and the potatoes au gratin. Andrew made those and brought them over."

"And don't forget—you made the salads, darling girl," Charlotte acknowledged.

Charli beamed. "And I made the salads."

"Who's Andrew?" Knox asked, plucking a warm roll from the basket and passing it to Hannah.

"Our chef," Charli piped up. "He cooks for us on Wednesday and Thursday nights. He brought by the side dishes."

Hannah smiled at Knox. At last, her daughter's chatty nature was coming out.

"Oh! We made chocolate chip cookies, though, didn't we, Mom?" Charli waved her fork. "There's a ton of them because we tried all different types of recipes, and different types of nuts and baking chips. The butterscotch was gross." She made a face, then flashed an apologetic look at Knox. "No offense, Mr. Munro."

"None taken." Knox's brown eyes twinkled. It was obvious Charli had charmed him. "And please call me Knox."

When Charlie swiveled her uncertain gaze to her mother, Hannah smiled and nodded.

Pleased, Charli went on. "Okay, Knox. We tried really expensive chocolate chunks from the little shi shi market down the street, and we even tried cranberries and white chocolate, but we always came back to the classic Toll House chocolate chip cookie recipe. It's the best."

She finally took a break long enough to take a bite of mashed potatoes.

"So where are all these cookies you baked?" Knox quipped.

"We filled the cookie jar and three tins—" Hannah started while Charli washed down her mouthful with a swig of cider.

"—and we froze the rest. You should see our freezer Mr., um, Knox. It's ab-so-lute-ly crammed with cookies."

"We'll be sure to send some home with you," Hannah told Knox, reaching for his leg under the table and giving it a squeeze. And when she added, "I'd hate for you to leave New York without getting your cookies," Knox's eyebrow twitched up, surprise at the bold comment plain in his expression.

Between what Charli referred to as their "gorgefest" and the easy conversation, the afternoon flew by. Knox told Charli and Charlotte about his life in Scotland and quizzed them about how they liked living in New York. When they finished eating, everyone pitched in to clear the table. The festivities continued in the kitchen while Hannah and Charlotte put away the leftovers and loaded the dishwasher, and Charli chattered about her new school to Knox.

As soon as the food had all been stowed in the fridge, Hannah released Charlotte from kitchen duty. Her mom had planned a holiday trip to California for a week of visiting friends. While there, she was also going to arrange to get the rest of her things out of storage and sent to New York.

"Go on," she coaxed, giving her mother a gentle nudge. "I'll take care of the rest of the dishes. You've got an early morning tomorrow. The driver will be here at five to take you to the airport."

Charlotte knit her brows. "I do have to finish packing, but I can't leave you to finish cleaning up on your own, especially when you have a guest." She inclined her head, gesturing at Knox.

"Charli has him entertained." Hannah smiled at her daughter talking animatedly with her boyfriend. "Look at her—she's got him eating out of her hand."

Charlotte gave a little laugh and had to agree. "Well, then, I guess I'll say goodnight and goodbye now, dear." She hugged Hannah and gave her a kiss, then squeezed Charli tight and kissed her, too. Turning to Knox, she said, "It was lovely meeting you. I hope we'll see you again soon."

"It was lovely meeting you too, Charlotte. Thank you for a scrumptious Thanksgiving feast." He stood and leaned down to kiss Charlotte on both cheeks.

When Charlotte had gone, Charli swiveled to face Hannah. "Mom! Can I show Knox how to make s'mores?"

"Honey, I think Knox already knows how to make s'mores." Hannah darted a bemused look Knox's way. He was busy stifling a chuckle. Looking back to Charli, she joked, "Besides, aren't you stuffed? We all ate our own body weight less than an hour ago. How can you possibly want something to eat?"

"I'm a growing girl," Charli retorted, as she pulled a step stool over to the cupboards near the fridge. "And I think my blood sugar is a little low. It's probably why I'm craving something sweet." She stepped up on the stool and started rooting around in the cupboard.

Hannah cast a helpless gaze at Knox. "Are you in the mood for s'mores?"

"Actually, it might be fun. As it turns out, I don't know how to make them, and I'd love it if the charming Miss Charli would show me how."

"Ha!" Charli gave a triumphant shout as she pulled the box containing a tabletop s'mores maker from the cupboard. "I found it. So, can we make them?" She turned on her most pleading look for Hannah.

"I guess so," Hannah acquiesced with a defeated smile and a shake of her head.

Charli got to work assembling the ingredients and lighting the little can of fuel gel. She explained the process to Knox and soon had him roasting a large marshmallow over the flame.

"Did you get enough of the milk chocolate on your graham cracker?" She craned her neck to inspect the s'more Knox was working on while she turned her own marshmallow over the heat. She smiled encouragingly. "Yeah, you did it! Well done, you. Especially for your first time."

Knox thanked her and beamed a proud smile at Hannah.

When a knock sounded on the kitchen door, Hannah went to answer it and found Lawrence standing outside.

"Dad! Happy Thanksgiving!" Charli dropped her blistered marshmallow on the table and ran over to hug him. "We're making s'mores. Do you want one?"

A slight frown creased Hannah's brow. "Lawrence. You're early. Why didn't the doorman ring to say you were here?"

Lawrence ignored her question and pinned Knox with a pointed look, then he gazed down at Charli, putting on a smile as easily as slipping on a mask. "No thank you, Peanut. We've got to get going. Do you have your suitcase ready?"

"Yeah—I'm all packed. I can't believe we're going to Martha's Vineyard for the rest of the weekend. I've always wanted to go there."

As Charli scrambled from the kitchen to retrieve her luggage, Lawrence went up to Knox and held out a hand. "Lawrence Vander Dussen. And you are...?"

"Knox Munro. Nice to meet you." He took Lawrence's hand and shook it.

Without taking his eyes off Knox, Lawrence said, "Hannah, can I speak to you in private for a moment?"

"Sure." Hannah slid an uneasy sideways glance at Knox, and he matched it with his own wary gaze.

Before following Lawrence out of the room, she whispered to Knox, "It's fine. I'll take him into the living room. You can come in and get me if we're not back in fifteen minutes."

Instead of letting Hannah steer him toward the living room, however, Lawrence strode to Hannah's bedroom and closed the door once she had followed him inside. Disregarding her protests, he heckled, "What the heck, Hannah? I walk in here, expecting my family to be celebrating a wholesome Thanksgiving, and instead I find you spending my hard-earned money entertaining some gigolo."

"You're overreacting," Hannah responded, struggling to stay calm. "Knox is my boyfriend and a good, responsible person."

"Boyfriend? Are you kidding me? Why am 1 hearing about this for the first time?" Lawrence demanded. "You know he's only after you for your money."

The notion was so ludicrous, Hannah almost laughed. "Ha! That's one thing I know he's not after, but I don't owe you an explanation. You're such a hypocrite. It was you who brought women into our home, into our bed, when we were married. You lost your privilege to adjudicate morality codes between us."

Lawrence stepped closer to Hannah, looming over her with a menacing glare. "Look, I don't appreciate you exposing that lowlife—" he jabbed a finger toward the door "—to my daughter. And his accent—he's not

American, and if things continue on between you two, I won't let you take Charli out of the country. I may have to file a petition to get more time with Charli.'"

"That's ridiculous," Hannah argued. "I haven't even considered taking Charli out of the country, and I've always said you can spend as much time with her as you want. Up until now, we've handled things decently, and Charli is much better off because of it. Why would you want to drag this through the courts? If you file a petition, I'll file a counter petition for sole custody and request to reopen the case for the acquisition of additional community assets. You know I gave up too much in the settlement."

"I know you told the mediator you knew about my real estate investments, and you gave them up." His voice was starting to rise.

"You are not as skillful of a trial lawyer as I am, Lawrence." Hannah smirked. "All settlement discussions are inadmissible in subsequent trials. The language was contained in the document we signed before the mediation. I have a copy of it if you'd like to take a look." Hannah gestured to the desk and small filing cabinet in the corner of the room. "Because I'm assuming you didn't read it."

But Lawrence continued unaffected, outright shouting. "You waived your rights! It's a done deal. Don't try to scare me with some trumped-up legal analysis. We finalized our money issues. This is about your behavior, not mine. You need to get your priorities straight. Focus on Charli instead of your personal life."

The bedroom door swung open, and Knox stepped in. Lawrence favored Hannah with one last scathing glare, then walked out, bumping Knox's shoulder with his.

Knox came to Hannah and put a hand to her cheek. "Are you alright?"

"Yes." Hannah gave a weary nod. "Let me go say goodbye to Charli, then I'll fill you in on what happened."

After seeing Charli off with a kiss and ignoring Lawrence's advice to use the weekend to think about what he had warned, Hannah met Knox in the living room. He had poured them both some wine and was waiting for her on the sofa.

When she plopped down beside him, he handed her a glass and revealed, "I caught the tail end of the conversation. Where does that leave us?"

"In the same place we were before my idiot ex-husband barged in and spoiled a delightful day," Hannah said, matter of fact. "I love you."

Knox's earnest gaze melted into relief. "I love you, too." He caught her chin and pulled her face closer for a kiss. When he pulled away, however, concern clouded his eyes. "If ya think my being here will affect ya being able to spend as much time as ya want with Charli, we can meet other places."

Hannah shook her head and swallowed the mouthful of wine she had taken. "I think he freaked out seeing you. He's used to me being compliant, both as a wife and ex-wife, without a personal life. We're divorced now, and he can't dictate the way I live my life anymore."

Knox grimaced. "He looks like a troll. I expected him to look different."

"I've never heard you say something like that. You're always so above the fray." Hannah laughed. "It's funny."

"You're my Achilles heel," Knox admitted, dropping his eyes to gaze into his wineglass. "Ya must know it includes a healthy dose of jealousy. Not that I'm jealous of that wanker. Besides, it's factual, not emotional—he looks like a troll. You are too good looking and perfect to have settled for him."

"I blame you," Hanna objected, fluttering her eyelashes playfully. "You have such a great bod and are so good-looking, you've set the bar too high. Everyone looks like a troll compared to you."

A smug smile crept onto Knox's lips. "Not everyone. Just him. He didn't spoil the day, though. I'll remember it as the best day I've had since Stuart passed." He took her hand and kissed it. "Thank you, sweetheart. Truly."

Too touched for words, Hannah gazed back at Knox, relying on him to know what she was thinking.

"So. What do you want to do now?" he inquired, holding her eyes with his as he took a sip of wine.

She arched a brow. "I want you to fuck my brains out, Mr. Munro."

"I think I can accommodate you there, Ms. Vander Dussen," he responded with a devilish smile. "Lock the door, close the curtains, take your clothes off, and meet me on the bed."

Chapter 19

Hannah left a trail of clothes through her apartment, frantically throwing them off as she locked the doors. Screw the curtains—there was no time to waste, and who could see into her high-rise windows anyway? When she breezed through the bedroom door, her bra hooked itself on the doorknob as she entered the room wearing only her panties.

Knox, who was standing near the bed still wearing all his clothes, gave her a stern look. "I thought I told you to take off your clothes."

Hannah bit back an excited smile. She peeled off her underwear and held them up for him to see, daintily gripped between her thumb and forefinger, before dropping them to the floor.

He gave a satisfied nod. "Better. Now, lay down on the bed," he instructed. "Put your arms over your head and spread your legs apart as far as you can."

She did as she was told, her excitement building as he moved into position between her legs and began licking and kissing her labia and sucking her clitoris.

"I love yir body," Knox snarled, his tone fierce and possessive. He placed a gentle kiss on the inside of one thigh, then nipped the inside of the other one with his teeth.

"Baby, can you take off your clothes, please?" Hannah pleaded, hungry for a glimpse of his body and needing to feel his skin on hers.

"In due time. I want to drink you in first," Knox replied, pushing his fingers inside her.

An involuntary moan of pleasure rose in her throat as she clenched around him. "We just got started, and you're already killing me." She pulled her knees up and spread them out as far as she could, arching her back to draw his fingers in further. When the cold metal of his belt buckle pressed against her ankle, she whimpered, "Baby, please take your clothes off."

He sat up and began unbuttoning his shirt. "Ya beg so prettily, how can I resist?"

While Hannah watched, Knox removed his shirt and slipped off his trousers, his engorged penis springing free from his boxers. At the sight of it, her tongue darted out and slicked across her bottom lip. Knox repositioned himself between her legs and commenced sucking with increased intensity. When Hannah moaned and pressed herself to his lips, Knox lifted his head. "You can't come until I tell you. And you can't yell my name tonight, because Charlotte is on the other side of the apartment. You'll stifle your scream. Do you understand?" He lowered his head and lapped at her slit once.

A blissful groan was the only sound Hannah was capable of.

Knox raised his head again, his mouth wet from Hannah's juices. "I didn't hear ya. Repeat what I said."

Hannah groaned once more, this time with the effort of speaking. "I can't come loudly, and I can't come until you tell me to," she gasped, "even though it's a total turnoff you mentioned my mom, and even though she can't hear anything that happens on this side of the apartment."

Amused, Knox cocked an eyebrow. His voice was stern when he scolded, "Now I'm going to have to spank you for yir sassy mouth. And you can't say anything out loud while I'm spanking ya, because of yir mam."

Knox turned her over his lap, his stiff erection pressing into her stomach, and proceeded to spank Hannah. He smacked her once on each butt cheek, followed by a brisk, soothing rub over the stinging spots. If she hadn't been following Knox's instructions, Hannah would have cried out, though she had to admit the pain of the slaps, and the pleasure of the rubbing, gave her a strange feeling. She was already so pent up, she wasn't sure if it turned her on more or not. It definitely didn't turn her off.

After the spanking, Knox flipped her over again. "You can come whenever ya want now, but it has to be when yir clit is in my mouth." Knox set to lapping at her seam in a forceful rhythm while his fingers tapped at her clit.

"Please, baby," Hannah panted, "suck my clit. Plleeeeeease! I want to come in your mouth so badly."

Instead of obliging her right away, Knox circled his fingertips around her clitoris, and stroked them back and forth with a feather touch. When at last he put his lips over her, he took her with such force it took everything she had not to scream her release.

"Ah, sweetheart, that was the best thing I've ever felt." Knox sat back on his haunches and gave her thigh a gentle squeeze. "Give me a minute to clean myself up, and I'll be back to give you another orgasm."

Hannah eyed his cock, still stiff and standing at attention. "Let me come with you," she cajoled. "I want you to fuck me in the shower."

"Do you?" A surprised spark twinkled in his eyes. "Then I'll be happy to grant your wish, but the same rules apply. You can't make a sound because yir mam is here, and ya can't come until ya feel me coming."

Hannah gave him a frowning smirk, certain he kept mentioning Charlotte only because she had told him it was a turnoff. Still, she nodded her agreement. Taking the hand he offered, she let him pull her up from the bed and lead her into the shower.

Under the steaming spray, they rubbed soap over each other, savoring one another at a slower pace. Their anticipation and desire built again with each gentle caress and with each deep kiss. At last, Knox interrupted. "I'll have to step out and get a condom."

"I can't wait," Hannah said in a petulant whisper. "Besides, it's unlikely I can get pregnant anyway. Let's go ahead without the condom."

"You're sure?" Though a slight frown creased Knox's forehead, the look in his eyes told her he was ready to take her whether she was sure or not.

In response, she nodded and pressed herself against him, pulling his face down for a lingering kiss. When he drew back, his eyes were dark with desire and only a hint of a smile curved his lips.

"Put your hands against the tile ridge there." Knox turned Hannah to face the wall and guided her into position. He pulled her wet hair aside and began kissing her neck as he reached around to rub her clit.

Already aroused, Hannah rocked her hips, alternating pressing into his fingers and back against his rigid shaft. Placing a palm between her shoulder blades, Knox gave her a gentle push forward and moved his fingers from her clitoris into the opening of her slit. He growled in approval at finding her as wet inside as she was on the outside, and she felt the silky head of his cock as he entered her from behind. She caught her breath as he slid deeper and deeper, and she gave a tiny whimper when he stopped, fully submerged inside her. He drew back and pumped into her once, then groaned.

"You feel too good from this angle, sweetheart. I'm not going to last long. You've got to come now."

As water rained down and steam swirled around them, Hannah could feel Knox inside of her, unmoving and hard. His skilled fingers went to work again, pressing her clit from the outside against the stiff length of him inside her. She rocked harder, and bit back his name as her release began rising in her core. Knox gripped her shoulder with his free hand, keeping the other clamped to her mound as he pumped in and out in hard jerks. Only twice more, and Knox groaned his own release.

Hannah turned around and they embraced under the hot spray as they caught their breath. At length, Knox knelt in front of her. He cleaned her again, washing himself from between her legs with a gentle touch, kissing her wrists, her breasts, and her stomach as he worked. When the water began running lukewarm, they stepped from the shower and dried off.

In Hannah's bedroom, Knox slipped into a pair of silk pajama pants from his duffel while Hannah put on a satin nightgown she had bought especially for his visit.

He smiled his approval and reached for her hand. "Come here," he called, drawing her to the bed with him. He turned down the comforter and slid between the sheets, pulling Hannah in beside him. Propping himself against her pillows, he pulled her to him and held her close.

"I feel happy," he said, giving her a squeeze. "It didn't seem I would ever feel normal again. I don't know how long it will last, but I'm going to wallow in it as long as I can."

"I'm glad. And I'm happy you're here—I almost can't believe it." Hannah snuggled into Knox's embrace. "I love you."

"I love you, too," Knox replied, pressing a kiss on the top of her head.

They fell asleep entwined in each other's arms, and Hannah awoke early the next morning with Knox still holding her close. Careful not to wake him, she eased herself from the bed and changed into an alexander-wang.t hoodie and matching sweatpants. She tiptoed into the kitchen and made coffee. As she was filling two cups, planning to take one to Knox in bed, he appeared in the doorway, sleep-rumpled and gorgeous. He still wore his pajama pants and had pulled on a sweatshirt. As he stood there, blinking against the morning sunshine, the hair on the top of his head sticking up in a few places, Hannah's heart gave a flutter. It thrilled her to see him just out of bed and so at home in her space.

She brought his coffee to him, giving him a kiss before she handed it over.

"I made coffee and was going to slip out to get us something to eat, but then I remembered the market and the cafe downstairs would be closed for the holiday," she told him as he took a sip of coffee. "There'll be something open somewhere. We'll have to walk, though."

"I'm fine eating anything you have here." Knox followed Hannah to the kitchen island. "If I remember right, there's half of a pumpkin pie in the refrigerator."

"Pie for breakfast," Hannah deadpanned. "You're as bad as Charli."

"What? Pumpkins are a good source of nutrition—fiber, potassium, and all sorts of vitamins I can't recall at the moment." A challenging twinkle danced in his eyes. "Or we could always break into your frozen cookie stash. Charli talked them up so much, I feel cheated no one offered to let me sample them."

Hannah shook her head, a fond smirk playing on her lips. "Cookies and pie and coffee. Breakfast of champions."

Knox grinned and slid his cup aside. "Truthfully, I'm not hungry after our 'gorge-fest' yesterday." He took Hannah's waist and lifted her onto the counter in one swift, effortless move, then placed himself between her legs.

Through a giggle, Hannah agreed, "Yeah, I'm not all that hungry, either."

Knox fed her a sip of his coffee from his cup before kissing her and taking a sip for himself. Leveling his eyes on hers, he inquired, "Last night you mentioned not being able to get pregnant. Is there an issue with your health?"

Hannah shook her head. "It's not that. It's just unlikely I could conceive at my age."

He studied her for a moment. "It's not probable, then, but it's possible." He put a hand to the side of her face and ran his thumb along her cheekbone with featherlight strokes. "A speeding freight train couldn't have stopped me from taking you last night in the shower, but we probably shouldn't risk it again."

A smile came to Hannah's lips. She had loved feeling him inside her, nothing between them. It sent her on a bit of a power trip knowing he had wanted her so badly even his better judgment couldn't have kept him from fucking her. "Agreed," she said. "Although I hope it doesn't scare you off to know I'd love to have a baby with you."

His brown eyes warmed, tiny lines crinkling around them with delight. "I feel the same way, sweetheart. I'm emotionally fragile right now. though. Counseling helped me see the reason I disconnected from ya was because I thought losing you would be unbearable, and I couldn't handle losing another person I loved. I know it doesn't make any sense. It was an attempt to protect myself from further pain." He searched her face, as if looking for evidence she understood. Bringing her fingers to his lips, he pressed a kiss on them. "If we were in a different universe, I'd love nothing more than to raise a pack of babies with you."

Hannah's heart pumped a happy beat. His declaration wasn't exactly on par with making future plans, but it opened up possibilities. "I know. Even though I love the romantic idea of having your child, the reality of a baby is crazy. Our lives are already complicated. I do have hopes for us, though, and I meant it when I said I love you." She kissed him, a kiss heated and deep for how quickly she cut it short. "I'm willing to take things a day at a time, and I'll enthusiastically take whatever you are willing or able to give."

"Sounds like a genius plan." He gave her hand a squeeze. "And as for seeing where things go, this may be premature, but there's a possibility I may be able to formulate some changes in my work schedule. If it pans out, I can spend more time with you here in New York." He paused, then added, "If it's alright with ya."

"Alright?" Hannah fought the urge to pinch herself to prove she wasn't dreaming. "I would love that! When?"

He gave her an indulgent smile. "Soon. I need to go back home and iron out some details."

The reminder he would be leaving deflated Hannah's elation, like a balloon with a slow leak. "Right. When do you have to go back?" Hannah tried to keep her tone light and carefree, though she felt certain her questioning eyes gave away her vulnerability.

"The original plan was to leave tomorrow, but I can delay my flight until Monday morning." He lifted a hand to coil a lock of her hair around his finger. "With yir mam and Charli away, we could have the rest of the holiday all to ourselves. How does that sound?"

"It sounds wonderful." Hannah blinked. "I don't want to pressure you, but I was prepared to beg you to stay, if it was an option."

His eyes lit up. "Beg me, huh?" He took her mouth with his and her breath along with it as he kissed her long and deep. Mischief played on his face when he pulled away and set her on her feet again. Taking her hand, Knox started leading Hannah toward the bedroom. "Let's exercise that option, shall we, *cuore mio?*"

Chapter 20

Hannah, I'm a grandfather!. Baby boy, 3.68 kilos, 51.7 cm. Alexander Stuart McGregor.

A week before Christmas, Knox's text took Hannah by surprise. They had talked on the phone that morning and though it had been a brief conversation, she hadn't expected a text at 7:45 p.m. New York time—nearly 1 a.m. his time in Scotland. She responded right away.

Hannah: How wonderful! Congratulations! How are mother and child?

Knox: Violet and the babe are doing well...Violet and Eric got married 2 weeks ago.

Maybe it was because Violet and Eric's marriage was expected, but Hannah felt unaffected by the news. If anything, she was relieved—a new family to focus on might be just the thing Eric needed. As Hannah was composing a reply to Knox, her phone began ringing, and his name lit up the screen.

"Hey you," Hannah greeted him. "I was just texting you back."

"I wanted to hear yir voice, in person." Knox's deep brogue flowed from the phone, caressing her ear and enveloping her like an embrace.

"Well, then, I'll congratulate you in person." Hannah laughed. "Congratulations! You're a grandfather!"

"And proud of it." His tone told Hannah he was pleased to be a granddad. "How have ya been, sweetheart?"

"Busy. Missing you," she admitted, trying not to sound too forlorn.

"I miss ya, too," Knox told her. "And it's another reason I called. What are your plans for Christmas?"

"It's going to be just me and Mom," she told him. "Lawrence invited Charli to stay with him for the two-week holiday break."

"Would you consider changing plans and coming to Glasgow to spend Christmas with my family and me?"

Thoughts of Charlotte were the only things keeping Hannah from blurting an immediate, ecstatic Yes! "I'd love to, but my mom—"

"Charlotte is invited, too, of course," Knox interjected.

"And you're sure we wouldn't be intruding?" As much as she wanted to spend the holiday with Knox, Hannah was well-aware this first holiday without Stuart would be a hard one on his family.

"Not at all," Knox said without hesitation. "Sam and Ma and Da want you to come, too. That's part of the reason yir getting a last-minute invite. I know I'm being a selfish prick, but I really want to spend the holiday with ya. I kept putting off talking with my family about it, then my mam brought it up this evening when we were all at hospital to see Violet. Everyone else chimed in and agreed I should invite ya. So, what do you say?"

"I want to spend the holiday with you, too," Hannah responded with enthusiasm, certain her mother would be happy to celebrate the holidays abroad. "I'll talk to Mom and see what she thinks."

As expected, it didn't take much convincing to talk Charlotte into going to Scotland for Christmas. And although their plans were spur-of-the-moment, Hannah was glad things had worked out the way they did. She was looking forward to the trip so much, she didn't think she could have waited more than a week. She felt like a child excited about a school excursion.

In the end, Charlotte, Charli and Hannah had their own Christmas celebration on Christmas Eve, before Lawrence picked up Charli. Andrew and Charlotte prepared what Charli called their "fantastic faux Christmas dinner" and, afterward, they sat around the Christmas tree, opened presents, and sang Christmas carols. The next day, after Charli left with her father, Hannah and Charlotte were on their way to Edinburgh.

Hannah: Mom & I just landed. xo H

Knox: I'm at baggage claim. Take ur time. Can't wait to c u. Love u, love u K

With all her focus on seeing Knox, Hannah barely registered de-boarding the plane and pushing through the crowd to get to the baggage claim area. As promised, Knox was there waiting. Hannah managed to refrain from jumping into his arms and showering him with kisses—but only just. Knox greeted both women with kisses on each cheek and an extra, secret squeeze for Hannah, before he grabbed their suitcases and whisked them off to his Range Rover.

"It was very kind of you to arrange for our flight," Charlotte told Knox once they were on the road to Glasgow. "The first-class tickets were nice, too. I've flown coach my entire life, though, so it wasn't necessary."

"It was no trouble at all, Charlotte," Knox assured her, meeting her gaze in the rearview mirror. "I would have sent the company jet for you if my partner hadn't taken it to Saint Bart's for the holiday."

Seated next to Knox, Hannah placed her hand on his leg, telegraphing her gratitude with a look and a squeeze of his thigh. His firm quadriceps tensed beneath her grip, and he took her hand in his.

As soon as they had cleared the city limits, Knox glanced in the back seat, and nudged Hannah to take a peek, as well. Charlotte was napping peacefully.

"I'm not surprised," Hannah affirmed, her voice soft. "Between the trip planning, our early Christmas celebration with Charli and our flight, it's no wonder she's exhausted."

"I've booked two rooms for ya at the Prestige in Glasgow." Knox spoke low, too. "My house in Glasgow isn't fit for company—well, for my company, at least. Sam has his mates and girlfriends of the week over there all the time." He flashed an apologetic grin. "All of Stuart's odds and ends are scattered throughout the house, too. Sam and I haven't had the heart to go through them yet, and Sam doesn't want Violet to do it, either."

"It's got to be hard on both of you." Hannah couldn't fathom letting go of anything of Charli's, even the smallest items like the hair clips and scrunchies she was always leaving lying about.

"It is, but we know it has to be done. Sam and Ma and Da are going to go through it all when they're ready, and I've asked Sam to set aside some of Stuart's things for the baby. I know I should help them with it but, God help me, I don't think I can." Although he spoke quietly, the crack in Knox's voice was unmistakable.

Hannah clasped his hand tighter. "It's still too painful, that's completely understandable," she assured him, her heart aching to comfort him.

"I've accepted that I'll miss Stuart every day for the rest of my life." Knox's fingers gripped hers, as if he was drawing strength from her. "However, I also know I'm getting a little stronger every day, thanks to you." He brought her hand up and pressed his lips to it.

Soon, the Glaswegian skyline came into view, all aglitter and glowing with red and green Christmas lights interspersed with twinkling white lights on many of the buildings. The River Clyde reflected it all back, doubling the impact and the beauty of the season. Hannah turned to comment on the sights to Charlotte and found her mother still sleeping.

"She's missing all this Christmas splendor," Hannah fretted.

"I'll take ya both on a Christmas lights tour while you're here," Knox said. "We'll add it to the itinerary, but Ma has spoken for tomorrow. She's thrown herself into creating a perfect holiday for everyone. Between decorating and shopping and meal planning with Wanate, she hasn't had time to be sad, and I think that was the ultimate goal all along."

"You of all people should know it helps to stay busy." Hannah gave him a fond poke with her elbow, then leaned over as far as the seatbelt would allow and rested her head on his shoulder. "I think a houseful of people for the holiday is exactly what she needs."

"It won't be too large of a crowd. Only the six of us— Ma, Da, Sam, Charlotte, you, and me."

Hannah sat up, her head cocked. "Won't Violet be there with the baby?"

Knox shook his head. "Violet and the baby will be spending the holiday with Eric and her family in Edinburgh." Though his lips were pressed in a grim line, he didn't sound regretful. He cast a quick side-glace Hannah's way, his thumb stroking rhythmically along hers. "You won't have to run into Eric McGregor at all, so no worries about that. Okay?"

"Eric is part of Violet's life, and she and Alexander and I are part of your life. I'll learn to deal with it." Hannah's lips curved in a rueful smile. "Still, I'd like to put off running into him for as long as possible."

Once at the Prestige, Knox ushered the two ladies to a private office behind the front desk. While the night manager made quick work of checking them in, Knox arranged a room-service feast for them when Charlotte mentioned having passed up the in-flight meal earlier. Watching Knox pamper her mother, checking with Charlotte to make sure she approved of everything he was ordering, made Hannah's heart swell. How was it possible for this man to make her fall even more in love with him?

When everything was settled, Knox walked Hannah and Charlotte to their rooms. After Charlotte had closed her door, Knox pressed a second key card into Hannah's hand. "Here is our room key," he said in a low murmur. "Meet me up there later."

"Aren't you joining us for dinner?" Hannah's brows dipped. "You ordered enough for an army."

"Not tonight." He shook his head and gave her a lingering kiss. "I have work to do. You two ladies enjoy your meal, and as soon as yir mom has turned in, come up to our room."

Hannah pressed into him and put her lips to his ear. "I can't wait."

Around midnight, Hannah let herself into Knox's room. Shirtless and wearing only pajama bottoms, he was studying paperwork at the small desk in the front room. He looked up, his eyes warming at the sight of Hannah. Immediately, he abandoned his papers and went to her, enveloping her in his arms and giving her an affectionate kiss. "God, I've missed you."

Hannah nuzzled at his neck, breathing in the citrus and amber scent of his cologne. "I've missed you, too."

Knox's hands rubbed soothing circles on her back. "Did Charlotte settle in alright?"

"Yes. She could barely keep her eyes open long enough to finish her soup and went straight to bed without touching the rest of her supper." She pulled back to look up at Knox, giving him as stern a look as she could muster. "You shouldn't have ordered so much—it will all go to waste, unless Mom feels like cold lamb and Foraged Salad for breakfast."

"Sounds delicious to me," Knox teased, hugging her tight.

"You're what sounds delicious to me." Hannah glowed, pressing herself against him and pleased to feel a growing hardness.

Knox chuckled. "You've had a long day, and I know ya're jet-lagged, so I'm not going to force myself on ya tonight. I would like to sleep with ya." He tilted back to meet Hannah's eyes. "*Sleep*," he emphasized. "And you'll have to sneak back into yir room, before Charlotte wakes up."

"Baby, you could never force yourself on me," Hannah insisted. "I delight in all forms of physical interaction with you. And how many times do I have to tell you my mom is not a prude? She encourages me to spend time with you, even if it includes doing the horizontal dance."

That brought a laugh from Knox. "I've missed yir wit, sweetheart, as much as anything, but it's not so much whether Charlotte would mind or not. It's a matter of respect for her." His expression grew earnest. "I want her to like me."

"She does like you. How could she not?"

"It's late." Knox shifted, leaving one arm draped across Hannah's shoulder. "You're dead on your feet. Let's go to bed."

Hannah couldn't argue with Knox on that point. She was, in fact, exhausted, even though she would happily do the horizontal dance with him into the early hours of the morning.

"Please do me the favor of setting yir alarm," Knox directed as he guided Hannah to the bed. "I won't bother ya during the night, so you'll get a few hours of sleep before ya have to sneak back to yir room."

"Fine," Hannah grumbled, pulling her phone from her pocket and jabbing at the screen to set the alarm. Once it was set, she showed it to Knox. "See? Happy now? It's set."

He gave a satisfied nod and thanked her before dropping a light peck on her lips. Then, to her surprise and delight, he stripped her, making quick work of removing all her clothes, and lifted her onto the bed. After pulling the duvet up to her chin, he went around to the other side and climbed in under the covers next to her, drawing her close to him.

As they lay there spooning and drowsing, Hannah teased, "I don't think all your body parts got the memo. Your brain might have to do a manual override to shut down a certain part of yourself, Mr. 'I-want-Charlotte-to-think-I'm-a-Boy-Scout.'"

"It's not my brain that's the problem, sweetheart." Knox's tone, though tired, was full of humor. "It's your sweet ass and big tits. Now get some sleep," he instructed, kissing the back of Hannah's head.

Chapter 21

In the early hours of Christmas morning, Hannah dragged herself out of Knox's bed, shuffled back to her hotel room, and promptly fell back to sleep in her own bed. What seemed like minutes later—although it was closer to a couple of hours—the ring tone on her cell phone sounded. Unable and uninterested in focusing on the caller ID, she fumbled to swipe the call-answer icon and mumbled a groggy, "Hello."

"Good morning, Darling," Charlotte chirped from the other end. "Knox is picking us up in an hour. I wanted to make sure you're up and getting ready."

"Thanks, Mom," she said through a yawn. "I was up earlier but fell back to sleep. I'll get moving."

She had dressed and was pulling a few curling tendrils free from the messy up-do she had twisted her hair into when a knock sounded at her door. A glimpse through the peep hole revealed Knox standing on the other side, a Roberto Cavalli wool overcoat draped over one arm, and carrying a load of gift-wrapped packages.

When she opened the door, Hannah noticed a set of Gucci GG Supreme luggage on the floor next to him.

"Sorry I'm early," he started. "I wanted to give your Christmas gifts to ya before we go to the house." Holding his armload of packages, he leaned down to kiss her full and deep. "Ya look beautiful," he told her when he had thoroughly taken the breath from her.

"Thank you." Hannah put her fingers to her lips, clutching the door with her free hand and leaning against it to steady herself while Knox stepped into the room. "You look quite handsome yourself," she swooned, admiring how he had accessorized his traditional Armani suit with a bright, festive Versace tie. "And I don't think there's anything you could give me to top that kiss."

He hitched an eyebrow as he set down the gifts on the bed. "If that's a challenge, we'll settle it later. For now—" he paused to bring the luggage into the room "—I didn't know how to wrap this. I wanted to give ya an incentive to keep coming back to Scotland. If it's too much to take back with ya, I can keep some of it at my house."

"It's absolutely gorgeous." Hannah ran her hands over the soft canvas, admiring the double-G trademark pattern. "Thank you so much. Now I can replace all the ragtag luggage I brought with me."

"I'm glad ya like it." Knox beamed. "Would ya like to open your other present now?"

"Of course, but open one of yours first." Hannah went to the dresser and pulled a wrapped gift from the top drawer.

When she handed it to Knox, he tore into the wrapping like a kid at, well, Christmas.

As he pulled out a pair of Tom Ford sunglasses, she remarked, "I thought you might start wearing American designers from time to time. You know—since your girlfriend is American."

Knox popped open the hinged case and put them on. "They're great—I love them," he said, turning his head from side to side for Hannah to see.

She congratulated herself on her own good taste, though she wasn't sure whether the sunglasses made him look good, or he made them look good. Either way, he was so hot.

"I'll think of ya when I wear them," he teased as he put them back into their case, "which isn't much of a promise, I suppose, because I think of you all the time." He shot her a flirtatious look, then produced a small gift box. "Now your turn."

Hannah sat on the bed and took more care than he had opening her gift. She pulled at the ribbon to untie the bow and slid a finger under the paper to gently pry it away from a little velvet box. When she opened the lid, she found a yellow gold locket on a delicate chain nestled inside. Engraved, scrolling characters adorned the front of the locket, and when she examined them, she realized they were numbers—Charli's birthday.

"Oh," was all she managed to say as she picked up the locket and opened it to reveal a tiny picture of Charli. Speechless, she looked up at Knox.

He sat down beside her. "Charlotte helped with it," he revealed, pleased at her reaction to the gift. "She provided me with the photo and Charli's birthday information."

Hannah's gaze turned to Charli's beaming face peering out from inside the locket.

"It's the best gift I've ever received." Her voice was thick around the lump in her throat. She threw her arms around his neck, hugging him tight so he wouldn't see the tears shimmering in her eyes. "Thank you. Thank you so much."

"I'm glad ya like it."

"I love it." She pulled back and placed the locket in his hand. "Will you help me put it on?"

She turned so he could fasten the clasp, then bounded up to admire it in the mirror.

"I have one more gift for you, baby," she cooed, drawing another parcel from the dresser drawer.

He showed a bit more restraint opening the second gift, though not much. Hannah watched with fond amusement as he pulled a small leather-bound book from the tatters of the gift wrap.

"It's original poems and translations by John Dryden," Hannah informed him when Knox only sat staring at the cover.

He nodded. "It's a First Edition. Thoughtful." His voice caught and when he looked up, his eyes were shining. "Thank you." He stood and took her in his arms, held her close without saying a word. She clung to him, too, feeling only a tinge of guilt at her wish they could forego the family get-together and spend the day alone in Knox's room.

Too soon, Knox announced it was time to get going. He had promised he, Hannah, and Charlotte would attend Christmas services with his parents. Sam would be bringing Francesca and Bruce to the church, and they would all go to the Munro's home for a dinner afterward.

The church was packed, standing room only. Amid the bustle of the congregation and the start of the service, there was little time for greetings and introducing Charlotte to Francesca, Bruce, and Sam. They sang hymns and listened to scripture readings. Although Charlotte attended church regularly these days, Hannah's parents hadn't raised her in any particular faith. Still, she wasn't anti-religion; it simply wasn't a part of her life. Here, though, seated beside Knox, Hannah felt a warm contentment she hadn't felt in a long time, and she found herself imagining attending holiday services regularly with Knox and his family.

When the service was over, the group convened at Francesca and Bruce's. Hannah and Charlotte had barely shed their coats when Francesca began passing out drinks.

"I made these California Meyer lemon and whiskey drinks for ya, Charlotte," Francesca beamed, handing the first glass to Hannah's mother. "Of course, I made them with the best whiskey."

Naturally, the family's obligatory "of course!" and "cheers!" followed her pronouncement. Familiar with the tradition, Hannah was pleased to call out along with them.

When everyone had a drink in hand, Bruce announced the front hall was no place for a Christmas celebration and suggested everyone gather in the great room. It, along with the entire house, was done up in traditional Christmas colors. Garlands of pine branches and cones decorated the mantle and stairs. Mercury-glass jars containing white lit candles were scattered throughout the house, giving it a festive glow. Classic lights glittered on a large Christmas tree, amid Munro and Campbell plaid ribbons. When Hannah inspected the tree closer, she could see Francesca had dedicated it to Stuart. Amid tinsel and garland, the branches were covered with photos of Stuart at all different ages, along with child's artwork signed with Stuart's name scribbled in a childish hand.

They all talked and laughed and pitched in, helping Francesca carry dish after dish of food to the long table, already laid with china, silverware, and wine glasses. Wanate had come in the day before to help Francesca prepare food, set the table, and finish up some last-minute decorating.

Once all the food had been brought in and Francesca had guided everyone to their seats according to her seating arrangement, Bruce stood up and declared, "I'd like to make a toast to the best lad there ever was, Stuart Gregorio Munro. Stuart is proof of the saying only the good die young because I'm here to celebrate, and he isn't." He lifted his glass higher. "We'll never forget you, laddie. You're in our hearts forever."

Tears stung Hannah's eyes as everyone raised their glasses. Francesca pressed a handkerchief to her nose and Sam stood and went to his grandfather.

"Well said, Grandda. Ya got one thing wrong though; you are good—it's why Stuart was good, too."

Francesca stood then, a wobbling smile on her lips. She held up her wine glass and said, "Hannah, thank you for putting a smile back on Knox's face. I can't tell ya how happy it makes his father and me. Stuart will live in our hearts forever, and you have come into our hearts as well. You've given us a reason to celebrate this Christmas season. Thank you, Hannah and Charlotte, for traveling so far to share the holiday with us and helping us remember the importance of this season."

As everyone drank to Francesca's toast, Knox took Hannah's hand under the table and gave it a squeeze.

After the meal, Bruce shepherded them into the great room to exchange presents. Hannah and Charlotte had brought "I Love NYC" t-shirts for everyone, and had purchased special, individual gifts for the family, as well. For Sam and Bruce, they had bought Prada dopp kits, and had decided on a red Prada textured leather wallet for Francesca. There was a wallet in black, too, for Violet, and Francesca set it aside to give to her later, along with the gifts for the baby Hannah had brought.

Everyone admired and exclaimed over the gifts and laughed when Sam remarked that the Munro Family

Christmas had funneled a small fortune to Italian designers. Seeing the Prada label everywhere, he chortled, "Bloody hell—Prada alone can afford a new summer palazzo, thanks to our clan."

At last, Francesca brought a final package from under the tree. Placing it in Hannah's hands, she said, "Please take this to Charli, and wish her a Happy Christmas for us."

Touched, Hannah took the gift and promised she would.

While the family sat chatting amid the scattering of gifts and crumpled Christmas wrap, the doorbell rang.

"And who can that be now?" Bruce jested.

Francesca jumped up and started toward the door, the corners of her mouth twitching. "It must be Violet." She leveled a delighted look at Knox. "I wanted to surprise ya with a visit from your grandson, so I asked if she could bring the baby over before it got too late."

She scurried to the door and flung it open. "Violet, Eric, come in, come in. Thank you for coming! And thank you for bringing Alexander. Christmas wouldn't have been the same without all of ya."

Although she spoke to Violet and Eric, Francesca had eyes only for her great-grandson. She took him in her arms and began cooing and speaking Italian to him.

Hannah sat frozen in place as she watched the young couple stroll in and shed their coats. She knew the family was greeting them—she could see their smiling lips moving. But she didn't hear a word over the white noise roaring in her ears at the sight of Eric McGregor.

He looked as he had the last time she had seen him, though he wasn't wearing the same desperate, manic look. He stood beaming and looking for all the world as if he belonged right there, his hand at the small of Violet's back, the proud patriarch of his little family.

Bruce came to his wife's side. As he stroked his hand over Alexander's head, the static in Hannah's ears began to subside. She heard Bruce say, "Violet, you know Knox's girl Hannah, and we need to introduce ya to her mam, Charlotte. And you, Eric. You've yet to meet them both."

Violet nodded at Hannah. "Of course. Nice to see ya again." She leaned in to kiss each of Hannah's cheeks. "Happy Christmas."

Hannah mumbled a "Happy Christmas" back and as Violet moved on to greet Charlotte, Bruce pulled Eric forward.

"Eric, I'd like ya to meet Hannah, Knox's girlfriend," Bruce said, adding, "Eric is Violet's husband."

Eric grasped Hannah's hand in his. He shook it and, not releasing his grip, pinned his eyes on hers. "Nice to meet ya, Hannah. You're visiting from the States? Is this your first time in Scotland?" His lip curled up in a sly smirk.

"No. It isn't." Knox put an arm around Hannah's shoulder and answered for her, guiding her away from Eric and the rest of the crowd. At the sideboard, he splashed some whiskey into a glass and handed it to her. "I'm sorry about this, Hannah. I had no idea Ma had invited them today."

She took the glass but didn't drink. "I'm fine," she insisted. "You don't have to worry about me."

He cupped his hands around hers. "Then why are ya shaking?"

She cut a quick glance at Eric and found him staring at her, a smug look on his face. She darted her eyes away. "It's just a shock, is all," she whispered, then took a sip of the whiskey, welcoming the warm, numbness spreading through her.

Knox spared Eric an irritated glare. "He's already being an ass. I'll have a talk with him."

"No—please don't." Hannah winced when her protest came out too loud. Lowering her voice, she said, "I can get through it without dragging you into this drama."

"I'm already a part of this drama. What affects you, affects me," Knox insisted, then softened. "It's not that I don't think ya can take care of yourself. It's just ... I might need to set Eric straight again, for everyone's sakes."

In the moment, there was nothing Hannah wanted more than for Knox to toss Eric out, as he had the last time Eric had caused her problems. It wouldn't be proper in this situation, though. The only thing she could do was avoid Eric as best she could and get through the evening. "Anything you say to him could be taken the wrong way," she told Knox. "And I don't want him telling anyone he, uh ... knows me. That would be embarrassing. Please don't spark a prob—"

"Knox," Francesca interrupted. She had come up behind Hannah, cradling Alexander. "Take a turn with your grandson. He's waited all day long for his grandfather to wish him a Happy Christmas."

Knox hesitated and his eyes drifted to the baby. He reached out and let the bright-eyed Alexander grip his finger in a tiny flailing hand. A melancholy smile stole onto Knox's face.

"I'd love to spend more time with the lad," he told Francesca. "But it's getting late. Hannah and Charlotte need to get back to the hotel now. I'll come back and help you clean the kitchen after I drop them. We'll visit more then."

"It's not so late," Francesca said with a quizzical expression. "Violet and Eric only just arrived with the baby."

"Mom's an early riser," Hannah interjected, "and we're still adjusting to the time change."

"Of course. Ya haven't even been here for a full day." Knox's mother seemed to buy Hannah's explanation, although traces of doubt lingered in her eyes. "Ring before ya make a trip back," she told Knox. "I don't need your help with the cleanup. It would be lovely if ya could spend some time with the baby, but if they've gone home before ya return, there's no sense in ya making another trip."

She accepted a kiss on the cheek from Knox and a hug from Hannah, who circled her arms around both great-grandmother and baby to give them a gentle squeeze.

When Hannah turned to search for Charlotte, a cold chill shot through her. She was standing between the Christmas tree and Eric, who was leaning too close for Hannah's comfort and intently questioning her mother.

"Really? A granddaughter," he was saying. "Ya don't seem old enough to be grandma to a teenager."

He leered at her with a predatory grin; Charlotte didn't appear to notice. Flashing a demure smile, she blushed and said something Hannah couldn't hear from across the room. Straight away, Hannah started toward her mother, angry determination overriding her discomfort. She had to keep Eric from flattering any more personal information out of her mother than he already had.

"Mom—it's time to go," Hannah urged, a harder edge to her tone than she had intended.

"What, so soon?" Eric turned his flinty gaze on Hannah.

"Yes. Hannah and her mother are still on New York time," Knox said, stepping between Eric and Hannah, "and I have a few things to wrap up before I spend the day in meetings tomorrow. There's no holidays in the hospitality business." Although his tone was friendly, the look he gave Eric was cold and hard.

While Hannah and Charlotte donned their coats, Knox thanked Violet for bringing Alexander.

"I know ya've got yir own family but thank you for letting us share part of Alexander's first Christmas with him." He gave Violet a hug and kissed Alexander's head.

After saying their goodbyes, they were on their way back to the hotel. Relief to have gotten out of the house without any further contact with Eric washed over Hannah as she buckled herself into Knox's Range Rover. At the same time, the last drop of her energy drained away. The day had been full of excitement, and not all of it had been pleasant.

Chapter 22

They drove back to the hotel mostly in silence. At first, Charlotte made some small talk about the wonderful time she had had, and how lovely Knox's parents were. She didn't seem to notice how agitated Hannah and Knox were or, if she did, she didn't mention it. As they drew closer to the Prestige, the tense knot in Hannah's stomach began to loosen, and the headache that had been threatening dissipated. By the time Knox had parked and was helping Charlotte and her carry their packages inside, Hannah's good mood had almost returned.

While Hannah saw Charlotte to her room and stashed her presents in her own room, Knox disappeared, saying he needed to check on something. But he told Hannah not to get ready for bed just yet and that he would be back shortly. Although it was a curious request, she didn't mind. After the night she had had, some alone time with Knox was exactly what she needed.

She had just kicked off her heels, reasoning he hadn't said she couldn't get comfortable, when a knock sounded at the door. Her lips curved into a coy smile as she went to answer it, but it faltered when she opened the door to find a bellman on the other side.

"Good evening, madam," he said, touching the brim of his hat. "Mr. Munro has asked that you join him downstairs."

"Oh?" Hannah questioned, confused.

"Yes. If you'll follow me, I can take you to him now." He gave a little bow and waved his hand, gesturing toward the elevator.

It made her a little uneasy, but Hannah had seen Knox talking to the man in a friendly way several times. Deciding there was nothing to worry about, she followed the bellman to the elevator and stepped inside the car.

He pressed the button for one of the lower floors, and as they rode down in silence, Hannah wondered what was up with all the mystery. When they reached their destination, the man took Hannah to a closed door with an engraved sign over it reading, "Terrace Ballroom."

"You are to go inside, please, madam," he said with a nod toward the closed door.

Hannah hesitated. "I'm confused."

"Everything will be clear once you walk through the door," the bellman replied.

Perplexed, Hannah watched him walk back to the elevator and disappear. Looking back at the ballroom door, her heartrate sped up and her nerves felt twitchy. In the end, her curiosity got the better of her.

As she held her breath, Hannah opened to door to find Knox standing there in full Scottish garb. He had on a kilt in the Munro plaid and a black kilt jacket over a white shirt with a turndown collar, French cuffs, and a long red tie. A Munro tartan crossed his chest and draped from his left shoulder, held in place by a large ornate brooch, and an embossed leather pouch Hannah knew was called a sporran hung about his waist. He had changed his dress shoes for Ghillies, customary Scottish thick-soled shoes with no tongues and long laces, which were wrapped around and tied above his ankles. And he had tucked a sgian dubh, a traditional knife, into one of the knee-high plaid stockings he wore.

Hannah exhaled, only to catch her breath again. Knox looked tall and magnificent, and he was staring at her as if she were the only woman on Earth.

In the background, there was a full orchestra with a beautiful girl in an evening gown standing in front of a microphone.

"I don't understand. What's going on?" Hannah asked as she came to him.

"After the night we've had, I thought a grand gesture was in order." Knox took her hands in his and brought them to his lips.

Tears welled Hannah's eyes, and she started to giggle and cry. What had she done to deserve such a thoughtful, amazing man?

"Will you dance with me, please?" he asked.

"I'd love to, but I'm not wearing shoes," she said through a teary laugh.

"You're perfect," Knox countered and turned to the woman, gesturing her to start as he led Hannah to the middle of the dance floor.

Pulling her close, he began to sway with her in a slow rhythm. "I don't care whether the song's slow or fast. I only want to dance in an embrace—slowly."

As Hannah stared up into his eyes, she listened closer to the lyrics the woman was singing: "You say we're gonna run away…"

"Oh my goodness. 'On Our Way.' It's a Lana Del Rey song," she exclaimed. "You do romance really well, big guy."

Knox pulled her in closer and rubbed her back as the singer crooned, "I love you more with each and every day…"

Together, they swayed, floating along in a dream, Hannah feeling like she was living the song.

They must have had a moment of truth, she thought, because there he was, holding her in his arms, dancing with her and loving her, whether or not it was the right thing for him.

Focus, Hannah, her inner voice commanded. *Enjoy this once in a lifetime moment. He gets you.*

And I love him, she found herself answering in reply.

When the song ended, Hannah came out of her trance to hear the next song start: "Because of You."

"There's no way you just pulled this together at the spur of the moment." Hannah smiled. "This obviously took a lot of planning."

"I may have set a few things up beforehand," Knox admitted.

Hannah sighed and burrowed deeper into Knox's embrace. "I've never been so happy. I love you so much."

"Good, because I feel like a bit of a tosser right now with the attention on us. Making you happy is worth everything. It's my raison d'être."

When the next song began, Hannah looked up at Knox. "'Lucky Ones.' I love this song. Is the repertoire all Lana?"

Knox nodded. "Yes, I asked them to play and sing the ten most romantic songs of hers. I don't recognize any of them, so I hope they chose correctly."

"They're perfect," Hannah confirmed. "You'll have to take my word for it—these songs are wonderful. The orchestra and singer are magnificent." She tilted her head and gave him an appreciative look. "You look ah-mazing, by the way. I'm going to blow your mind when I get you alone."

"My mind, sweetheart?" Knox grinned.

Hannah laughed. "I won't scold you for that comment, because you can do or say nothing wrong for at least the next twenty-four hours."

"Good. I'll start my stopwatch." Knox pulled her closer.

Since she had left her heels in her room, Hannah's head barely met his chest. Knox ran his hand through her hair. He fingered her bangs back and kissed her forehead.

Plastered to each other, they slow-danced through the next songs: "Young and Beautiful," "Lust for Life,"

"Because of You," "Old Money," "Love," and finally, "Never Let Me Go."

When the last note faded, Knox thanked the singer and musicians, and they exited the room, leaving their instruments behind. Knox took Hannah's hand and led her to the side of the ballroom to a small table laid out with an assortment of hors d'oeuvres and champagne. He expertly popped the cork and filled two elegant crystal flutes.

Handing a glass to Hannah, he declared, "Here's to you, Hannah. I'll love you forever."

"I'll love you forever, too," she responded, clinking her glass to his.

They drank, and after a moment, Knox set his glass aside. "Remember when ya said you'd take anything I was willing to give, including marriage? Did you mean it?"

Mind racing in sync with her heart, Hannah blinked. "Y-yes ..." she stammered.

"Good," he said, giving a relieved chuckle. "I'm a coward. The question was my way of hedging my bet." He stepped back before sinking to one knee.

Hannah put a hand to her mouth. "Oh my God," she mumbled.

"Hannah Marie VanDer Dussen, will you do me the honor of marrying me?" He looked up at Hannah with such hope and love, it overwhelmed her.

"Yes!" she managed to choke out. "A thousand times, yes!"

She bent to throw her arms around Knox and at the same time, he stood. Their mouths crashed together as he lifted her up. He took two steps to press her against the wall, kissing her as he went.

"I love you," Hannah repeated between kisses.

"I love you too." With one hand, Knox held her in place while his other hand caressed her body, tracing sensual circles here, gliding up and sliding away to tease her there. "I bought you a wedding ring," he revealed, bringing her fingers to his mouth and sucking the tips before setting her down. He lifted the flap on his sporran and produced a glittering ring. "It's for now, or for later, if you prefer, but I thought I'd take you to Milan on a shopping spree, so you can pick the engagement ring you want. How does that sound?"

"Heavenly. Do you mind if I wear it now?" Hannah asked, holding out her hand.

Knox shook his head and handed the ring over.

"And now I'm yours," she mused, paraphrasing Lana's lyrics. She slid the ring onto her finger, examining the narrow white gold band encrusted with sparkly diamonds all the way around. "It's perfect. I can wear it as an engagement ring now and wear it as a wedding ring later. Is that okay?"

"Yes. If it pleases you, it pleases me."

"It does," she said, beaming. "Can I tell everyone?"

"Of course."

Standing on tiptoe, Hannah put her arms around Knox's neck. "I can't believe we're making plans together for our future. It's a dream come true."

Knox hugged her close and placed a gentle kiss on top of her head. "We should be going. The staff needs to clean up the room and get it ready for an event in the morning. I had to twist some arms to get everything together for tonight."

"It's good to be king."

"Yes, it is," Knox agreed, taking Hannah's hand. "Let's go."

They walked arm in arm down the hall and once they were in the elevator, Knox pressed the button to take them to his room.

Hannah's eyes narrowed. "I thought you wanted to keep up the pretense of an innocent relationship," she said, one corner of her mouth quirking up.

"I do. But Charlotte was asleep on her feet. I'm sure she's well asleep by now."

"Definitely," Hannah agreed. "And it gives us the rest of the night to celebrate our nuptials."

"More than that," Knox corrected. He stepped from the elevator when the doors opened and led Hannah down the hallway. "We have three whole days until you leave."

"Don't mention me leaving yet," Hannah protested as Knox swiped the key card to unlock the door to his room. "I'm in a euphoric bubble, and I don't want it to burst."

Seeing Knox's expression fall, she gave him an apologetic smile. "Sorry. Your stopwatch is probably exploding about now. Apparently, you are the glass-half-full member of this couple." She pumped her fist in the air. "Woo-hoo! Three whole days!! Yay!!"

Knox laughed as he closed the door behind them. "I find you to be the most delightful person I've ever met. How did I get so lucky to have a woman like you fall for me? Your love for me has been unconditional." He pulled her to him. "Is it wrong of me to say I've never loved anyone like I love you? I love my parents and children, of course. I loved—still love—Jayne, but not with the same intensity as you. We were kids who found ourselves with responsibilities too soon. This love is so strong. It's already withstood a horrible tragedy."

Hannah gazed up at him. "I know. I feel the same way. I walk around like a lovesick fool day and night."

Knox bent to kiss her, then beckoned, "Let's go into the bedroom, sweetheart. I'd like you naked with just the ring on tonight."

"That sounds perfect."

Their hands clasped, Hannah preceded Knox into the bedroom, then turned to face him. "I've made a decision. I'm going on the pill," she told him. "It's not fair for you to always have to use a condom. I'll see my doctor as soon as I get home."

Knox was silent for a beat, seeming to consider her words. "What do you think about not going on the pill, and not using condoms from now on?"

"Are you asking what I think you're asking?" Hannah held her breath.

He nodded, a shy smile on his lips. "You said yourself the chances of getting pregnant are slim. Nothing happened when we went bare last time. Why don't we let the fates decide?" He tucked a strand of hair behind her ear.

The prospect of having a baby with Knox set Hannah's insides fluttering. Still, she bit her lip.

"We could," she agreed. "But what if it's wrong to want a baby so much with you? Are we setting ourselves up for disappointment?"

His hand cupping her face, Knox stroked his thumb along Hannah's cheek. "I'll be happy no matter what the outcome. What about you?"

Hannah nodded and grinned. "Yes. Glass half full—how can I be disappointed when I'm engaged to be married to you?"

"Wonderful," Knox said, his dark eyes shining. "And now that's sorted, I'm afraid I'm going to have to rip that pretty dress apart if you don't get naked and on that bed now."

Without hesitation, Hannah undressed, taking off everything but the ring Knox had given her. As she lay down on the bed, she told him, "I'm ready. Your turn to strip."

"You're getting the full Scottish treatment tonight," Knox told her with a wicked glint in his eye. "I'm going to fuck you with this kilt on."

"Go for it, my Scottish hunk of a fiancé," Hannah said with a delighted laugh.

"Remember what a Scot wears under his kilt." Knox lifted up his kilt, revealing he wasn't wearing underwear.

Hannah's eyes grew big at the sight of his semi-erect penis.

Knox grinned. "What do you expect when you're lying there naked, woman?"

"Well, then, get busy, ya macho skirt-wearing stud. I can't wait any longer for the full Scottish treatment," Hannah cajoled, affecting a strong Scottish brogue.

"Damn." Knox faked a disappointed look. "I wasn't going to use the gag tonight, but the wee cock blocker is at it again. I'll give ya a reprieve because you've promised to be my wife."

"Fine with me, chatty Cathy. Get to it. Hurry up, slow poke. Make me come while you've got that sexy skirt on. Oooh, I love me some hairy Scotch legs," she teased, still using the heavy brogue accent.

With a surprised laugh, Knox shook his head. He opened a drawer and pulled out a gag. "I'm going to have to invest in more of these, fiancée," he replied as he put the gag in Hannah's mouth. "Ya know I hate it when Americans call me Scotch. I think ya said it on purpose, so I'd gag ya because it turns ya on."

Hannah could only smile in response.

Knox's brow went up. "Ah, my fiancée definitely has a kinky submissive side to her."

With a shrug, Hannah nodded.

"Alright," Knox relented, leaning over her to trail a finger between her breasts and down her torso. "I'll stop talking and get to it. You look sexy as fuck." He continued to caress her body as he climbed onto the bed and lay on top of her. Still fully clothed, he kissed and sucked on her from head to toe. When he reached the junction of her thighs, he gently tapped and kissed her clitoris, then spread her legs wider and leaned into her. Inserting his penis, Knox pumped in and out, while pushing against her clit with his thumb.

Hannah moaned.

"I'm going to come soon. You feel so damn good," Knox groaned as he stroked and pushed on Hannah's clitoris in a rhythmic and steady motion. Through a labored breath, he commanded, "Come!"

As Hannah screamed through the gag, she felt Knox coming inside of her.

He grunted and softly called out, "Hannah."

They lay there, Knox collapsed on top of Hannah, for so long, she felt herself starting to fall asleep.

At last, Knox removed the gag from Hannah's mouth before shifting and rolling to the side. Weak with exhaustion, she half-heartedly worked her jaw, then said, "I don't have the energy to take a shower. Will you clean me up, and we'll cuddle?"

Knox didn't answer. He merely kissed her cheek, and said one word, "Fiancée," and walked into the bathroom. He returned with a warm washcloth and cleaned up Hannah, finishing with a kiss on her lips.

"I'm glad we were on the same page for the grand gesture, sweetheart," he said, looking deep into her eyes.

Hannah gazed back dreamily. "Me too. Goodnight baby."

"Goodnight."

Chapter 23

The next morning, Hannah woke to find herself in Knox's room. She hadn't outright forgotten to set her alarm to sneak back into her room; in addition to wanting to spend the night wrapped in her fiancé's protective, loving arms—God! She couldn't believe he had asked her to marry him!—their private celebration had exhausted her. In the end, she had bargained with herself that if she happened to wake up early enough, she would go back downstairs. And, if not, she didn't care. They were all adults here—Charlotte, Knox, and herself. And now they were engaged, so there was even less reason to fake a chaste relationship.

Slipping from the bed, Hannah wrapped Knox's robe around herself and went to find him. He wasn't in the suite's living area, though she smiled when she saw pastries, hard boiled eggs, cheese and sausage laid out on the kitchen counter. She had certainly found herself a thoughtful man, she mused as she poured herself a cup of coffee. The fact that he lit her insides on fire and continued to reveal new and exciting ways to give her orgasm after orgasm was more than icing on the cake.

Hannah took her coffee and settled in on the sofa with her phone. She would check in with Charli; first, though, she wanted to track down her amazing man. It didn't take much. When she opened her messages, a text from Knox was at the top.

Good morning sweetheart. I've taken Charlotte to ma's to spend the day. Since u didn't set ur alarm to go back downstairs like u were supposed to, I told ur mom that u were still asleep in ur room, and we shouldn't wake u. C what a bad influence u are on me? lying to the sweetest woman on the face of the earth. Not u—ur mother

He had punctuated his message with a grinning emoji.

Hannah shook her head and typed a response.

Good morning. I'll let it slide that u think mom is sweeter than me, b/c of course, it's tru. TY 4 the best Xmas I've ever had, certain company excepted. Everything w/u is the best!

Knox's reply pinged back within seconds

Knox: YW

Hannah: Look at u w/ the acronym! Ur moving into the 21st century at a glacial pace. rotfl

An eyerolling emoji appeared.

It's got to be global warming...I've got a meeting to get to but I'll c u IRL later. ILY

Delighted and impressed, Hannah typed:

Damn, ur a quick study. Love u 2

As she closed her messages, a knock sounded at the door. Still in a bubble of happiness, Hannah set her phone aside and drifted across the room to answer the door. It was likely room service, come to collect the unfinished breakfast food and dishes. The bubble burst when Hannah opened the door to find Eric standing on the other side.

"Good morning," he said, his eyes raking over her body. "Happy Boxing Day."

Hannah flushed, as much with anger as with self-consciousness. She clutched at the robe to pull it closed and cut off his view of her cleavage.

"What are you doing here?" she demanded.

"Aren't ya going to invite me in?" He tilted his head and adopted a concerned expression. "We didn't get much of a chance to catch up with each other yesterday."

Hannah lifted her chin in a bid to display confidence she didn't feel. "We have nothing to talk about." She began to close the door.

Eric pressed forward and stopped the door from shutting with his foot. "Oh, but we do. And I have something I need to show ya. It's important."

Hannah swallowed down her rising panic and opted for bluffing him. "Let me get Knox. He's in the shower now. You can show us together."

Eric gave his head a mournful shake, his eyes full of sardonic sympathy. "Hannah, we both know Mr. Munro isn't here. He'll be in meetings most of the day. He said so himself last night." In what seemed to be an effortless move, he pushed the door open, forcing Hannah backward, and stepped inside. "And I rang his office before I came up to double-check his schedule. He won't be available for hours." The sympathy drained from his expression, replaced by wicked satisfaction. He closed the door behind him and advanced toward Hannah. "Besides, what I have to say, what I have to show ya, is for you and you only."

Heart racing, Hannah fought to remain calm as she backed away from Eric. If he only wanted to talk, maybe he would leave after he had his say. With sweating palms, she readjusted her robe, pulled the opening at the neck closed, and said, "Okay. What is it?"

He looked her up and down once more, the darkness in his eyes more dangerous than the lust she had grown accustomed to when Knox looked at her. Striding to the sofa, he sat down and patted the cushion next to him. "Come. Sit here."

Her eyes flicked to her phone on the end table at his side. If she had only kept it in her hands. Maybe she could have surreptitiously dialed Knox's number.

Eric followed her gaze and scowled. "You won't be needing this," he growled, sliding open the table's drawer and pushing her phone inside while he took his phone out of his shirt pocket. "Let's take a look at mine, shall we?"

When Hannah didn't move, he grew agitated. "Now, Hannah," he demanded.

Hannah sat down, leaving some space between her and Eric, but he wasn't having it. Stretching out an arm, he hooked it around Hannah's shoulder and yanked her to his side. When her robe gapped open on her lap, she tried to pull it closed over her legs again. Eric wasn't having that, either. "Don't worry about that, Darling." He gave her hands a hard smack. "Nothing I haven't seen before, right?"

Unable to answer him, Hannah sat stiff and still, her eyes averted so she didn't have to look at him.

Unfazed, Eric brought his cell phone up with his free hand and tapped a video icon with his thumb. "This is a little PDA with you and Knoxie at Loch Lomand," he narrated, showing Hannah the phone. "Look at him stroking your tits for everyone to see. It's a little blurry, but it looks like he got you off." He pulled the screen to his face, as if inspecting the video closer.

Hannah's stomach turned. So Eric had followed them that day. No wonder she had felt uneasy the entire time. He had been watching them.

"I have to tell Knox about this."

"Wait, there's more. You'll want to see the rest." Eric seemed to be enjoying himself now.

"Not much else interesting after that in Glasgow because you kept to hotel rooms. *However,* then I had the great idea to get a P.I. in New York when I found out Knox was going there. They're not as expensive as you'd think." His tone was casual while he scrolled through his phone.

"The first trip was a bust. I thought it was a fifty-fifty chance Knox had gone to seek comfort in your loving arms when he was having such a hard time. You know. With the death of his beloved boy." He shook his head and clucked his tongue as if feeling truly sorry for Knox's loss. "I actually thought things might be over between the two of you then," he went on, showing Hannah a picture of her and Knox outside the coffee shop she had met him at when he had told her he had nothing left to give her. "But! Then my P.I. friend told me Knox was back in the States for the holidays, and I told him to go ahead and keep watch. It's a good thing I did. He didn't catch you two sneaking off to a hotel but, ah, ya forgot to close the curtains at least once." He cackled.

Nausea washed over Hannah, and she thought she might be sick right there. The man was obsessed, and she was starting to see he could be dangerous, too.

"Look at these," he said, starting another video. "I could look at you walking naked across your flat all day long, although I think the best ones for YouTube will be the ones of you giving Knoxie a blow job. These videos are better than the dirtiest porn I've ever watched. Lots of fucking in different positions." He paused, the glee turning to despondency when he said, "Maybe if you would have sucked my cock, you would have stayed with me."

Realizing she was trapped alone with a man walking the edge of insanity, Hannah struggled to remain calm. Her head was spinning, and she couldn't seem to control her breath.

"This is the way it's going to go from now on," Eric announced, tossing his phone aside. "When you're here, you will make yourself available to me."

Revulsion rippled through Hannah in waves. "Never," she said, surprised at the strength in her voice.

Eric shrugged. "The alternative is breaking up with Knox and staying on your side of the pond. Either choice is fine with me. If you don't pick one or the other, I'm going to release these videos publicly. Do you understand, Hannah?"

Pictures of Charli, her mother, even Lawrence passed through her mind, and how something like that could affect them all. "Please, Eric. Don't do this."

"I'm in charge now." Eric leaned forward and slid a hand inside her robe. He gave her breast a painful squeeze. "I'm going to give you twenty-four hours to make your decision. And before I leave today, I want a taste of what I've been missing this year."

He pushed Hannah back, grinning when he pulled her robe aside. "Och—I can see you must have been expecting me. Good thinking. No panties to get in the way."

With a quick flick of his hand, he had pulled his cock out and stroked it once, showing it to Hannah. "Ya remember how much your pussy likes my cock? Lucky you—you're getting it again."

Before she could call up anything she had learned in her rape-safe class, he had nudged a knee between her legs and was pushing inside her.

Too numb to cry or react in any way, Hannah lay there, her hands at her sides and mumbling weak protests.

The ordeal didn't last long. After only a few thrusts, Eric grunted his release and got off her. As he was stuffing himself back inside his pants, the door to the suite opened and Knox stepped inside.

"What the fuck is going on?" he demanded, his eyes going first to Hannah, then to Eric.

While Eric finished righting his clothes, Hannah scrambled to sit upright, pulling the robe closed around her.

"She was begging for it," Eric said, straightening his shirt cuffs before looking at Knox. "I told you she was a whore."

Fist cocked, Knox flew at Eric. "You raped her, you motherfucker! I'm going to kill you!" His fist met Eric's jaw with a hard crack.

Eric cupped his chin, a mean smile playing on his bloodied lips. "Careful now, Mr. Munro. We don't want this to end in a messy lawsuit, do we?"

Shooting a scathing glare at Eric, Knox went to Hannah and sat down beside her. "Are you alright?"

Filled with a numbing horror, Hannah couldn't look at him. "He didn't rape me," she said quietly, her eyes pinned to the floor. "I just want to go back to my room. I don't feel well."

"You heard her," Eric said. "I didn't rape her."

Hannah closed her eyes. "Please just leave," she pleaded.

Knox stood and pointed to the door. "Go!"

Eric smirked, then came near the sofa to retrieve his phone. As he bent to pick it up, he whispered to Hannah, "Keep behaving or those porno tapes go on the Internet."

When he stood up, he slugged Knox in the gut. "That's what you get for making assumptions," he said.

Caught off-guard, Knox took the blow, though he managed to keep from doubling over. He glared at Eric, watching him leave the room. Once they were alone, Knox sat down next to Hannah again. "Sweetheart, please. Talk to me."

It seemed like an eternity before Hannah could answer him. When she did, her words sounded distant and robotic. "Nothing to explain. You saw what happened."

"I'll tell you what I saw." Knox's tone was quiet, but strong. "You were lying there terrified. He raped you."

Hannah blinked and turned toward Knox, though she didn't meet his eyes. "Mom and I will get a driver for the airport tomorrow. I don't want you to worry about taking us."

Knox gusted out an incredulous half-laugh. "Hannah. We must go to the police. You know for a fact most sexual assaults go unreported because the victims are too scared to come forward. You can't let him get away with this. What would you counsel people you work with?"

She could feel his pleading eyes on her and knew she wouldn't be able to make this work if she stayed near him much longer. Standing, she walked toward the bedroom. Knox followed her.

"Please, sweetheart, we can get through this." His words broke as he choked back a panicked sob.

Hannah pulled on her dress from the night before and gathered up her underwear, shoes, and stockings.

She pushed past Knox and started for the door. "I don't want to see you again. Please don't try to contact me." She stopped and turned back, taking off the ring he had given her. Setting it on the table by the door, she met his eyes one last time.

"I'm sorry," she said, and walked out the door.

Chapter 24

New Years came, although it didn't bring the shining hope it should have. Hannah was glad Charli was with Lawrence for the holiday; at least she had most of the week after Christmas to try to figure out how to function without having to put on a happy face for her daughter. It was hard enough for Hannah to convince Charlotte their sudden change in plans to fly back to the States early was a reasonable choice influenced by nothing in particular. She had told her mother something important had come up with Knox's business, and since she couldn't see him for the rest of the week, she would rather go home. She felt guilty about cutting her mom's first trip to Scotland short. But her need to get away from Eric, and stay away from Knox, was stronger than any pressure from her conscience.

For the next couple of weeks, Hannah moped around the house, not sleeping and unable to eat. She was fatigued and had no appetite—sometimes just the sight of food made her nauseated. Still, she tried to throw herself into the life she had had. She put on a pleasant front for her family, although she knew both her daughter and her mother could see right through it. But, sticking to their routine and keeping things as normal as possible for Charli was what Hannah felt could get her through the dismal, depressing existence her life had become. Losing Knox the first time around had been miserable, she reflected glumly, but pushing him away on purpose was hell.

Although it was a struggle, she forced herself to get up each morning, shower, dress, and do her makeup and hair. She took advantage of working from home for several weeks. Her plan was to be back to a regular working schedule by the end of March. Knowing Eric had had her watched before, once home, she couldn't shake the feeling her every move was being monitored. Even so, although she had agreed to his terms by breaking things off with Knox, she couldn't let Eric completely control her life. She needed to find a way to get back to some kind of normal. Other than her daughter, work was all Hannah had now, so getting that part of her life back seemed like the logical next step.

And the entire time, she sent Knox's calls to voicemail and deleted his texts without reading them. It would have been smarter, she knew, to block his number. She wasn't ready to do that, though. Not yet. Seeing his name on her phone's screen was, in a strange way, both painful and comforting. When he called or texted, Eric's threat kept her from responding, heartbreaking as it was. Still, there were days when the thin thread of a connection with Knox was what kept her going.

One bright March morning, when spring was making an early appearance, Hannah strolled out of her building headed for the office, to find Knox waiting for her. Dressed in an impeccable gray Armani suit and black cashmere turtleneck under a charcoal trench coat, he was leaning back against a town car parked in front of her co-op. He pushed to standing, hope flooding his dark eyes, when he spotted her.

The sight of him stopped Hannah in her tracks. Before she could tamp it down, joy flooded her heart, causing it to skitter as it always did when she saw him. When he took a tentative step in her direction, the consequences of letting him back into her life rushed in and shut everything down. Blinking, Hannah turned and walked away from him, as fast as her short strides would go.

"Hannah!" Knox called, coming up behind her. He reached her side before she had gotten halfway up the block. "Hannah, I'm sorry to waylay you like this, but you haven't returned any of my calls or texts." He didn't take her arm or try to stop her; he only matched her pace to walk beside her.

Jaw clenched, Hannah pinned her lips between her teeth and shook her head. *No. I can't talk to you*, she thought, wishing he could somehow understand.

"I texted a couple of days ago, when I found out I would be coming to New York. I don't even know if you've been getting my messages, or if you've blocked my number."

Hannah closed her eyes. She had missed Knox so much. Missed his voice, his touch—having him this close, hearing him speak soothed her like nothing had over the last few months. Yet, it wasn't enough to drive away the raw anxiety over the danger of breaking her agreement with Eric.

"I'm so sorry I hurt you." Her words were thick with emotion. "Please. Just leave me be. You deserve someone better."

"Hannah, sweetheart." Knox lightly touched her arm. "You're the only woman for me."

The tenderness in his voice broke her heart all over again. She sucked in a breath to choke out the sob rising up her throat and quickened her steps. "I'm late for work," she said, her eyes hot with tears she was determined not to shed.

This time, he didn't let her get away. Hooking her arm, Knox drug her to a stop and turned her to face him.

"If you can't talk now, please, meet me later. You never said goodbye when you left. We didn't get a chance to talk things through."

She hadn't allowed herself to look at him or meet his eyes. Now, though, as he spoke, her gaze traveled up. He had lost some weight, she noticed. His handsome chiseled face was wan, and there were bags under his eyes. He looked older, and so weary, but he was still beautiful. Her throat tightened with the words she wanted to say.

"Please. Sweetheart. Just give me a few minutes. Now, later—whenever you can spare them. I know there has to be more to the story than you've said, and all I'm asking is to understand. Why you left and why we can't be together." He released his grasp on her arm and huffed a defeated sigh. "Give me that, and I won't bother you again if you don't want me to."

Hannah dropped her eyes to study the grimy sidewalk. At last, she looked up. "Fine. Let's do this now. I'll call in to work and meet you at the same Starbucks near Columbus Circle where we met before."

The tension drained from Knox's face, replaced by a tentative smile. "I hired a car. We can take that." He pointed back down the block to the car he had been leaning against when she had first seen him.

Hannah shook her head. "I'll walk. I need a few minutes to gather my thoughts. Besides," she glanced around, trying not to look fearful or suspicious, "it's probably not a good idea for us to be seen together."

Knox's brow creased, but he only gave a slow nod. "I'll meet you there, then," he said carefully.

By the time Hannah stepped into Starbucks, Knox already had a table. It was tucked away toward the back of the shop, isolated from the rest of the seats behind a set of shelves displaying branded merchandise. He met her at the counter, looking pleased and relieved.

"Thank you for coming," he said, leaning in as if he meant to kiss her cheek, then stopping himself. "Would you like something to eat or drink?"

"No. Thank you. Let's just get on with this. Okay?" She sounded impatient and emotionless, Hannah knew. She had made a decision on her walk to the coffee shop, however, and she was afraid if she didn't jump right into it, she might lose her nerve.

Knox pointed the way to their table, and Hannah took a seat, placing her hands in her lap. She pinned her eyes to a spot on the tabletop where the faux woodgrain had worn away with use. This was harder than she had thought it would be, and now she wasn't sure she was doing the right thing.

"So. Uh," Knox cleared his throat and broke the tension. "About three weeks ago, Sam found me in a drunken, sorry state at home. As I said, I know there's something you haven't told me. It's been eating me up and between losing you and not knowing why, I was spiraling down fast again. Sammy sobered me up. He spent the weekend with me, talking about old times, reminiscing about his brother. He asked me if I really wanted to go back to the dark place I had been in after Stuart died, and I don't, Hannah. God help me, I don't." He reached a hand across the table, placed it palm-up over the spot Hannah was staring at.

She clenched her fists in her lap, restraining herself from taking his hand. It would be a comfort for them both. But, as much as her heart ached for him, she had no right to console him, and didn't deserve his reassurance.

After a moment, he gave a soft, defeated chuckle and went on. "When I realized that, I knew I had to talk to you. Even if it's one last time, I can't move forward until I understand what happened. I know everything went off the rails after ..." He left the rest unsaid and mercifully continued, "... well, I have strong suspicions about what happened that day. But, even if I'm right, I can't believe it's why you broke things off with me." His tone was growing harder as he spoke, almost taking on a tinge of desperate anger. "I know you were afraid—it seems like you still are. If you won't let me help you, at least help me understand."

Hannah drew in a breath. It was now or never. She closed her eyes and started talking. She told him how Eric had waited until Knox was tied up with work to come to his suite and corner her. How he had spied on them the entire time they were in Glasgow, including following them to Loch Lomand and taping their private tryst on his phone. She told him how Eric had admitted to hiring a P.I. to keep tabs on her after she came home, and about the footage the investigator had gotten of them during Thanksgiving weekend.

Knox listened, taking in everything and not seeming surprised. "Is it possible he's bluffing? He could have followed us in Glasgow and to the Loch without having actually filmed anything."

Hannah shook her head, heat rising in her cheeks at the memory of seeing herself in those surreal videos. "I saw the videos, unfortunately. He showed them to me," she told him. "And then he gave me an ultimatum. I was either to make myself available to him whenever I was in the country, or I had to stay on my side of the pond, as he put it, and break off all contact with you. If I didn't pick one or the other, he threatened to put the videos on the Internet." Tears stung at her eyes again, and she looked away, her next words coming out in a whisper. "It would devastate my mother. Lawrence would be livid, and I'd lose Charli. God, Knox, I could even lose my job."

Compassion and grief chased across Knox's face. "Why didn't you tell me?"

"I shouldn't be telling you now," she said, stealing a glance around the café. Not entirely convinced they weren't being watched, she lowered her voice. "If Eric finds out I met with you, it's all over. My family will be destroyed."

Knox scooted his chair closer and grasped her hand beneath the table. "Sweetheart. If I'd have known, I could have done something."

The physical contact felt too good. She soaked it in like parched soil drinking in water and she gave herself permission not to pull away, even as she argued, "But that's the problem. If you say anything to him, he'll release the videos. You're in them, too. They'll affect everyone we love. We can't let that happen."

It was a relief to have shared the burden with someone, especially with Knox. However, the relief didn't quite chase away the unsettling feeling of Eric's eyes on them at that very moment. Anxiety building, Hannah glanced around again. What if the P.I. was in the shop right now? She had already spent too much time with Knox and had said way too much. Pulling her hand from his grasp, she stood, slamming her chair into the wall behind her with a loud "clack."

"I have to go. Please, don't do anything, and don't contact me again. You know everything now. You have your closure. I hope you use it to move on with your life, because—" she poured the love she still had for Knox into the look she gave him. "—I truly do want you to be happy."

"Hannah, sweetheart. Wait." Knox clutched at her hand, but she moved too quickly for him to stop her.

Head spinning with what might happen now she had told Knox everything, Hannah rushed out of the coffee shop and down the sidewalk, losing herself in the midday crowd. She felt as if she was being chased, and she quickened her pace, not sure whether her pursuer was Eric, Knox, or a figment of her imagination. When panic overtook her, she darted into an alleyway and slumped down onto the ground, her back against a cold brick wall.

The tears came then. Tears she had suppressed for months, washing out the grief and the guilt and the frustration and everything horrible Eric had brought into her life. Her sobs flowed as freely as the tears, although she tried to stifle them. She didn't want to attract attention; she simply wanted to have a good, ugly cry and get it all out.

Oblivious to everything but her own raw emotions, Hannah didn't notice the man stepping into the alley with her. Only when he laid a gentle hand on her shoulder did she looked up to see Knox crouching beside her, his eyes filled with sympathy and pain.

Chapter 25

When Hannah registered it was Knox's hand on her shoulder, she made to get up, but he stopped her. Taking a seat on the ground beside her, he pulled her into his lap. Exhausted, Hannah could only let him hold her. As her sobs built up once more, he stroked her hair and whispered to her.

"*Shhh, tesoro. Stai bene. Tutto andrà bene. Non piangere amore mio.*"

Although she didn't understand the words he spoke, they comforted her, nonetheless. When her sobs subsided to hiccupping breaths and gradually to sniffling, Hannah said, "I should have fought him. I didn't even say no. I let him do it."

Knox rested his cheek against her hair. "Don't do that to yourself. It's not your fault. He blindsided you with blackmail and took advantage of you before you could wrap your mind around what was happening."

Her face pressed to his chest, Hannah closed her eyes and shook her head. "You were right, though. I should have gone to the police. The videos might have gotten out anyway, but I wouldn't be in this mess now."

Knox inclined his head to look down at her. "First, you're not in this mess alone anymore. I'm here in it with you. And second, it's not too late. You can still go to the police. The case won't be as strong, but you were threatened."

"He didn't really threaten me," Hannah said with reservation, meeting Knox's eyes. "That's why I feel so stupid for letting him ... do that to me. It's not like he had a knife at my throat or a gun to my head."

"Ah, but he did threaten you," Knox assured her, wiping a stray tear from her cheek. "He gave you two impossible choices—break up with me or make yourself available to him. And he threatened to go public with the videos if you didn't comply with one or the other. You panicked."

Hannah considered Knox's words and gave a conceding nod. "The thought of the consequences of those videos going public—I was frozen with fear. It was like watching myself in a horror movie and not being able to change the channel."

Knox listened, grim remorse settling over his face. "This is my fault. You were such an innocent when we met, and I got you into all the kinky stuff. The videos wouldn't exist if I didn't push you to do those things with me."

"You didn't force me to do anything I didn't want to," Hannah told him, her lips turning up on one side.

"I loved every minute with you, everything we did. All things considered, I don't think I would change any of it."

"I wish you would have trusted me enough to tell me, though." Knox pulled her back in. "It would have been easier going through it together."

As good as it felt for Knox to hold her again, Hannah couldn't agree. "I don't know how. You would have confronted him—"

"Of course I would," Knox interjected.

"—and made things worse," Hannah said with a frown. "But going along with his blackmail scheme isn't an option either. Neither of us wants me to be Eric's play-thing, at his beck and call whenever I'm in Scotland." She blew out a defeated sigh. "It was better with me dropping out of the picture."

"You dropping out has not been the better choice," Knox disagreed. "Whether you'll admit it out loud or not, I can see you're miserable. And I've missed ya so much. I carry your ring around in my pocket. See?" He reached into his trousers' pocket and produced the little velvet box with her ring in it. "It's the only thing I have left of you, the symbol of our bond. I guess I've been hoping you'd change your mind."

Hannah ran a finger over the tiny box's soft lid. "I can't believe you have this," she murmured.

"It's with me all the time," he said, matching her tone. "I meant it when I said I'll love you forever."

Tears welled in her eyes again. "I don't deserve you." Her voice hitched with a sob.

"It's me who doesn't deserve you." His words came out thick with emotion. "Do you still have any feelings for me? Do I have any chance at all?"

Hannah tensed. "I don't know what to say."

"Good. Don't say anything. It's better than a no." He rubbed her shoulder. "If you'll give us another chance, I'll do anything you want. We'll handle this together."

Hannah shifted on Knox's lap. As bad as the blackmail was, there was more she hadn't told him. "There's a complication." She spoke so softly, she couldn't be sure he had heard her.

"How could it be more complicated than it is?" A smile warmed his voice as he continued to stroke his hand up and down her arm.

"I'm pregnant."

He stopped rubbing. "So much for statistics on the decline of fertility after the age of thirty-five."

Hannah sat up to look at him. "It's still early days. I suspected right away, and I took a home pregnancy test last week."

"And you want the babe."

She nodded, unable to articulate her tangled emotions.

"Were you going to tell me?" Knox asked, obviously struggling for control over his feelings about the matter.

"I'm not sure." Hannah shrugged. "The chances of having a miscarriage at my age are high. If I told you and upended your world, then something happened ..." She let her words trail off. There was more to it. "The real problem ... I don't know who the father is. See? Complication."

Knox shook his head, a hopeless smile tugging at his lips. "Hannah, I love you, and I love the baby inside you. If he—or she—comes out six feet tall, with red hair and Eric's face, I will still love it."

Hannah's arms went around Knox's neck. "Do you mean it?"

He squeezed her tight. "Of course I do. I'd love to have a baby with you. It doesn't matter whose DNA it has."

When Hannah pulled back and their eyes locked, the familiar spark sizzled between them, as strong as ever. Knox bent, keeping his gaze on hers until their lips met.

Hannah could feel Knox holding back his desire, and had to rein in her own, as well. As tender as it was, it gave her everything she needed, everything she had been missing over the past few months.

When he broke away, Knox inclined his head. "So how about it? Are we a team again?"

"I guess we are." Although she was still afraid of what Eric could do to her, it felt better to have Knox back in her corner.

"Then there's just one more matter to address." Knox picked up the box containing Hannah's ring and held it out to her. "You don't have to put it on, and you don't have to promise anything right now. I'll take anything you're willing to give me—a kiss, marriage, a text—" he cocked an eyebrow, "—sex."

"Nice." Hannah smirked. "Use my own words against me."

Knox kissed her forehead as he put the little box in her hand and closed her fingers around it. "Just hold onto it, okay?"

Hannah pressed the box to her chest, then slipped it inside her purse. She wasn't sure how far she could let Knox back into her life, and wearing his ring could be the thing to set Eric off. For now, however, having it in her possession gave her hope.

"I think it's time to take you home," Knox said, brushing Hannah's tousled hair away from her face. "Let's get a cab."

He took her hand to help her up and looked toward the street. "There's a taxi now. Let's see if we can grab it before someone else snatches it up."

Happy to have Knox calling the shots again, Hannah followed him out of the alley and into the back seat of the cab. He gave the driver Hannah's address, then sat back, putting his arm around Hannah, pulling her to him.

For the first time in months, Hannah felt safe again. Even so, she couldn't see past today, past the present moment.

"What are we going to do?" she asked Knox, her tone melancholy.

"I don't know yet," he admitted. "My resources are better than Eric McGregor's. I'll find out what he's up to. Who this P.I. of his is. Maybe I can hire someone to find out what videos he's got and where he's keeping them. It should be an easy job for a talented hacker to get into his phone or computer and get rid of them."

Hope pulsed through Hannah's heart. "Do you think so?"

"I don't see why not. And once he no longer has anything to blackmail us with, you can go to the police."

Hannah deflated. She didn't want to revisit Eric's assault on her. If only it could just go away.

When she didn't respond, Knox squeezed her shoulder. "It's all up to you, sweetheart, but you know if it was anyone else, it's what you'd advise them to do."

She gave a half-hearted nod. He was right.

"Have ya seen a counselor?" His question took her by surprise.

"No." She blinked, uncomfortable to admit it.

He shook his head in dismay. "God, what am I going to do with you? Didn't you learn anything from my experience? Do you think you're invincible? Regardless of whether you fought him or not, he raped you. That alone would be enough to require professional help, and you're still going through a lot." He held up a hand and started counting off on his fingers. "You're suffering from PTSD. You are under constant stress from fear that psychopath may release the videos. You're pregnant. And you're madly in love with me." He smiled and tweaked her chin. "Go talk to a counselor about it. Make the call first thing in the morning. Promise?"

After everything, Knox still loved her and worried about her. Hannah rolled her eyes, hiding how much his concern touched her. "Yes, I promise, Mr. Tall, Dark and Bossy."

Hannah stiffened when the cab turned onto her block. If she hadn't been followed earlier, there was a good chance there were eyes on her building at this moment.

Knox picked up on her mood shift and removed his arm from around her shoulder. "Do you think he's having your building watched?" Knox's suspicious gaze swept over the street, the cars, and the windows in the surrounding buildings.

"I'm not sure," Hannah said with a shiver. "Truthfully, I've felt like someone's watching me ever since I came home from Scotland."

"It's no wonder," he said, his sympathetic eyes finding hers. "You've got a sociopath obsessed with you. If he doesn't have his P.I. following you twenty-four-seven, I'm sure Eric at least puts him to work when I'm in town." He glanced around again. "Listen, I want you to slap me when we get out of the cab."

A bemused smile crept onto Hannah's face. "I didn't think you were into the pain stuff."

Although he favored her with an amused look, his tone was all-business. "We'll talk about that later. For now, I'm serious. We'll have a few words, and you'll slap me, in case anyone's watching."

"Okay," Hannah agreed as the cab pulled to a stop in front of her building. "And I thought I was paranoid."

Knox stepped out of the cab and came around to open Hannah's door. When she got out, neither of them reached for each other, and they kept neutral expressions on their faces. Hannah went as far as the sidewalk, stopping short of her building's entrance. She turned to face Knox, who was following solemnly a few steps behind her.

"So, what now?" she said, thinking if she was keeping her feelings from shining through the look she was giving Knox, she deserved the Academy Award.

He shrugged. "We'll be careful. After today, we may not be able to be together until I can do something about McGregor." He looked around again, as if he expected Eric to stroll up any minute. "I know a couple of guys in the city, Steven and John Milakovo. They're brothers who work as bodyguards. I'd like to hire them to watch over you until I can do the job myself."

Hannah didn't have to fake the annoyed look that flashed across her face, but Knox stopped her argument before she could start it.

"Don't be angry. It's only until we get this sorted out and can go on with our lives. I'll call you every day and I'm expecting you'll answer now, right?"

She lifted her hand to scratch a non-existent itch and hide the smile on her lips. "Yes," she mumbled, exasperated.

"Good," he said, managing to confine his amusement to his eyes. "I'll have them introduce themselves soon, within the next day or two. They should be able to start right away. I think it would be easiest if they acted as employees. I know you're attached to your driver, but one could take his place for now and the other could step in as your personal trainer."

"Fine," Hannah agreed. "Is there anything else?"

Knox raised an eyebrow. "Only one more thing."

Hannah pursed her lips and tried to look indignant before reaching up to strike Knox across the face.

"Bloody hell!" His hand went to his jaw, but his eyes told her he was impressed.

As he stood there stunned, Hannah turned on her heel and marched into her building.

Chapter 26

Two days later, when Charli was at school and Charlotte was lunching with friends, Hannah's doorman buzzed to ask if she'd hired a new driver and personal trainer.

"I suppose I have," she admitted reluctantly, and told him to send them up.

When she opened the door, two short, stocky men were on her doorstep. They introduced themselves as the Milakovo brothers, and Hannah invited them in.

She served them coffee in the living room, and they filled her in on the plan they had worked out with Knox. The brothers seemed to be made of solid muscle, with John being a little less thickset. He informed Hannah he would be her personal trainer and Steven would be her driver for the time being. They went over schedules and gave Hannah their cell phone numbers. The brothers also provided a list of codes she was to use to text them in various situations, like if anyone was following her or if she noticed someone seemed to be taking pictures of her.

"We do some private investigating, and we're keeping an eye out for the guy hired to follow you," Steven told her. "McGregor might have brought him in from out of the country, because all our inquiries so far haven't turned up anything."

Although the brothers' presence eased Hannah's anxiety, the news that Eric's P.I. could still be out there watching her pushed her unease back up a few notches. And they seemed to take the job Knox hired them to do seriously—to an extreme, in fact. After John and Steven left, Hannah dialed Knox.

"Hello. I didn't expect to hear from you this soon," Knox said, sounding warm but stilted. "I'm walking into my office right now, and we can talk in a moment."

Hannah held her breath, exhaling only when she realized even if Knox wasn't alone, no one there could hear her end of the conversation.

"I hope it's okay I called," she said hesitantly.

The sound of a door closing came down the line, then, more relaxed, Knox said, "Of course it is. I'm glad you called. How are you?"

"Good. I just met my new employees," Hannah told him. "They're a bundle of laughs, aren't they?"

Knox chuckled. "They're professionals and they're good at what they do, sweetheart. I hired them to protect ya, not entertain ya."

"Well, they certainly have the serious, no-nonsense tough guy thing down."

"Then they're doing their job," Knox said, satisfied. "So—did ya make an appointment with a therapist?"

Hanna was pleased to be able to report not only had she made an appointment but had already had her first session the previous afternoon.

"It thought it was going to feel like cutting open a vein having to tell a stranger everything, but we went over her confidentiality policy, so that made me feel safer. I know one session won't be enough. The experience was somewhat cathartic, though. Thank you for suggesting it."

"I'm glad it went well," he said. "It's going to help you a lot, you'll see." He paused, then released a contented sigh. "It's good to talk again. I've missed ya so much."

"Me too. Have you recovered from the slap I gave you?"

"Mostly," Knox chuckled. "Good thing I didn't tell ya to punch me. Shane Mosley couldn't have delivered a better slap."

"It had to look real," Hannah said, feigning defensiveness.

"And I'm sure anyone watching believed it was."

"I have something for you that might make up for it," Hanna told him. "I'm going to text you a photo."

"Ah, sexting photos? Aren't we having enough trouble with dirty pics and videos?" Knox joked.

"Not funny."

"Maybe just a wee bit funny?"

A smile tugged at Hannah's lips. "Maybe a wee bit," she said begrudgingly. "I'll talk to you soon. Bye, baby."

After ending the call, Hannah snapped a picture of her left hand, the beautiful ring Knox had given her displayed on her finger. She had been wearing it since the night before, when she had decided to go all-in on getting back together with him. He had shown her he had never stopped loving her, and she had failed miserably at trying not to love him. They belonged together, and she couldn't think of a better way to show it.

Attaching the picture to a text message, she typed:

Thank you for waiting for me. xxH

Knox's reply was immediate:

Always X

Once it was official, Hannah was able to relax a bit. Not that her world was back to normal yet, although it did settle into a new type of normal. At least one of the Milakovo's were always nearby so, although she still felt like she was being watched, she didn't live in a state of anxiety. And, there were the regular weekly appointments with her counselor. Charlotte and Charli both commented on her improved mood. While Hannah knew the therapy was helping her emotionally and Knox's bodyguards were making her feel safer, she gave Knox all the credit for returning the joy to her life.

Hannah and Knox had decided as happy as they were to be back together, they wouldn't be sharing the news with anyone. Knox had hired an investigator of his own, Aldis Grant, who had been following Eric's every move, and had been able to access Eric's phone calls, texts, and emails. Although Grant had corrupted the video files on Eric's phone, he'd told Knox it was likely Eric kept copies on a flash drive or computer. He suspected they were on a laptop he had seen Eric carrying. Knox told his investigator to "do what it takes" to get access to the laptop but, after several weeks, the P.I. hadn't reported success.

"With his phone's videos destroyed, I'm sure he'll suspect something," Knox said when he updated Hannah during one of their nightly calls. "Aldis corrupted a few random photos and other videos for good measure, but we can't be sure of anything when it comes to a mental case like McGregor."

A shudder ran down Hannah's spine. "So I guess I'll be working from home and keeping Charli out of school for awhile," she said, downcast. It had felt good not carrying the weight of her family's safety by herself. She knew she had let her guard slip a little, relying on Steven and John more than she should have.

"It's the safe thing to do." Knox's tone was gentle. He had told her how pleased he was to see her getting a little closer to her old self, the joking, lighthearted woman he had fallen in love with. Hannah knew he would never do anything to undo all the progress she had made, but she also knew he had her and her family's best interests in mind. "You should probably arrange to have your counseling appointments over the phone or online, if it's an option," Knox went on. "And, is Charlotte still working part-time at the senior center?"

It was obvious where he was going with the question. Hannah closed her eyes and shook her head. "She is. I supposed I'll need to come up with a reason for her to quit or at least take a leave of absence." She hadn't told Charlotte anything about the blackmail or the danger they all might be in and hated it was affecting more than her and Knox.

"Hopefully this won't go on much longer. Aldis is watching Eric's every move. He'll find those videos soon, sweetheart, and this will be all over."

Hannah inclined her head, leaning into the sound of Knox's comforting voice and wishing it was his arms she was sinking into. "I can't wait until it is," she said. "When do you think you'll be back in New York?"

"Permanently? Not for awhile. I can arrange a visit anytime, though. It's been far too long since I've slept with my beautiful fiancée curled up against me." The warmth of his words brought a smile to Hannah's face, although a hint of apprehension curbed her delight.

"There's, uh, something we should probably discuss." Hannah's mouth had gone dry. She wasn't sure this was the best time to bring it up. On the other hand, she reasoned, she couldn't imagine any good time to talk about it.

"Sounds ominous." Knox kept his tone light, and Hannah silently thanked him for it. She just hoped he would still be in a jovial mood once she said what she had to say.

Taking a deep breath, Hannah plunged in. She told him she missed him so much, her heart literally ached sometimes. Hannah told Knox she couldn't wait to see him again, to share a bed and wake up with him wrapped around her. But she was concerned about their sex life going forward.

"I don't feel desirable," she confided. "And I don't know if I can be as responsive as I was before ... before the, um ... attack." She still couldn't bring herself to say *rape*.

There was only the slightest pause before Knox responded. "I've been thinking about it, too, sweetheart. I'm glad you brought it up because I wasn't sure whether I should or not." He sounded relieved. "Look, I want you to know I have no expectations. I will forego having sex altogether if that's what it takes to be with you. You can dictate our sex lives, or I can, if you prefer. We can even go to counseling together if you think it will help."

Exhaling, Hannah pressed her palm to her heart. How could she have doubted he would be supportive? "The trouble is, I don't know what I want. My therapist says what happened could impact me for the rest of my life, even in ways I don't realize right now." She paused. For all the uncertainty she felt, there were a few things she knew to be true. "I do know I'm still attracted to you," she affirmed. "That hasn't changed. Maybe we can take it slow."

"Of course we can. The important thing is for us to be together, whatever form it takes."

The sincerity in his voice brought her back to a place of calm. A place she had try to come back to, if not stay in as much as possible, she vowed to herself as they ended their call.

Knox had said he would see about moving a few of his business obligations around so he could come for a few days' visit. The school year would be over soon, and Charli would spend the first six weeks of the summer break with Lawrence. A trip back to California to visit friends would be a nice Mother's Day present for Charlotte, Hannah mused as she walked out onto the terrace off her bedroom and surveyed the glittering nighttime cityscape. With a private airplane at his disposal, Knox could get to New York covertly enough, and the Milakovos could bring him to her co-op undetected, she was certain. Then, she and Knox could have a few glorious days together, however long he could stay.

A siren sounded in the distance and the skin on Hannah's arms prickled with gooseflesh. She hated all this sneaking around, looking over her shoulder all the time, and manufacturing excuses to manipulate her daughter and mother's schedules. She hated even more that she was the one who had brought the situation on all of them. With a shiver, she turned to go back inside, praying this whole ordeal would be over soon.

Chapter 27

"I find it hard to believe you can't get bagel chips in Martha's Vineyard," Hannah groused. She was standing behind Charli in the corner bodega, watching her daughter piling bags of snacks into the wicker basket dangling from her arm. With Charli's back to her, Hannah heard the eyeroll in her daughter's response instead of actually seeing it.

"Ugh, Mom—I told you. The market there doesn't carry this brand." She thrust a bag of Everything Bagel chips over her shoulder and shook it at Hannah before placing it in the basket. "They're my favorite, and since I'll be at Dad's for the next six weeks, I need to stock up. Sheesh."

Hannah shook her head. The school year had ended two days before, and Charli was packed and ready for Lawrence to pick her up the next morning. However, about thirty minutes ago, she had flown into the kitchen in a panic over not having anything to snack on while she was away. And, since nothing Hannah had on hand in the cupboards would do, Hannah had reluctantly brought her daughter to the little market on the corner for a supply of her favorite noshes. Hannah reached out a hand to stroke the back of Charli's head. She had to admit to the ulterior motive behind dropping everything to make a trip to the store—sending a little piece of home with Charli would be a comfort to them both.

With nervous distraction, Hannah glanced out the window at the growing dusk outside. In the moment, it hadn't seemed a big deal to dash down to the bodega to pick up a few things. She had texted Steven to let him know where she and Charli were going, but she hadn't asked him drive them. Now, however, it was getting late. Not being in the safety of her co-op after dark always made Hannah edgy, whether one of her two bodyguards was with her or not.

"I think you've got enough, sweetie," she said to Charli, forcing her tone to stay casual and light. "I can always send you a little care package if you run out."

She put an arm around Charli to draw her toward the checkout counter, then froze in place when she turned to find Eric at the end of the aisle.

He stood there, beaming and holding one perfect long-stemmed rose. "Hello, Hannah. I've missed you," he said, his voice unnervingly normal, as if they were long-lost friends.

Hannah felt the blood drain from her face. She pushed Charli behind her as she groped in her bag for her phone. A tiny cry of dismay rose in her throat when her hand closed around it, and she looked up to see Eric advancing toward her. She fumbled to pull up a text to send out an S.O.S. to

Steven. Her skin was clammy, and panic vibrated through her, setting every nerve on edge. Before her fumbling fingers managed to tap out a full word, Knox was grabbing Eric by the shoulders from behind.

"You get any closer to her, and I swear I will kill you." Knox's threat came out in a low growl as he pulled Eric back.

The rose went flying when Eric's hands went up, and he shook Knox off. "I knew there was a chance you'd be here somewhere," he said, his eyes narrowing. "Your ma and da said they thought you might still be hung up on her." With a casual toss of his head, he gestured toward Hannah. "They think she's trash, you know. They think you need to move on. Have they told you that?"

"Shut the fuck up, and stay away from her," Knox responded, struggling to keep his anger in check.

Eric smirked. "You hate the power I've got now, don't you? I'm da to your grandson and your family has taken me in as one of their own. I even have your mam wrapped around my little finger. Has she told you she's agreed to give Alex her share of the whiskey company? Naturally, as his legal guardian, I'll be in control of it until he's of age."

"We'll see about that." Knox's jaw muscle ticked, and his fists clenched.

Eric didn't try for any level of control. His voice rose, bitterness and hatred spewing out with every word. "You think you're so high and mighty. You threw me out of your bar last year—well who's on top now? I've fucked your fiancée, I'm taking over your family businesses, and you can't do a thing about it." He turned to glare at Hannah. "I've been very patient, but I told you what would happen if you didn't break things off with him. You've left me no choice—before the night's over, your videos will be collecting views on YouTube."

Hannah gritted her teeth, blinking hard. She would not let this bastard break her down here in front of her daughter. As she opened her mouth to speak, John came through the door brandishing a laptop.

"McGregor!" he called out. "Is this yours?"

Eric's eyes went wide. "Where did you get that?"

Steven came strolling in behind his brother. "We were out taking a walk, saw it sitting in your unlocked car. You really should take better care of your valuables."

"It was in the trunk, and the car was locked," Eric ground out through his teeth.

John feigned confusion. "It was? Hmm. I don't think so." He looked at Steven. "I don't know nothin' about gettin' into a locked car trunk, do you?"

Steven shook his head. "That would involve breaking and entering."

Eric pushed past Knox to snatch at the computer. "Give it to me!"

In one fluid motion, John tossed the laptop to Steven, keep-away style, and grabbed Eric's wrist, spinning him around. Before Hannah realized what was happening, Steven had set the laptop down and had handcuffs around Eric's wrists. Steven looked at the clerk behind the counter, who had been watching the entire encounter in mute astonishment.

"Did you call the cops?" he asked the clerk.

Unblinking, the man shook his head.

John nodded. "Good. We'll see justice is served." He turned to Eric. "Why don't we go somewhere private and have a little discussion about the distasteful content on your computer?"

Eric didn't go quietly. He continued to shout threats, trying to draw attention and get the authorities involved. However, the brothers shoved him out the door and toward a waiting vehicle.

"What's going on, Mom?" Charli asked, emerging from behind Hannah once the coast was clear. "Who was that man? And why is Knox here?"

Hannah took a shaky breath. "He's someone who's been trying to hurt me," she said, her eyes going to Knox. "And I don't know why Knox is here. It's lucky he showed up, isn't it?"

"Not luck," Knox touched her arm, examining Hannah as if to assure himself she was okay. "I'll fill you in later. Are you both alright?" He looked at Charli and assessed her as well.

"We're fine, I think. Just a little shaken," Hannah said.

"That guy's a creep, but I think we're okay," Charli piped up. "Fill us in on what? Is there something I should know?"

Hannah and Knox exchanged a look and chuckled. The incident didn't seem to have rattled Charli out of being Charli.

"Let's go home," Hannah said. "Knox and I need to talk, and I'll tell you if there's anything you should know."

Knox saw Hannah and Charli home safely and waited in the kitchen while Hannah got Charli settled for the night. When she entered the room, worn out from the evening's events, he was sitting at the table with two filled wineglasses waiting for her.

Weary, she sat down next to him and took a long fortifying drink before reaching for his hand.

"I don't know if I've ever been happier to see you than I was tonight. What in the hell is Eric doing in New York?" Just saying his name had Hannah on the edge of frightened tears.

Knox gave her hand a reassuring squeeze. "It's a bit of a story," he said, his tone grim. "While he's been keeping tabs on you, Aldis has been keeping tabs on him. It turns out McGregor came here on legitimate business, a convention or conference or something for his fishing supply company, and he decided on making a personal visit to you. When I found out he was in New York, I moved heaven and earth to get here. I've been in contact with John and Steven all day. Apparently, Eric tried seeing you here, but he couldn't get past your doorman—"

"What?!" Hannah cut in, almost knocking over her wine glass. "That psycho was in my building? Why didn't anyone warn me?"

Knox righted her glass and took both her trembling hands in his. "Sweetheart, calm down," he soothed. "We were certain you were safe here in your home, and I didn't want to upset you. I told the Milakovos not to say anything to you but to stay close. We didn't count on you taking a bonny jaunt to the corner market." His expression was a mixture of reproach and bemusement. "You should have had Steven drive you."

Hannah frowned. "To the corner? That's ridiculous," she huffed. "Of course, if you'd kept me in the loop and I realized what was going on, I would have handled things differently."

Knox brought her hands to his lips and kissed them. "I'm sorry, truly. I should have told you Eric was in town, but I didn't want to alarm you." When Hannah opened her mouth with a retort, he hurried on. "I was on my way, though, and as soon as Steven got the text about you and Charli heading to the market, he and John were fast behind you. They spotted McGregor following you in his rental car and waited for him to go inside the store. I arrived as they were liberating his laptop from the car's trunk, and I came inside to head Eric off before he could get to you and Charli."

Brows knit, Hannah considered his words. She didn't like the thought of Eric having gotten so close, especially since her daughter had been with her. And she would have been happier if the altercation with him had never happened. Still, Knox had shown up in time, and John and Steven had his laptop and had taken him away—hopefully far, far away.

"What will happen now? What are Steven and John going to do with him?" Hannah asked, almost afraid to hear the answer.

"I spoke with Steven while you were seeing to Charli, and there's good news and bad news," Knox said, the line of his lips turning down. "The good news is the laptop did contain the original videos, and they've already been destroyed. Aldis has done a thorough search and believes there aren't any copies stored anywhere else. Eric's confirmed it to Steven and John. The level of his rage when they deleted the files, scrubbed the drive, then took a sledgehammer to the hard drive makes them believe him."

Relief washed over Hannah. "That's wonderful! Then we're finally out from under his thumb?"

Looking uncertain, Knox shrugged. "I hope so, yes. I'd have liked to kill the bastard for everything he's done, and the Milakovos wouldn't have any qualms about carrying something like that out."

The image of Knox's hired men fitting Eric with cement shoes made Hannah's stomach turn. Although she wished he'd never come into her life, she didn't think she wanted him dead.

"I couldn't bring myself to order someone's death, though." Knox looked past Hannah out the kitchen window into the dark and sparkling Manhattan night. "Maybe it makes me weak, but I'm just not that guy. John and Steven will turn him loose. I've instructed them to drive him to the airport and put him on the next flight to Edinburgh." He brought his gaze to Hannah. "And now that we've taken away the thing he was holding over us, he has no power."

"You're not weak," Hannah protested. "You're a sexy, wonderful man with a conscience. It's far more than I can say for Eric McGregor." She tilted her head to the side. "But what was all that about your parents giving him part of the whiskey business?"

Knox grimaced. "My mam's a soft touch. She's made no secret about her intention to split her part of our whiskey business between Sam and Alexander. However, Violet's been pushing to have Alexander's inheritance signed over now, probably at Eric's urging. Of course, she and Eric would have custodianship of it until he's of age. Sam and I are upset about it, although we haven't let on why it's a bad idea. My da thinks it's best to have it pass down through me. What Violet and Eric don't know is I'm the majority owner of the business. They'd be gaining a lot if they got their hands on my mam's part, but it wouldn't be the vast control Eric thinks it would be."

Hannah shook her head. "I am so sorry I brought him into our lives."

"Och, now, donna go there." He put out his arms and pulled her onto his lap. "Who's to say he wouldn't have found Violet and ended up exactly where he is anyway?" He smoothed Hannah's hair away from her face. "At least we're past the worst of it, and I'll figure out a way to deal with him if he winds up custodian of Alexander's interest in the family business."

As Hannah looked into Knox's eyes, her heart was full. She could believe the worst of it was behind them. "I love you." She spoke the only words on her mind at the moment. "The baby and I need a future with you."

"It's what I want, too. Patience is a virtue in business and in life, but I can't wait much longer for us to be together officially."

"Then let's not wait." Hannah's heart beat an excited rhythm in her chest. With Eric's threat out of the way, she had new hope for herself and Knox.

He did a double-take, searching her eyes as if wanting to make sure she wasn't joking. "Are you saying you want to get married?"

"Yes." She smiled. "The sooner, the better, as far as I'm concerned."

Surprise and eager delight played across Knox's face. "You'd better be serious, sweetheart. I can book tickets to Las Vegas right now." He held up his cell phone.

"Actually, do you mind if we have a small ceremony here? I'd like my mom and Charli and Grace to be there."

Knox leveled his dark gaze on her. "If that's what you want, nothing would make me happier."

Chapter 28

The wedding took place on a warm mid-June day. Hannah hired a planner to take care of arranging a tasteful but modest celebration at her apartment. The woman also arranged for an officiant to perform the ceremony there among the intimate gathering of friends and family. Because Hannah's baby bump was growing more obvious by the day, she and Knox explained the spur-of-the-moment wedding was because they were expecting. Only Grace knew the truth, and Hannah knew she could trust her bestie to take her secret to the grave.

So, within weeks, Francesca, Bruce, and Sam flew in for the wedding, and since Knox's partner, Tom, couldn't make it, Sam stood up beside Knox as his best man. Of course, Charlotte and Grace were there for Hannah, and Charli returned from Lawrence's for the occasion. The turn of events didn't thrill Lawrence. He insisted on keeping Charli an extra week over the summer to make up for the two days she spent with Hannah for the wedding. It didn't matter to Hannah. She was in a glossy bubble of joy nothing could break. At last, she and Knox were going to be together—and this time, it was forever.

If there was one weed in their happy little garden, it was that Knox still had to spend a good deal of time on business in Scotland. He and Hannah had rushed into marriage, and neither of them regretted it. But even though he had already planned on transitioning to work from New York, he hadn't had time to make it happen. Tom was understanding and took on a large amount of Knox's work for a few weeks, to give Knox and Hannah time together as newlyweds. And Sam stepped up, too. It had always been Knox's idea to have Sam join the hotel business alongside him. It more than pleased him when Sam brought it up himself before Knox had a chance to ask him. Everything seemed to be falling into place, and Hannah said a prayer of thanks almost every day upon waking, tucked safely in her big, sexy Scot's arms.

One morning in late July, however, Hannah awoke feeling nauseated. Before she was fully awake, she was already throwing back the covers, stomach churning, and running for the bathroom. After rinsing with mouthwash and splashing water on her face, she dragged herself back into the bedroom to find Knox standing in the doorway. He wore slacks and a shirt and tie, and was holding a tray, looking concerned.

"Seems like it's getting worse, not better," he said, sympathy in his eyes.

Hannah shook her head and gave a halfhearted laugh as she climbed back into bed. "It wasn't this bad and didn't last this long with Charli. Dr. Slaton says it could be because I'm older. Pregnancy isn't one of those things that gets easier with age." She sunk back against the pillows and let Knox tuck the comforter around her.

He had followed her to the bed and set the tray aside, and now he picked it back up and set it across her lap. "I made you breakfast. Only tea and toast, but it might be all you can hold down at the moment." He smoothed the wayward waves of hair from her face.

Hannah clasped his wrist and leaned her cheek against the coolness of his hand. "No. I don't think even that will stay down right now."

Knox sat on the edge of the bed next to her. "I'd feel a lot better if you ate something before I have to leave."

A quizzical look came to Hannah's face. Within seconds her mental fog cleared. "Oh, right. You're leaving for Glasgow today." Her heart sank.

When Knox told her he had to go back to Scotland for three weeks to tie up some loose ends with the hotel there, Hannah had planned to go with him. As her morning sickness held on and grew worse, though, and because hers was already considered a higher risk pregnancy, Dr. Slaton had grounded her.

"Just stick close to home," she had counseled Hannah. "You're already past twenty-eight weeks. It's better to err on the side of caution when it comes to your baby's health and well-being."

Now, faced with almost a month without Knox, Hannah considered disregarding her doctor's orders.

"You're taking the company jet. Maybe I could tag along." She lifted her eyebrows hopefully.

With a shake of his head, Knox gave her an indulgent smile. "I'd love to have you with me. It's going to be torture being away from you—"

"For three weeks!" Hannah cut in to remind him.

"Right. Don't remind me. It only makes it harder. But you know what the doctor said. I can't have anything happening to you or our babe. It would end me." His solemn look told Hannah he wasn't exaggerating.

"I know." She tried not to sound too disappointed. "I just don't like the thought of being away from you."

Knox set the tray on the floor and nudged in beside Hannah, stretching his long legs out on the bed and putting his arm around her to pull her close. "I don't like it any better than you do." He tilted his head to the side to catch her eye. "With your mam visiting friends, it's only you and Charli. You're not afraid about being alone, are you?"

Although they both knew what he meant, from all appearances they didn't have anything to be concerned about. Eric hadn't tried to contact Hannah since the incident in the bodega months ago. What's more, he had been behaving in an almost exemplary way, as far as they knew. Living most of the time in the States now, Knox didn't have much contact with Violet or Eric. But reports from Sam and Knox's parents all spoke of a nice, thoughtful guy settling into the role of doting family man. He was polite and cordial when he and Violet brought baby Alexander to visit Bruce and Francesca. And it had been months since he had brought up the subject of the whiskey business to Francesca or Bruce.

Hannah sighed, not sure what to say. The truth was, she was still dealing with the trauma of Eric blackmailing her and stalking her. She couldn't help looking over her shoulder wherever she went, and the constant feeling of being watched hadn't gone away. Deciding against giving Knox more to worry about, she shook her head. "We're not alone. Jonnie will drive us wherever we need to go, and Andrew is in twice a week to cook for us. We'll be fine." She snuggled closer to him, but he knew her too well.

"I can have Steven and John back on the payroll this afternoon," he said, wrapping both arms around her. "I pay them enough. They can bloody well drop what they're doing to watch over my wife and child."

Hannah smiled into his shirt, breathing in his scent and loving how safe he made her feel. "I'll be fine," she insisted. "I'm just being a baby about it because I can't go with you." She pulled back to look up at him. "Go. Get on your plane and fly to Scotland and take care of business so you can come back to your family."

The relief she saw when he smiled at her made it worth the extra effort Hannah put into the grin she gave him.

"I'll be back a week before the baby's due, and I am going to miss you both every second of every moment from the minute I walk out the door," he said, pointing at the doorway.

"And I am missing you already," she told him.

He bent to kiss her with a softness that soon deepened to sizzling and had her stomach fluttering with desire rather than the queasiness she had awakened to. Too soon, he broke away, returning twice more for shorter but no less passionate kisses, then said, "If I don't get going, I'll wind up spending the day in bed with you."

"Sounds like a good idea to me," Hannah teased.

Knox placed the tray back on her lap, instructing her to eat something and to drink the tea while it was still hot. He shrugged into his suit jacket as he walked toward the door, then stopped before stepping through and turned back to blow Hannah a kiss.

"I'll see you in a few weeks, *amore mio*."

Chapter 29

Hannah juggled her mail and an armful of shopping bags as she let herself into her co-op. When a padded envelope slipped from her grip, she groaned. At just over thirty-three weeks pregnant, it was a challenge to pick up anything off the floor. The thought of the contortions it would take to retrieve the dropped envelope had her wishing she had let her driver accompany her inside. Jonnie was back on the job and, after a morning of shuttling Hannah and Charli on errands and to an appointment with the obstetrician, he had offered to carry Hannah's bags inside. But she had declined, asking him instead to deliver Charli to a friend's house for a weekend sleepover. The doctor's appointment had run late which, in turn, had made Charli late and she had fretted all the way across town about being the last one to arrive.

"I mean, it's bad enough to get there before anyone else," she had explained with a worried expression. "No one wants to be the loser who walks in after everyone else is there."

She had been tempted to alleviate her daughter's anxiety and have Jonnie drop off Charli first, but Hannah was drained and wanted to get home to lie down. What's more, Dr. Slaton had given her a prescription for her morning sickness, and Hannah was eager to start taking it.

Tired and frustrated, Hannah gave the envelope a gentle kick, sliding it across the threshold and into the entry hall. Then she flicked on the light and deposited her bags on the entryway bench before closing the door. Taking a seat next to her bags, she slid the errant envelope closer with the toe of one of her Ferragamo flats and leaned sideways to pick it up. *If only Mom was here,* Hannah thought, as her fingers scrabbled to grip the envelope's edge. She had encouraged her mother to go on a seniors' singles' cruise with friends without considering all the little ways Charlotte was helpful around the house. Breathing heavily, Hannah sat up, a triumphant smile on her face, and placed the envelope with the rest of the mail on the table next to the bench. She would sort through it all later, maybe after she had a nap.

Taking the small paper pharmacy bag, Hannah got to her feet and headed for the kitchen, pulling a little bottle from the bag and reading the dosage instructions as she went. She was so absorbed in calculating when to take her next pill if she took one immediately, she didn't see the man seated at the table in the breakfast nook.

Her blood froze in her veins when the familiar Scottish brogue softly said, "Hello, Hannah."

Stopping in her tracks, Hannah's head came up and she whirled around.

Eric sat, casually sipping from a glass half filled with amber liquid and ice cubes. He had helped himself to Knox's scotch and although he wore a faint smile on his lips, his eyes were flat and cold.

"What ... how did you ...?" Hannah stammered, unable to take in a full breath or think straight.

Eric's smile widened. "It's good to see you again," he said, getting up from his seat and coming toward her. "After what happened the last time I was here, I hope you weren't afraid we wouldn't see each other again."

Unaware she had been taking one step back for every step Eric took, Hannah let out a little gasp when her back hit a floor-to-ceiling cupboard.

Reaching out, Eric cupped her face in his hand. "I'm sorry I couldn't make the wedding. I think my invitation must have gotten lost in the mail." He chuckled. "Ya know how the international post can be. I didn't even find out about the happy occasion until after the fact, when Francesca was raving about the 'bride's beautiful dress' to Violet."

"Eric, you can't be here," Hannah said when she managed to find her voice.

The smile on his face faded, turning sad. "I almost wasn't, but I've come so far, I couldn't not pop in to say 'hi.'"

A cold chill snaked up Hannah's spine. She had been so preoccupied when she had taken her mail from the box downstairs, she hadn't noticed the doorman's absence. Jonnie had been the one to hold the building's door open for her. She had gone straight to her mailbox, fumbled the key into the lock, and taken everything out, the entire time her mind on getting upstairs and taking her medication.

She gulped. "Eric. What did you do? How did you get in here?"

"I'm a resourceful guy." With a mysterious grin, he dropped his hand from her face, and his gaze traveled down to Hannah's swollen belly. "And what's this?"

When he reached out and caressed Hannah's stomach, she shuddered.

He looked her in the eye again. "Now let me think … I'm no expert on pregnancy, but if I were to guess, I'd say you're about …" He cocked his head as if doing the math in his head. "… eight or nine months along. Am I right?"

Bile rose in Hannah's throat. She blinked and swallowed hard, fighting the sob that wanted to break free.

Delight danced in Eric's eyes. "Ah. I'm close, then. And I wonder. Who's the proud daddie to your wee babe?"

"Knox," Hannah said, her voice cracking. "Knox," she repeated, her voice stronger. "It's Knox's baby."

Eric's eyes narrowed. "Och, you're a liar and a whore, aren't ya?" He had leaned in and the heavy scent of whiskey on his breath told Hannah the drink on the table probably wasn't his first.

A buzz sounded from Hannah's sweater pocket and her hand jerked in an automatic response. She wasn't quick enough, though. Eric beat her to it, pulling out her phone as it buzzed again. He glared at the screen, then bared his teeth in an unhinged grin. When he turned the screen to Hannah's face, she saw Knox's name.

"Well, there's the alleged baby daddie now." There was a sharp, nasty edge to his tone. "Too bad he wasn't home when I got here. I would have loved to say hello. And to be truthful, I do have a score to settle with him."

The phone stopped buzzing and Hannah's heart sank. "Please," she said, reaching for her cell. "He'll call back if I don't answer. You have to let me talk to him."

Eric shook his head. "You're done talking to that bastard," he spat. "He thinks he's so rich and powerful, he can just take whatever he wants—" He bent, getting in Hannah's face. "—whoever he wants."

Hannah's head spun with fear. God, why hadn't she let Knox call Steven and John? She should have trusted her gut feeling. A lunatic like Eric would never give up. She searched her mind for something to say to calm him down, maybe buy her some time or put him off guard so she could get away. If she could make it to a neighbor's door, get inside before he had a chance to follow her ...

Her phone pinged with a text. Eric's lips curled in a sneer as his eyes zig-zagged across the screen, reading the message.

"Ah, how sweet," he said, his tone mocking. "Lover Boy misses you and the babe and hopes you're feeling better. But it looks like there's been a delay, and he'll be gone a week longer than expected." His face fell in false sympathy, and he clucked his tongue.

Hannah choked back a sob as she watched Eric turn the phone off and toss it onto the counter out of her reach.

"He was going to fill you in on the details when you talk later, but we both know that conversation isn't going to happen." He held out a hand to her. "Come on now. We need to get going."

Gooseflesh prickled Hannah's skin. "G-going where?" she stammered.

"Away. We need a fresh start. You and me and the babe …" His fingers trailed across her abdomen once more.

When Hannah recoiled from his touch, Eric wrapped his hand around her wrist in a painful grip.

"I think you've been under a bad influence too long. Have you forgotten how much you enjoyed my hands on you?" Flattening the palm of his free hand on her belly, Eric ran it up her side and squeezed her breast. "It'll all come back," he said with a cruel chuckle. "You'll remember."

Giving her no time to respond or think, he tugged her toward the kitchen door, leading out to the building's back hallway. Although she tried to resist, the soles of her ballet flats slid along the polished hardwood floor. She had the momentary frustrated thought that they almost made it easier for him to take her against her will. When she yelled, "No! I'm not going anywhere!"_he turned and drove the back of his hand across her face.

"Shut up!" he demanded through clenched teeth. "Keep quiet, unless you want your baby to pay." He shot a pointed glare at her stomach.

"I'm, I'm sorry," Hannah sobbed, sick with fear. "Please, don't. I'll be quiet. I'll come with you. Anywhere. Please, just don't hurt my ba—"

"I said shut up!" He took her by the shoulders and shook her hard, putting an end to her babbling and her crying.

When she pressed her lips between her teeth, her eyes wide, Eric seemed satisfied. He took her wrist, not quite as tightly, and tugged her through the door. He started for the elevator at the far end of the hall and Hannah's mind raced ahead, anticipating what would happen next. This elevator would take them to the lobby, just as the one on the other side of the building outside her front door would. The back elevator, however, opened in an alcove across from a door opening to the alley. If Eric had a car waiting, she thought with a fresh surge of panic, he would shove her inside and spirit her away from the building without a trace. Her mind raced, trying to think of how to get away from him.

As Eric dragged Hannah along the corridor, she prayed one of her neighbors would come out as they passed by, but no one did. When Eric punched the elevator's button, the doors opened right away, as if it had been waiting for them. He dragged her inside and jabbed at the ground floor button.

Chapter 30

Hannah held her breath and slid her eyes to the side to try to judge where Eric's attention was. Fractions of seconds ticked by as she fought to remain calm and still. Even as the elevator doors began closing, she kept her breathing steady. But at the last moment, she pulled free from Eric's grasp and darted through the doors.

"Wha—" Startled, Eric didn't respond fast enough. Through the closed doors, Hannah heard him swearing and hammering his fists on the elevator walls.

She dashed back down the hall, beating on doors as she went. To her distress, no one came out. When she reached her own door, it was locked, of course. The safety feature meant it was always locked from the outside, even when the latch was disengaged on the inside.

"Damn it!" She groaned and pounded once on the door. Her keys were inside, right on the entryway table, where she had left them. Fear and dread filled her as she glanced toward the elevator. It had stopped a few floors down. Was he rerouting the lift? She glanced at the stairwell door. Or would he come up the stairs?

With quick steps, Hannah went to the stairwell door and pulled it open. It was inky black inside. The lighting had gone out months ago, but the super had an excuse every time one of the tenants asked when he would fix it. Hannah cocked her head and listened. No doors creaking open, no feet pounding up the stairs. Just silence. She looked over her shoulder, adrenalin shooting through her when she saw the elevator coming back up. This was it. She had no choice. As the elevator doors slid open, Hannah stepped into the stairwell. She pulled the door closed behind her, taking care to ease it shut so the clicking of the latch wouldn't give her away.

Turning, she realized that, although the overhead lights weren't working and the shaft was windowless, an emergency light illuminated the sign above the door displaying the floor number. It cast a weak, greenish glow over the number "10," giving Hannah a scrap of hope she had a chance of getting to the ground floor safely.

As she began down the stairs, Hannah went as quickly as she dared while still trying to keep from making noise. The corridor was all concrete and metal, and even the smallest sound seemed to echo loudly. Round and round, down and down she went, wondering where Eric was. If he had been on the elevator, surely he would have checked the stairwell once he had realized she couldn't have gotten back into her apartment.

When she stepped onto the fifth-floor landing, a hand snaked out of the dark to clutch her arm and another hand came over her mouth before she could scream.

"What took you so long, sweetheart?" Eric whispered into her ear as he stepped behind her and pulled her against him.

She whimpered against his hand, and he tightened his grip. "Remember what I said about keeping quiet?" he hissed.

Hannah nodded, relieved when he eased his hand away. She wiped her mouth with her hand, then brushed at her ear where his lips had been.

Without another word, Eric took her wrist and began dragging Hannah down the steps; she tripped and scrambled to keep up with him. Rounding a corner too sharply and several steps ahead of Hannah, Eric pulled her into the handrail. She cried out when the pointed metal edge jabbed into her belly. A sharp look from Eric kept her from saying anything more. Her pace slowed further, though, as the spot where the handrail had dug into her throbbed and an ache began spreading through her abdomen. A new harsh terror seized Hannah. The thought of something happening to jeopardize the little one inside her, the baby she and Knox thought of as theirs, was too much to bear. As the dim light above the fourth-floor doorway appeared below, Hannah began struggling and trying to pull away from Eric's grasp.

"Let me go," she pleaded. "I'm hurt, and I need help!"

Eric tugged her to him, his hand coming over her mouth again. He walked her backward until her back hit the wall. "I told you what would happen if you don't shut the fuck up!" He punched at Hannah's belly. In such close quarters, the impact wasn't as hard as it could have been. Still, her stomach muscles clenched as a cramp seized her, sending painful pulses through Hannah's womb. She bit down on his hand as hard as she could, then doubled over when he jerked his hand away from her mouth.

"You bitch! You fucking cunt!" He cursed her out, breaking his own rules about keeping the volume down.

While Hannah was bent in pain, Eric grabbed a handful of her hair and jerked her upright, holding her at arm's length. She flailed her arms in a fruitless attempt to fight him. His limbs were longer, though, and her fists only swiped through the air. The fact that it was dark as a tomb didn't help; she couldn't see well enough to aim a good shot and land it. When Eric began shoving Hannah toward the stairs, she figured there was nothing to lose. If she didn't fight tooth and nail, she had no hope of escaping him. And, even if she didn't succeed in getting away, she intended on doing as much damage to this psycho as she could.

With that resolve in mind, Hannah lashed out with her leg, hoping to connect with Eric's knee or, better yet, his groin. Instead, her leg tangled in his and he stumbled. Unwilling to let go of Hannah, he leaned toward the handrail, apparently hoping to catch his fall. However, in the dark, he must have misjudged where it was. He began tumbling forward, taking Hannah with him.

Together, they bounced and rolled down the stairs, smashing into the wall to ricochet off it and careening with fresh momentum down the next set of stairs. As they went, Hannah struggled to disentangle herself from Eric while trying her best to shield her belly from his flailing arms and legs. If she could just angle herself in a certain way, she might be able to spin off in a different direction than him. Pushing with all her might, she shoved him with her hip right as they toppled into the dim glow of the fourth-floor landing. Hannah landed with a smack onto the concrete floor. Eric tried to get his footing and continued to lurch backward, his eyes so wild with panic, they were visible in the hazy darkness. He landed with a sickening wet crunch when the back of his head struck the handrail's sharp corner.

Hannah lay there, her drive to escape waning as she realized Eric wasn't moving. What's more, once she did try pushing herself to sit, the pain wracking her body and stabbing cramps in her abdomen had her lying back down fast. Glancing toward the dark shape of Eric's motionless body, Hannah thought of checking his pockets for a cell phone. He had left hers upstairs, but he would have his on him, wouldn't he? Horror movie images of countless villains coming back to life right when the hero looms over them snuffed out any thoughts of searching him.

That left only one option. Afraid to even roll onto her back, Hannah angled to the side to take her weight off her belly, then inched her way toward the door. It was at her back, so she wasn't facing it, but she couldn't reach the knob from where she lay, anyway. Breathing hard against the pain, she made a fist and began pounding on the door behind her. Although the thumps sounded feeble, it was the only thing she could do. When her arm grew tired, she only let it rest for a moment. When she started to lose consciousness, she roused herself with a painful jolt, and started pounding again.

At last, the door shoved open, sliding Hannah forward and bringing light from the hallway spilling into the stairwell.

"Oh! My dear! Hannah—is that you?"

Hannah recognized the voice of her neighbor from the fourth floor.

"Mrs. Huntley," was the only thing Hannah managed to croak out in a weak voice before the darkness enveloped her.

Chapter 31

Hannah awoke achy and groggy and wondering why every part of her seemed to hurt. Her eyelids were heavy, and she lay there trying to place where she was and how long she had been out. The strong smell of industrial disinfectant and the gentle "bong" of an intercom followed by a woman's voice calling a Dr. Upton to the nurse's station told her she must be in the hospital. When the memories of Eric came flooding back, her hand went to her now-flat stomach and her eyes popped open. Heavy as they were, they drooped shut again, but she forced them open a second time and looked around the room. Bunches of colorful flowers and balloons lined the wall near the window. And there was Knox at the bedside, hunched over in his seat, his elbows propped on his knees, his face in his hands.

When Hannah opened her mouth to say his name, the only sound she made was a weak rasp. It was enough, though. Knox's head shot up, his weary eyes hopeful, and he smiled.

Hannah swallowed and tried again, but her mouth was dry. She put out a hand to Knox as he stood and came closer.

"Hey. How are ya feeling?" he asked, clasping her hand in both of his.

She opened her mouth to answer, then sighed and shook her head.

"Would ya like some water?" he asked, already reaching for the plastic pitcher and cup on the tray next to her bed.

He held the cup to her mouth and let her drink, then wiped her lips before bending to kiss them. It was a tender kiss and Hannah wished she could dissolve into it and remain in its loving protection. She managed to bring a hand to his face. He took it in his own, pulling away to look at her as if he needed reassurance she was awake and okay.

"Knox ..." Rallying her voice, she searched his eyes, afraid to ask the question playing on her mind.

He answered her with a smile. "The babe is fine. A healthy wee lass, considering she's a few weeks early. They're keeping her in an incubator when she's not being held or fed. She's shown no signs of anemia or apnea, though, and she seems to have taken to the bottle like a natural. The doctors want to keep the both of ya for awhile, so ya can recuperate, and she can grow stronger. But they say neither of you is worse for the wear."

Hannah's heart soared. After all she and the baby had been through, it almost seemed too much for them both to have come out alive and well.

"How ...? I mean, did they have to ..."

"The fall must have triggered labor. By the time you arrived here, you and the baby were both in distress. Dr. Slaton was on call, and she performed and emergency Cesarean."

Hannah nodded, her hand going to her abdomen where she felt a bumpy row of sutures.

"What day is it?" she asked, wondering how long she had been a new mother without knowing it.

"It's Saturday. Evening." He nodded to the setting sun through the window. "You were in and out last night and they've had ya sedated today."

Hannah's brow creased. "You must have flown right out. How did you know to come?"

Knox cocked his head to the side. "I arrived home right as the ambulance was pulling away to bring you here."

"But, your trip ... you were delayed. I thought you'd be away for another week."

It was Knox's turn to look confused. "Delayed? Why would you think that? I wrapped up business early so I could come home sooner."

"But you called and—" Hannah cut herself off. Eric had been the one to read Knox's text. Angry tears sprang to her eyes. "Eric took my phone. He wouldn't let me answer your call. And after you texted, he relayed the message. Or, rather, he told me what he wanted me to hear."

"I'm sorry." Knox squeezed her hand, fury chasing the haunted look from his eyes. "I should have been here. That bastard wouldn't have tried anything if I had."

Remembering the deranged look on Eric's face, she couldn't say she agreed. "I don't know," she said, tugging on Knox's hand, pulling him to sit down beside her on the bed. "He might have gone after you first, then come for me. As long as he's alive, he'll never leave us alone."

Lips pressed in a stern line, Knox nodded his head as his arm tightened around her. "Probably not, but at least we won't have to worry about him anymore. He didn't survive the fall."

When Hannah exhaled, it felt like she had been holding her breath forever. The entire episode had been terrifying. Was it too much to hope they were free of Eric McGregor at last? As she was contemplating not having to live life looking over her shoulder, a distressing thought occurred.

"What about Violet? And Alexander?" The poor girl had lost two husbands, and the baby two fathers—and all in the span of Alexander's short life.

"Violet may not see the blessing of it. She has her family, though. And the Munros will support her and Alexander, no matter what. Sammy's never been fond of her, but he loves his brother's child, and plans on being as involved in the baby's life as he can. The same goes for my parents. They're a doting grandma and grandda—they'll make sure Violet and Alexander want for nothing."

Hannah laced her fingers through Knox's and snuggled into his embrace. "And what about you? Don't you want to be a part of your grandson's life?"

The twinkle returned to Knox's warm dark eyes when he smiled at her question. Planting a kiss on the top of her head, he replied, "Of course I do. But we have a babe of our own to focus on now. When she's a bit older, we'll take her to Scotland to visit her family. In the meantime, Violet and Alexander can visit us here." His expression softened and his tone grew quiet. "Stuart's son will always be a part of our lives."

As they contemplated navigating this newest twist, a nurse entered the room. Her eyes were on the clipboard she carried, and they nearly popped when she looked up to see Hannah sitting up in bed.

"Mrs. Munro—you're awake." The nurse sounded equal parts surprised and pleased. "How are you feeling?"

A soft chuckle escaped Hannah's lips. "I've been better. Everything hurts, inside and out, and I'm exhausted. I think I'm okay, though."

The nurse came to the side of the bed across from Knox and placed two fingers on Hannah's wrist. After recording Hannah's pulse on the clipboard, she smiled at Hannah. "You've been through a lot. It's not surprising you're still feeling tired—especially with the sedatives in your system. They'll wear off after a few days, but it will be awhile before you're feeling like yourself again. It's going to take a lot of rest and TLC to get you there." Her eyes went to Knox, and she lifted a brow.

"No worries." He gave Hannah's hand a squeeze. "She and the babe will have only the best care around the clock from here on out," he promised.

"Good," the nurse responded with a satisfied smile, then turned to Hannah. "You aren't due for another dose of painkillers for a few hours. Can I get you anything now?"

"Can I see my baby?" she asked, looking from the nurse to Knox and back again. "She's almost a full day old and I haven't even held her yet."

"Of course you can." The nurse beamed, then checked her watch. "Actually, it's almost feeding time. I'll have someone bring her in with a bottle so you can do the honors yourself."

As the nurse left the room, Hannah turned to Knox. "Have you seen her yet?"

"I have, and she's beautiful," Knox said, pride and love evident in his expression. "Just like her mother."

Although Hannah smiled at his words, a thin stream of uncertainty trickled through her thoughts. She and Knox had decided he was her father, regardless of what her genetics were, and had chosen not to go through DNA testing. Now, on the verge of seeing the baby for the first time, Hannah instructed herself not to look for any trace of Eric McGregor. This baby was not his. There could be no doubts Knox was her true father.

"Oh!" Hannah had a sudden thought. "What about Mom and Charli? Has anyone contacted them?"

Knox nodded. "Once you and the baby were out of the woods, I called them both to let them know about the newest member of the family. I left out the part about the intruder and the tumble down the stairs, and the emergency c-section of course." The face he made said he felt a little guilty about sweeping so much under the rug.

"Thank you." She breathed a sigh of relief. "I don't want them to worry, but I'm glad you called them."

A gentle knock sounded on the door and a different nurse peeked in. "Are you ready to meet your daughter?" she asked.

Hannah gave an eager nod and beckoned her in.

Pushing the door wider, the nurse stepped into the room holding a tiny baby in her arms, all bundled in pink. She carried a bottle of formula in one hand and let Knox take it from her while she handed over the baby to Hannah.

"I'll leave you alone for some bonding time. Just press the call button if you need anything," the nurse said, making a quick and quiet retreat.

As she gazed down into the small perfect face, a lump rose in Hannah's throat. The baby's skin was the most delicate ivory, her chubby cheeks and perfect rosebud lips as pink as the little cap covering her head. "Oh," Hannah whispered, her heart full to overflowing. "She looks like Charli did when she was born. A perfect little porcelain doll."

The baby stirred at the sound of Hannah's voice and her sleepy blue eyes blinked open.

Knox crooked a finger and ran it along the baby's soft cheek. "She has your eyes, sweetheart."

Hannah chuckled. "I think you're right." To the baby, she cooed, "Hello, little one. I'm so glad you're here."

"We both are," Knox added. He held out the bottle to Hannah. "You want to give it a try?"

Taking the bottle, Hannah touched the nipple to the baby's lips. Straight away, her little mouth opened, and she began sucking. Hannah smiled up at Knox.

"See?" He grinned back at her. "A natural."

Hanna dropped her eyes to her baby again. As the infant settled into a rhythm of sucking and swallowing, Hannah said, "You know, we never settled on a name."

"We didn't know if we'd be naming a boy or a girl." He shrugged. "Besides, I think it's best to meet your baby before you name it. Both Stuart and Sammy were going to have entirely different names before they were born. Then, once they got here, we realized the names we'd picked didn't seem to fit."

Hannah nodded as she gazed down at the baby. Secretly, she had come up with the perfect girl's name. She hadn't mentioned it to Knox because, at first, she had been afraid she wouldn't be able to carry the baby to term. Then, once Dr. Slaton assured her the pregnancy was going fine, Hannah worried picking a girl's name would ensure she would have a boy. Superstitious, she knew, but she had had too many worries this time around. It seemed safer not to get her hopes up. Now that her daughter was here, though ...

"Well, she's obviously a girl, so if you don't have any ideas, how about Francesca Grace?" She let the name hang in the air for a moment, her eyes sliding to give Knox a sideways glance.

A slow grin spread on his lips. "A perfect name for a perfect lass," he agreed, reaching to stroke Francesca's head. The movement skewed the little cap she wore, revealing a line of fine, downy hair.

Hannah's brows dipped. Slowly, she pulled the bottle from the baby's mouth and handed it to Knox. When Francesca began fussing, Hannah didn't hear her protests. With gentle care, she slipped the cap off the baby's head and stared at the strawberry fuzz hidden beneath. Although it wasn't the deep copper Eric's hair had been, it was unmistakably red. Hannah looked up at Knox.

His eyes shone with a sheen of tears and a fierce, deep love. It was the reassurance she needed and more than she could have hoped for.

"You saw her last night," she said, her voice thick. "You already knew ..."

Francesca's little arms were flailing, and her cries had become more distressed.

"Yes." He blinked and put on a serious expression as he took the baby from Hannah. He rested her against his shoulder and began rubbing circles on her back. "I already knew how beautiful *our* daughter is. And anyone who says different will answer to me."

Hannah shook her head. "How did I get so lucky to wind up with a man like you?" She tugged fondly at his shirtsleeve.

He smiled at Hannah and looked down at Francesca, who had produced a tiny burp and was now calm and dozing. Laying her gently in Hannah's lap, Knox bent over his wife, planting his hands on either side of her. Looking her in the eye, he said, "It's me who's the lucky one. You've given me everything—a second chance at love, and a baby."

As he kissed her deep and long, Hannah's heart filled and spilled over, flooding her body and soul. Knox had given Hannah her life back. Better than that, it felt like her life hadn't really started until he came along, and she couldn't ask for more.

The End